SO SHORT

*Sometimes, Murder Is
The Only Option*

By

Mark Coryndon

Copyright © Mark Coryndon 2020
This book is sold subject to the condition that it shall not, by way of trade or otherwise, be lent, resold, hired out, or otherwise circulated without the publisher's prior consent in any form of binding or cover other than that in which it is published and without a similar condition including this condition being imposed on the subsequent publisher.
The moral right of Mark Coryndon has been asserted
ISBN: 9798623510846

This is a work of fiction. Names, characters, businesses, organizations, places, events and incidents either are the product of the author's imagination or are used fictitiously. Any resemblance to actual persons, living or dead, events, or locales is entirely coincidental.

To Pooch.

CONTENTS

PROLOGUE	1
CHAPTER I	8
CHAPTER II	17
CHAPTER III	51
CHAPTER IV	74
CHAPTER V	96
CHAPTER VI	125
CHAPTER VII	143
CHAPTER VIII	173
CHAPTER IX	186
CHAPTER X	225
CHAPTER XI	252
CHAPTER XII	274
CHAPTER XIII	301
ABOUT THE AUTHOR	324

PROLOGUE

No.

A flat no.

The word echoed in my ears. It was not what I was expecting. I gazed up at her from one knee, searching for the words that might now fill the gaping silence, and I finally saw what my friends told me they saw. I saw her disdain. I saw the sharp curl of the lip. And despite the raw emotion of my proposal, despite the glorious setting and obscene diamond in the ring I was holding; her eyes were cold.

There was nothing there.

I had been confident. Perhaps a little too confident. For some time, I thought she had been ready. It was, after all, natural. It was how relationships of people our age played out and, as time had ticked by, I sensed it was our time. Opulent white weddings had long since turned from the carefree receptions of reckless revelry, to more serious, stifled affairs. The mood had soured. The fizz and pop and excited ambience had given way to dinner timetables of sober eyes and talk of adult life.

It had turned into a race down the aisle.

'We're thinking about moving to Zone 3,' a girl had whispered at a recent affair, the tempura prawns going cold on her plate. 'You know you get so much more than Zone 2. And the schools are really very good.'

I had stared back at her not knowing what to say, conscious that my eyes had started to widen at the implications of talking about schools: children.

Only grownups had children.

'Oh no, thank you. I'm driving,' she said, as I offered her the numbing comfort of a crisp white Burgundy.

My career had been going well at a big multinational corporation. I was, at the time, all in on the corporate Kool-Aid and, after a few years, whilst still a junior on the intranet's organisational chart, I was also senior to a whole load of juniors. I was in the middle, but on my way up; my hands grappling at the greasy pole, my feet forever floundering for the heads of my peers.

I was playing the game.

'You've come a long way this year,' my boss had told me in my most recent year-end appraisal.

My boss with the sharp elbows and sharper tongue.

'You can't ease up though. Next year is a big one. Promotion is a possibility,' he had added without looking up, the words laced with meaning. Dark. Possibly even a threat. Easing up, I sensed, was not an option.

I sat and fidgeted in my seat, my palms sweaty, weighing a response.

But my lips were too dry.

Promotion.

It was going to be a big year. Time, I knew then, to ask the question. To propose. To finally grow up, find a mortgage, and start looking at semi-detached houses in the leafy surrounds of suburbia.

All I had to do was buy a ring and ask the question.

SOLD SHORT

And so, one wet weekend I went out and bought a ring. I scuttled up to the chichi arcade where young men, I was told, went to buy such things. And I saw them, the other startled looking young men, scampering this way and that, chased by the implications of real grown up life. All alarmed at the bright lights and gaudy smiles and soft words of reassurance from the assistants in their expensive looking suits.

As I stood in the entrance to one shop and stared at a ring with a brilliant blue stone in the middle and a price tag I couldn't quite see, there was a muffled cough behind me.

"That one, Sir, yes, a good choice. I suppose it is more than adequate. But perhaps the lady would care for one of these?"

The voice was sugary and warm.

I spun around to see him holding a small box with three rings nestled in the soft green baize, holding diamonds far bigger than the one I had been looking at, diamonds that were all glistening with intent.

'Is she, umm, with you?' he asked, looking around, 'or are you on your own?'

I shuffled my shoes and stole a glance at the door and, in an instant, he knew. I saw him lick his lips, and then he went for me. The verbal assault was fierce, and I stared hard at the three rings. His tone, on discovering I was alone, had turned blunt.

'A man of your obvious means,' he finally whispered, his words tight and clipped, 'would not want to disappoint.'

He had been there many times before and knew what words to emphasise. His job was to make sure that I knew what was at stake too.

Silence.

The phone behind the till rang, but he did not move; he just stood and stared at me, a ring – the one with the biggest diamond - now clamped between his forefinger and thumb, inches from my nose.

'Beautiful,' I mumbled.

It was all I could say. My voice sounded hollow, but I knew I had no choice. I could not risk disappointing my fiancée. And so, I bought the ring and scampered home on the bus, the box bulging in my trousers, my pocket unaccustomed to such wealth. Having slipped in through the door I stuffed the ring into my sock draw where it brooded for several weeks, playing havoc with my dreams.

I started to take to the downstairs loo where I'd look in the mirror and practice the question. I'd try different voices, different tones. I'd change my expression. With time the words grew familiar and the question lost its edge. Saying it started to feel natural, easy even, amidst the soft hum of the extractor fan.

'What ARE you doing in there?' she'd shout, hovering outside of the door.

'Flossing,' I'd say, and smile, knowing what she did not yet know.

And then one morning, impulsively, I decided I was finally ready. All I needed was to plan the proposal. After much mulling, I finally came to a plan. The ruse was neither tight, nor clever. But hopefully effective.

The plan was to lure her up to the top of the hill in the local park one evening after work. With the sun setting I would then do the deed. The view, I knew, was the perfect backdrop for such a momentous occasion. I had Max too, hiding in the bushes with his cello, cursing the tight nylon pants of the dinner suit I had made him wear. Max ready with his bow and a piece of music to suit the scene. And I had the hamper too. Of course. A hamper subtlety hidden under the bench. A hamper full of the deli's finest, with a special punnet of her favourite stuffed olives.

'And which champagne would you like?' the man in the deli had asked, a little breathless, as I gazed at the shelf.

It seemed he too sensed the occasion.

I ignored him and continued to gaze at the shelf, unsure where to go.

There were so many bottles.

Reaching for one, the man made his move. The hand, as it gripped my arm was firm. It was a hand that also chopped up pigs for a living in the deli's small butcher, and I knew I needed to tread carefully.

'I think you'll find the sixty-four was a far better year,' he said, guiding my hand to the top of the shelf.

'The sixty-four, yes, that sounds perfect,' I had muttered, unable to look at him as his hand gripped my wrist. I slowly placed the bottle on the counter and he finally smiled, a thin smile, as he ran the champagne and assorted eats through the till.

I had even asked her father, a wild, eccentric man, who lived alone in a remote cottage on the Norfolk broads. He had long since divorced and checked out of mainstream living shortly after. I had asked him one morning as we walked the wetlands, looking for skylarks.

'What was that?' he muttered, stopping, sticking his binoculars on to his formidable brow as the mist lifted to expose a thick section of reeds.

I repeated my question.

'Fine by me,' he muttered, leaning into the bitter wind, gripping the binoculars harder.

I stood and looked at him, unsure if he had heard me.

'Surely not?' he whispered, almost under his breath.

'Well, yes,' I said, somewhat surprised at his question, to my question. 'I think we're ready and...'

'Ooh hello gorgeous', he cooed, cutting me off. 'You're back early this year.'

The man couldn't care less, and I knew then, I was in the clear.

And so, I had waited for a clear evening and messaged her at work during the slow grind of the early afternoon, suggesting an evening walk and then maybe a quick drink in the pub. I left it open, deliberately nonchalant and vague, knowing all too well that we would be drinking late into the night, breathlessly toasting our future, teasing each other, debating when to announce our 'news'.

I had got to the park early and briefed Max. I hid the hamper under the bench and messaged her to say I'd meet her at the entrance. I waited, lurking by the gates, as sweaty runners and bearded dog walkers slipped past. Finally, she arrived. She was talking to her mother on the phone and so we walked up the hill together.

And as she talked, I fell into a stew of anxiety with each step.

The lonely passage of every man.

When we got to the top, she said goodbye to her Mother and stopped. The air was clear, the capital stretched out into the distance now bathed in the soft light of a tiring sun. It was perfect. And yet she started to talk; to talk about her day, about the meeting that had ended in a row with her biggest client. About the email she had written and left unsent in her outbox. I listened attentively, as is advised in the magazines; I knew she needed to air her day.

I needed to time my run.

Eventually she stopped, and I paused, savouring the moment, knowing I would look back on it fondly in years to come, before stooping down on one knee and asking my girlfriend of five years to marry me.

And she said, 'No.'

And that was not all she said. She then said it was all over. Us. We were finished. As I stared at the ring, not knowing where to look, she got up a full head of steam and said that she was amazed that I had got it so wrong. How did I not know? She said she had been unhappy for months, unsure of how to end it. All the engagement parties and weddings and long Sunday nights in front of the TV, she had realised that we had no future. The only thing keeping us together, she said, was the sticky break clause in our landlord's contract.

And with that she turned and walked away back down the hill.

I would never see her again.

'Do you still want me to play?' whispered Max through the brambles, having heard her every word.

'Go on then,' I said, staring at the hamper, 'it seems a pity to waste it all.'

I didn't know it then but, as I sat and stared out across the Cityscape eating a punnet of stuffed olives and drinking vintage champagne, all to the sound of Max's discordant cello; that was the day it all started to go wrong.

The day my life turned.

That said, quite how it ended up with murder, remains to this day, a real surprise.

CHAPTER I

'I just love the way they smell,' Phil yelled at me over the relentless thump of the house music.

I slowly sipped my beer and nodded.

Given Phil had just emerged from behind a velvet curtain that led to darker and more intimate parts of the club, I feared he wasn't talking about his tomatoes.

Phil was a client of ours, a very large and profitable client and Gerald, my boss, had organised a social. A night out. This had included a meal, at which Phil and I were sat next to each other. It was at the meal where Phil had spent a long time talking about his vegetable patch, specifically his home-grown tomatoes.

We were now in a strip bar, in a tight booth, with a bucket of bottled beer on the table, and a thrilling succession of ladies, leaning ever lower, and wanting to know if we were having 'fun'.

I worked for a bank.

I had never heard of the bank growing up, but it was one that had offered me a job at a time of mounting debts and few other options. And so, I took it. I joined the bank a long time ago though. It was a different time in my life. It was young and shiny; an age when I was still buying my girlfriend lacy underwear and corporate life was fresh and exciting.

'Have you…?' Phil asked, leaning in on me as he reached for a bottle of beer.

'Have I….?' I asked, once it became clear there was no more to the question.

'You know…'

He grinned and nodded the way of a passing hostess; one whose lithe and exaggerated movement suggested her tips did more than cover the rent.

'Oh…' I said, 'umm, no, err…. still warming up!'

I raised my beer and we toasted something, I am not sure what.

'Here, let me…' he then said, seemingly unable to think of anything else to say, before fumbling in his pocket for the fake cash that was the currency of such places.

'No, no,' I said, 'I couldn't possibly! We're taking you out. You're the client!'

There were unspoken rules.

'I insist,' he said, awkwardly stuffing the monopoly money into my hand.

I grinned back as best I could, knowing my options were narrowing fast. With an unsolicited loan I was now obliged to disappear behind the velvet curtain myself and indulge in fifteen minutes of awkward small talk as a naked girl I had never met before contorted herself on my lap.

It had been months since my failed proposal and emotionally I was still at sea. My girlfriend had moved out and taken half the furniture with her. There had been no discussion. My flat was now cold and empty; much like my life. I didn't like strip clubs, reeking as they do of stale middle-aged desperation, but there I was in a tight booth drinking overpriced Japanese lager with a man I barely knew.

I was in a bad place.

'Everything ok here?' a voice said, and I looked up to see my boss.

Gerald.

He too sat down and took a beer, and we all sat smiling and nodding, the music too loud to chat as a group and the scene, perhaps, too vivid to talk earnestly about the recent cautious comments from the Bank of England.

'Oh my God!' Gerald then exclaimed, squirming in his seat as the main stage changed shifts and the compere announced the arrival of an Amazonian beauty who quickly showcased a move on the pole that left little to the imagination.

Phil, fortunately, had lost his train of thought and I quietly squeezed out of the booth and announced I was going to the bar to buy more champagne. It was either more champagne or fifteen minutes behind the curtain desperately trying to avoid eye contact.

Champagne it was.

*

I had liked Gerald the moment I met him at my interview.

I had turned up for the interview at the bank lacking confidence that my CV had enough grit in it to yield a job. I lacked any sort of relevant experience but somehow, I had landed an interview and fully intended to make the most of it.

This despite having turned up to the interview in a suit, but no pants.

I was wearing no pants, as my pants were still wet on the rack in the kitchen of my dark and dingey ground floor flat. Riddled with a late bout of anxiety on the sticky prospect of being grilled on financial matters I knew so little about, I had forgotten to unload the washing machine in the feeble light of dawn. I had decided later, over a slice of dry toast, that no pants, were better than wet pants.

After pushing through the imposing revolving door and sliding past the dead eyes of the security guard, I stopped in the middle of the mock marble lobby and stared. The scene was a sea of business, stuffed full of serious, busy-looking people; all scrolling on their mobile phones, with harried looks and taut chops. The air was thick with the fog of expensive cologne and the walls were adorned with the bold, brassy prints of 'modern' art.

I had swallowed hard and approached the main desk.

'Good morning,' I said to the receptionist.

The face that looked up was efficient, pinched and without any trace of mischief. I was shown into a waiting room no different to the soulless space of the airport lounge. There were newspapers and bowls of free jelly babies. The air was scented with lavender and there was more artwork that lacked structure.

I sat and waited and, as I was thinking they had forgotten about me, a man appeared. He oozed the indifferent manner of an individual who had spent years struggling to fully get to grips with humility. His hair was slicked back, and he had his initials stitched on his shirt just shy of the pocket like you would if you wanted your friends to think hard about staying in touch.

This man thrust out a hand.

'Sorry, busy day,' he said. 'Busy making...'

'...money!' I said, a wicked grin spreading across my own chops.

I had seen the films.

I knew the script.

He looked at me with cold eyes.

'Making calls,' he said.

I immediately wanted to clarify that calls made money, perhaps even apologise, but the man, whose name I had forgotten, had set off for the lifts.

Clip, clip. Clip, clip.

Time.

Money.

I followed, an itch in the crotch slowing my pursuit.

We rode up the three floors in silence and then the lift door pinged open and we walked out on to the trading floor.

It was huge.

Hollywood has portrayed trading floors of investment banks to be noisy and chaotic places, full of testosterone and yelling. Noise. Wild places. Capitalism distilled into its purest form. I scanned the floor for any awkward looking dwarves, but there were none.

Hollywood lied.

The man ushered me into a glass office overlooking the floor and once I had been left alone, I peered out across the sea of screens. The crisp conditioned air was, I suspected, already on its third trip round the building, but the decks of screens, all showing the constant, colourful ebb and flow of the financial markets, offered a glimpse into an exciting new world.

I scratched my groin as there was a loud rap of knuckles on the glass door and jumped and spun around and turned to face him for the first time.

'Gerald,' he said and thrust out a hand, a gold bracelet hanging loose off his wrist.

He had a deep tan and piercing blue eyes.

He oozed confidence.

I shook it and remember thinking his hands were so soft.

So very soft.

*

By now it was late, how late I didn't know. Time had an uneasy habit of moving at a different speed when so far underground in Soho's clubland.

Phil was back behind the velvet curtain and, as far as I was aware, the two other clients, whose names I had forgotten, had gone home.

Gerald sat opposite.

The table was littered with empty glasses and bottles. It was a mess. So too was Gerald. His lips were wet and loose, his eyes told their own story. A dark story. I could only guess what they had seen. He was a different man to the polished executive who sat in front of his screens and directed traffic at the crossroads of high finance.

The music made it hard to hear, but what he said next – seemingly so innocuous – would change my life forever.

'Listen, can you pick up the tab, I'm going to slip off.'

I sat up in my seat and he leant forward and put his hand on my arm.

'And use your personal card, not the corporate one. You know what the fun police are like. Don't worry, you know who signs off your expenses...'

He winked and grinned.

I felt uneasy. I didn't know what the bill would be. I didn't even know what had gone on the bill and whilst I was doing well at work, the mean-fisted credit team at my bank still liked to keep a tight hold of my finances.

The student debt had taken a long time to clear.

But I knew I had no choice.

'Sure boss, no problem,' I said.

'Good lad.'

And with that he disappeared.

When the bill did arrive, in a surprisingly bland wooden bowl, I took it and, as nonchalantly as was possible given its size, offered my card to the now indifferent hostess. A bill paid by card offered no immediate financial upside for her and, as I was clearly the last man standing, she had her mind on a cup of cocoa and a hot bath.

'Do you have another card?' she asked.

I did my best to stay professional.

'Has it not gone through?' I mumbled.

'No.'

'Maybe you could try it again?' I suggested, 'the other one is the family joint account.'

I grinned, but she and I both knew my heart wasn't in it. She eyed me coldly, as the machine tried to find the broadband signal, taking me at face value. In her eyes, I saw, I was a bad person.

The machine finally started to whirr, and I let out a whistle of air.

'Thanks,' I said, as she handed back my card, 'and you get back home ok.'

She half smiled, perhaps thinking I was just another lonely man, before dropping the receipt into the bowl and returning to the safety of the bar.

I looked at the receipt.

BESPOKE TAILORING, CONDUIT STREET.

It made sense.

The bill would have matched the receipt for a couple of tailored suits.

The owner was clearly clever and knew his clientele.

And it was the owner of that tawdry, velvety den of stale sexual frustration who, after an unsavoury twist of events, I would later try to kill.

CHAPTER II

When I first started working at the bank, I found it daunting. I didn't know the routine. I didn't know the people, the politics, or the unique language. In a bank, one which I quickly discovered was packed full of salty ambition and epic egos, it took time to feel the mood and figure out what was what. As the months and years flicked by though, far from the feelgood principles of the company's earnest mission statement, what I found was a hot house of human conflict.

And the pace was intense.

Whilst I started knowing nothing, I quickly learnt that to survive I needed to smile and nod and look serious. Very serious. Making money was a serious business. We all sat in long rows, hemmed in by screens, stuffed tight, cheek to jowl; all with the sole purpose of making money. Gerald would sit in front of his own bank of screens that flashed with stock prices and scrolling news headlines. He'd sit and bark at people, his eyes narrow, never leaving the screens, his knees jiggling up and down.

Always jiggling.

Up and down.

After the late night in the Soho strip joint watching brittle middle-class morals getting smashed by bottles of beer and six-inch stilettos, I was feeling fragile. Physically and emotionally. I nursed a large cup of coffee and hoped for a quiet morning.

BANK OF ENGLAND SLASHES GROWTH FORECAST

The headline lit up the tape.

Gerald jumped.

It was a surprise.

We, like the market, had been expecting the Bank of England to grin, and tell us that economic growth was looking peachy.

It turned out; it wasn't.

'SELL BANKS! Gerald yelled. 'Pick up your phones and tell your clients to SELL THEIR BANKS!'

I scrambled for my phone and dialled, frantic and wide eyed. I needed to be seen to be verbally pulling the fingernails off my clients. They needed to trade, and trade through us so we would get to the ring the commission.

I dialled a familiar number.

'Hello?' said my mother.

'Do you own any banks?' I shouted.

I shouted, as I needed to be heard.

'You have to stop this,' my mother said.

I ignored her, as I always did.

'Growth is slowing,' I said, 'bad for banks. Sell them!'

'Stop it. I have had enough!'

'How many do you want to sell?' I raised my voice a turn.

Gerald cocked his head.

'Ten million?'

'The cat's gone missing.'

'You want to sell ten million RBS?'

'I think your father has killed it.'

'No, speak to the trader. Call him. Yes, the price on the screen!'

Gerald winked.

'He hates it. It craps on his vegetable patch.'

'And Barclays?'

'Oh, *THERE* you are!'

'You own some Barclays?'

'The cat's alive!'

Gerald was now smiling.

Smiling at me.

'Yes of course! Sell them too! Rotten loan book. Sell all of them!'

I heard a voice shouting at my mother in the background.

'It's him again,' she said, 'I don't know… he's saying he wants me to sell all the banks.'

'Happy to be of service,' I said.

I smiled back at Gerald.

'Your father says you're a disgrace and an

embarrassment to the family,' my mother muttered.

'Lunch? Yes, of course. Send me some dates,' I said.

'I will. Maybe Sunday? I also need you to fix my Wi-Fi.'

'Sounds great!' I said.

My mother sighed.

'Why couldn't you have been a vet?'

I hung up and grinned at Gerald.

I knew it was wrong. I knew my father would walk me round his raised beds and talk about his disappointment in what I had become, but Gerald's intensity was frightening and all consuming. For him, nothing mattered but the market. He rarely ate. He would tell his assistant that he needed coffee, and a stray underling, sometimes myself, would be dispatched to the kiosk to buy him a double macchiato.

Always a double macchiato.

One day, a day when the market was in freefall after a bank sheepishly admitted that they had run out of money, I lost count of how many macchiatos he drank. Sleep would have been impossible. Not that he did. He came in early the next morning with blood shot eyes and told me, in a hurried, furtive manner as I sat at my desk flicking more inadmissible receipts into the bin, to buy guns and gold.

I nodded.

'Yes, gold and guns, of course,' I had said.

As the day wore on, activity on the desk waned. The share prices of the banks steadied, and lunch beckoned. With the receipt from the strip club in my hand I knew I needed to pick my moment. I picked up a report on the reasons why some feverish analyst thought our clients ought to be buying a retailer who overlooked the opportunity offered by a decent website and sat and spun on my chair. This way and that, watching Gerald.

When he hung up the phone, I moved quickly.

'That was some night,' I said quietly, standing next to his desk, knowing that I was being watched. Anyone who spoke to Gerald would be watched by shiny eyes from across the trading floor, liable in the corridors and musty air of the print room to later be the topic of idle gossip. That I knew, but I also needed my expenses paying.

I slipped the receipt onto his desk.

His eyes glanced down and then returned to the screens.

'I'll see to it,' he said, just as quietly.

With nothing more to follow, I knew if I loitered it would grow awkward.

'Thanks boss,' I muttered, the words both grubby and thick. He and I had bonded. We were on the same side.

Or so I thought.

*

A few days later, I decided to take the day off. I needed some space. I needed to escape the heat and muscle of the trading floor and so I took an early train down to the coast. I walked the cliffs sucking in the fresh, salty air. I had fish and chips for lunch with a flock of beady-eyed seagulls for company, and then

I got the train back to town.

Food for the soul.

In wanting to escape the desperate rat race of City living, I had left my phone behind. When I got back to my flat, I took a shower and, with my spirits refreshed and my complexion ruddy and weather-beaten, I put a large lasagne in the oven and finally felt ready to log back in to life.

It was then that I discovered the news.

I had messages from work. From friends. There were missed calls from numbers I didn't even recognise. I don't know how many messages there were, as I stopped looking after I had pieced together what had happened.

After fetching a gin and tonic, I sat down at my small kitchen table, opened my laptop, took a deep breath, and started to read the stinging tabloid 'splash'. It wasn't, what I'd call, a balanced piece. The photos were unbecoming, as the picture editor intended.

My phone rang.

It was an old school friend.

'You dirty *dog*!' he said without introduction.

I thought I'd be irritated, but in my time of public humiliation I found it reassuring to hear a familiar voice, despite that voice seemingly trivialising my sticky predicament.

'Did you know there were cameras in there?'

'No,' I replied.

'Did you speak to the reporter?'

'No.'

'Is it all true?' he asked.

'No, it's not all true,' I said.

'Was it better than Budapest?' he asked, tentatively.

Budapest.

That was a long time ago, when we were both young and naive to the darker ways of the grown-up world. We had gone inter-railing during the summer holiday after leaving school and Budapest had opened our eyes to what was possible with hard currency.

'No, it was nothing like Budapest,' I said, letting the words drift a little. 'Listen I didn't even want to go to the club.'

'Of course, you did,' he said.

'What?'

'Sure, you did. How long have you been single now?'

'A few months,' I replied.

'Have you been on any dates?'

'No.'

'Have you spoken to any girls outside of work?'

'Umm…'

I thought about saying something but didn't. I didn't want to get into an argument trying to defend myself, not to him.

Of all people: Manilla Mike.

I hung up.

HANDS IN THE TILL! yelled the headline.

The article went on to explain the *'shocking behaviour'* of two *'greedy financiers'* who *'went crazy'* with girls and champagne. The photo of me wasn't good. I was in the booth and appeared to be leering at a passing hostess. The angle was awful. Phil was next to me, but you couldn't see his face and so the world did not know it was Phil. Enough of the world clearly knew it was me, but for those who didn't, my name appeared in the first paragraph. I had, according to the *'frightened waitress'* paid with a card from a *'posh private bank'*.

I finished reading the article and it appeared my name was the only name mentioned. The photos also had just the two of us – Phil and me – Gerald and the others were not in the frame, any frame and, as far as the reporter was concerned, were not even in the club.

It was just me, and Phil.

There was, in addition to the main piece covering off events *'in the early hours of the morning'*, an interview with the girl Phil had spent several hours with behind the velvet curtain. She was photographed at home in slippers and a cardigan. Her house was bright and clean and tidy, with enough bric-a-brac of driftwood and small ceramic dogs to open a shop. Her cat lay curled up on a bed in the corner.

It was suburbia at its best.

'He wanted to touch me,' she was quoted as saying.

Neither she, nor the reporter, had felt it necessary to make it clear whether she was talking about me, or Phil.

'And he said I smelled nice.'

I closed my eyes.

This was bad.

I didn't know how bad, however, until the next morning when I arrived at work. I kept my head down as I walked across the floor, but there were wolf whistles from the traders who were in early, flicking through the Racing Post and waiting for the market to open. I waved back but didn't look up.

The desk was empty, bar Gerald.

'We need to talk,' he said, before I had even sat down.

It was inevitable.

'How did this happen?' I asked him, after we had slipped into one of the glass-fronted meeting rooms adjacent to the trading floor.

'I don't know,' he said, tapping a finger on the table.

'The club must have tipped off the reporter,' I said, thinking aloud. 'They must have known we worked for a bank, or something, and then tipped the guy off.'

He stared back at me.

'Yes, I suppose they did.'

Silence.

'Listen, the brass is in a right stew on this,' he said leaning forward. 'Although the bank is not named in the article, it probably won't take long for it to get out given they know your name. And you know the rules about client entertaining. This sort of thing is just not allowed. New York has seen it and they want blood.'

I feared there would be repercussions.

'Have you spoken to Phil?' I asked.

Phil was his client.

'Yes, I did,' he said. 'He's very worried.'

'Why? You can't tell its him from the photo. And he's not named.'

'You haven't met his wife,' Gerald replied.

'He's married?'

'He is, and she buys his shirts.'

I wondered what supper at Phil's had been like last night. At least I was single and lonely and so, perhaps, with an understanding audience, could explain why I might end up in such a moral pickle in the early hours of weeknight.

He had no safety net and it was a long way down.

'You need to see HR,' Gerald went on. 'There is a Tribunal scheduled for this morning.'

'On my own?' I asked, frantically trying to assess the implications.

'No, I'll come with you,' Gerald said.

'But you weren't named in the article?'

'As your line manager,' he said, dryly.

I then started to see the picture. It was me. Just me. I was being singled out. As far as HR was concerned, it was all me. I shifted in my seat and Gerald fiddled with one of his cuff links.

'What about you?' I said, 'you were there…'

'Listen, we can't go there,' he snapped back. 'We

need to contain this. I'll do what I can. I know Head of HR well, and I'll put in a word. Don't worry. The Tribunal is just a box ticking thing. The bank needs to be able to say that you have been disciplined.'

'They only had my name because you asked me to pay the bill,' I said, sharply.

'You should have paid in cash,' he shot back. 'Always pay cash, and then there is no trail.'

He then offered his hands up in the air, palms facing up, his expression light and innocent.

'What time is this Tribunal?' I asked, needing to get out before I said something I would regret.

'11am,' he said, 'and don't worry, I have your back.'

He reached forward and squeezed my arm, just like he did in the club.

I looked up and nodded.

'Thanks, boss.'

*

I was drunk.

I knew I was drunk, as I was talking to a stranger in a bar. I didn't know the man, we had no history, and yet I was talking to him, at the bar, just like they do in America. As it turned out this man was American, which explains why he was willing to talk with me in a bar, despite not knowing me.

'I can't believe he said that?' drawled the man, shaking his head 'and he was there all night?'

He threw his neck back and lobbed another peanut

into his open mouth.

'It was his idea,' I said softly, staring into my pint of beer, 'they were his clients.'

'So, they fired you?' he asked.

'No, not yet,' I replied, 'I've been suspended, but I think they will. It's inevitable.'

The words felt loose in my mouth.

After the Tribunal I had stumbled out of the building and walked the wet streets as dusk fell. I ended up in a small, traditional pub, gripped by the slow tick-tock of an old grandfather clock. It had curled beer mats pinned to the walls, stale sausage rolls on the bar, and this American man from Wisconsin who was sat at the bar wondering why no one wanted to talk to him.

Welcome to England.

The Tribunal had been a shock. It was not what I expected given Gerald's sugary pep-talk before it. Having waited outside at the allotted time, Gerald and I had been called into the small stuffy room where we sat down in the two vacant chairs facing the panel.

The panel consisted of one man in a grey flannel suit and two intense women who positively hummed with excitement. The opportunity to fire bankers who went to strip bars was, possibly, the reason they worked in HR in a large bank.

There was no time, or appetite, for small talk.

'This is very disappointing, and obviously unacceptable,' the man began, his voice a little hoarse. He spoke slowly, deliberately choosing every word. He had clearly done it all before. He then paused and took a sip of water, letting the silence do its thing.

I sat and concentrated on breathing through my nose, like the self-help books tell you.

This man then went on to describe the lurid details that appeared to have been lifted straight from the newspaper and digressed into a long and rambling description of the expected standards of employee behaviour. One of the ladies then went through the compliance manual, picking out numerous articles that had been breached. The other lady just sat and stared and played with a curl of her dyed blue hair, radiating passive aggression.

Eventually they stopped.

'Have you got anything to say?' asked the man, finally looking up from his pad, flexing his long, cold fingers.

I stood up and rubbed my chin and coughed to clear my own throat.

'I have thought hard…' I started.

'Not you,' he said, cutting me off abruptly, 'Gerald.'

I sat back down slowly, looking at Gerald. Perhaps he had squared it all already. Lined the ducks up. He said the Tribunal was largely for show; only the Tribunal panel didn't look like the sort to just tick the boxes.

Gerald stood up.

'I am appalled at this behaviour,' he started, 'and I am deeply embarrassed a member of my team would go behind my back like this.'

The panel nodded in agreement.

'I have always been very clear with them with regards to their behaviour and their responsibilities…'

I couldn't believe what I was hearing. My chest started to tighten and the air thinned. I struggled to breath. I swore at him, as best I could, under my breath.

'…the bank has a reputation, and one we all need to protect. I know the client involved, I know him well, and I have already apologised to him, for being put in such an uncomfortable position.'

Far from having my back, Gerald was throwing me under the bus.

When he finally finished, he had the panel where he wanted them. I was told I was suspended for two weeks, pending a final decision, and ushered out of a side door where Bob, the friendly security guard from the lobby, was waiting to escort me out the back of the building.

Bob said nothing all the way down in the lift but, as he opened the door he whispered, 'Crazy place that club, brother. I hope you saw Cleopatra.'

I looked back at him, but his eyes had glazed over. Bob didn't see me go. He was behind a velvet curtain of his own.

'You know what?' said the American, after I had returned from the loo.

'Know what? I asked, fumbling with my flies.

I sat back down at the table, to which we had moved.

'Sue,' he said.

'Sue?' I asked.

'Yes, sue!'

I stared back at him, but the drink had blurred his edges. I was at a level of drunk where I needed to concentrate hard on what he said. His accent didn't help.

'I don't know Sue,' I finally muttered, shaking my head.

'Are you serious?' the American asked.

'Yes, I've never met her.'

He then roared with laughter. Spit flew from his open mouth. Spit and little bits of half bit peanut. He slapped the table hard and started to choke. I reached out a hand to grab his shoulder.

'Are you ok?' I asked.

'You British.... you're so *naive*!' he wheezed.

I didn't follow him. He too must have been drunk. Two drunks talking, but neither knowing what the other was talking about.

'Lawyer,' he finally wheezed, 'get yourself a lawyer and threaten to sue.'

He gasped once more before sucking down half a pint of warm bitter.

'Sue as in *sue,*' I said, my brain slowly putting the pieces together.

'Threaten them,' he said, his tone lower, 'banks don't like this kind publicity. So, threaten them. Any half-decent lawyer should get them running hard with a case like yours.'

I then saw it like an American would. It was brilliant. I'd threaten to drag them down into the gutter with me.

'Leak their name to the newspapers,' I said, placing too much emphasis on the last word. I leaned in and tickled the man's tight beard. 'Of course. Yes. What a brilliant idea!'

He stared at me, and then started to laugh again.

'Not the bank, you limey fool. The client!' he said.

Phil.

He was right. There was no way Gerald would want Phil compromised, not when he bought so many of the bank's flabby deals.

It was now my turn to laugh. And how I laughed. After seeing a long, dark tunnel, I now saw light, a brilliant white light; and the American and I hollered, and fist pumped like it was the half-time show of the Superbowl.

'Can you two keep it down, please?' called the barman, a man with the sad, jowly face of a Basset Hound. 'Have some consideration for the other customers,' he added in the flat tone of, perhaps, a basset hound explaining to his owner why it was not such a good idea to leave the cheese board out at night.

The American and I peered around the now, empty bar.

Tick.

Tock.

'Jesus Christ, I LOVE this country,' he howled,

banging the table, tears starting to roll down his cheeks.

It all got a little hazy after that. The high didn't last, as it never does. The drink soon took hold and exposed my fragile mental state. I was still sore from my split with my girlfriend, and the events at work had stuffed me further into the emotional weeds.

I remember being outside the pub, hugging the American, promising to visit him in Wisconsin.

I remember crying on the tube.

But that's about it.

Still, I left with a plan.

All I needed was a good lawyer.

*

It was cold in the bus shelter and I hopped from foot to foot trying to get warm, my eyes never leaving the door. It was late, and there was no longer a queue, but the security man was still there, standing. Watching. Ready for action.

I had been into the club earlier, just to check she was there. Which she was. I made sure I kept my head down though and avoided eye contact. I nipped in and nipped out, and then took up my post in a dark bus shelter on the opposite side of the road and waited.

I had found a lawyer. It didn't take long. I asked around a few friends and got the name of a man who supposedly knew how to grab employment tribunals by the balls. I had gone to see him too, in his plush office off Green Park, and he had sat and listened and scribbled in his big yellow legal pad as I told him my story.

'In my opinion, you have a strong case,' he said confidently, after I had finished.

I took a sip of my water.

'But you need to get a witness, to back up your story. Otherwise they'll deny it. They'll squeeze you. And squeeze you until your pips pop.'

I put my glass slowly back down on the table. I didn't want my pips to pop. I gazed at the lawyer with his features that were all a bit too close together. There wasn't enough room on his face. He also had the tight look of a man who liked bleach and cling film. And didn't like loose ends. Spontaneity, I would have wagered, was a strict no-no at home.

Still he was my guy and he was confident I had a case.

The only witness I could think of was the stripper Phil had taken a shine too. Hence, I was outside the strip club at 3 a.m. waiting for her to leave. The plan was to follow her home, and then I'd know where she lived. My lawyer said he knew a man who could do all this for me, but I wanted to see it through. And I was angry. I was also single and needed something to do at night. I needed to keep busy.

Eventually the bouncer started moving the ropes inside, and I could see the lights had gone on in the club. Girls started leaving. I moved closer, crossing the street and taking advantage of a large parking meter. I loitered, pretending to read the details of how much it would cost me to park for an hour, and then I spotted her, talking to the bouncer. I ducked down as she came out of the club and then followed her as she set off down the street.

At the next junction she stopped and hailed a passing taxi and jumped in.

I swore and ran, frantically searching for a taxi of my own. I couldn't let her get away. The lawyer said I had a small window to sue the bank, otherwise my case would go cold.

As the lights at the junction turned green another taxi popped up from a side street. I almost missed it but flagged it down and jumped in.

'Where to Guv?' the driver asked, in the genial tone of a seasoned cabbie.

'Follow that car!' I yelled, jabbing a finger at the black cab pulling away from the lights.

'Good one mate!' he said, laughing, 'haven't heard that one in a while.'

He grinned.

I growled.

'Just drive,' I spat.

Traffic was, as you'd expect for the late hour, light and it was easy to follow her car. We headed south, hitting a main artery and picked up speed. Large box retailers flashed past, full of billboards selling stuff we don't need. The road signs quickly had names of places that I knew lived far beyond the tube map. Eventually we hit the suburbs and the car turned off and into the dark warren of streets.

We followed it through slumbering neighbourhoods until it parked up in a quiet cul-de-sac. We rolled to a stop at the curb, keeping a safe distance and both watched as she got out. The driver whistled as she leaned in through the passenger window to pay the fare and her coat ran up her thighs to expose, through her leggings, a tight pair of professional buttocks.

'Oh-la-la,' he whispered.

She then tapped the roof of the cab and turned and walked up the drive to number three.

Number 3, Squirrel Close.

So easy.

I thought about going in after her, but I knew it was too late. I needed to talk to her, I needed to persuade her to rat on Gerald and save my job. I needed her to be on my side.

'Take me back to town,' I said, slumping in the back seat.

I saw the driver look at me in the rear-view mirror, a face as full of questions as faces get, but he said nothing. I knew optically, it didn't look very good, but I didn't care.

By the time I got back home, dawn was breaking.

Fortunately, I didn't have to go to work.

*

The lawyer said he could post it, but I insisted. I wanted to deliver it by hand. I wanted to see the man's eyes as I served him with my writ.

The letter contained the legal details of why, unless the tribunal brushed the whole sorry affair under the carpet and I could return to work, I would be suing the bank. It also, in clever legal speak, offered a sinister suggestion that Phil's name was very close to appearing in a Sunday tabloid splash of his own. The language used was sharp and uncompromising, full of clever structures and varnished with confidence.

Holding it as I waited outside the bank, I felt charged.

'What are you doing here?' a voice said from behind me.

I turned around to see Bob, the security guard who had shown me out. Bob who kept Cleopatra in mink gloves.

'Ah, morning Bob,' I said.

'You shouldn't be here,' he whispered, 'I ought to call you in.'

'Call me in Bob?' I said, 'what are you, the LAPD?'

Bob laughed.

'Anyway, I won't be long, I am just here to give this to that slimy stoat who runs HR.'

I tapped the letter in my hand and grinned a grin that lacked any warmth or mirth. It was the menacing grin of the African warlord or gimlet-eyed racketeer, or neighbour who dumps his grass cuttings in your wheelie bin.

Bob knew the game.

'He's in the shop next to the tube,' he said, nodding his head. 'I just saw him go in.'

I squeezed his shoulder.

'God bless you Bob.'

This was even better: neutral ground.

I walked quickly back to the tube station and stopped outside the shop that stood next to the steps that led down to the rattle and grime of the trains. I peered through the glass and there he was in his cycling gear, zipped and clipped with enough high visibility kit to divert passing aircraft. He was stooped over by the counter and so I slid in and idly flicked through the tie rack, watching my quarry. He soon stood up, a pair of grey socks and a three-for-two box of pants in his hand.

Impulsively I struck.

A man buying pants was vulnerable, that I knew.

It was very basic behavioural psychology.

I moved quickly and ghosted up behind him and, as he fumbled for his wallet muttering to the sleepy sales assistant that he'd packed in a hurry and forgot the 'essentials', I slapped the letter down hard on the counter.

Both jumped.

'See you in court,' I said, leaning in on him, like the bailiffs do.

He started and recoiled, his lip wobbled, and his bike helmet slipped back to leave him with a slightly startled look.

I turned to the sales assistant and flicked a look at the pants.

'Same deal on ties?' I whispered.

He shook his head.

'Shame,' I muttered and then turned and left, without looking back.

*

I felt too conspicuous. There was nowhere to hide,

nowhere to lurk. And indeed, if I did lurk, given it was Saturday morning in a residential area, it wouldn't be long before a curtain twitched and a couple of fresh-faced, community officers appeared.

I was back at Squirrel Close.

The plan was to wait for her to leave the house, then follow her and find an opportunity – perhaps in a coffee queue or empty train carriage – to speak to her and explain my desperate position.

A couple of boys were kicking a ball in the street and after I had thumped it back for the third time, one of them approached me.

'You don't live round here,' he said, dancing about like small boys are prone to do.

'No,' I said.

'What are you doing then?' his friend asked.

Hop.

Hop.

I looked around at the nearby houses. They were all so close together and I was consumed by the feeling of being watched. I needed to get away from them. The last thing I needed was a scene.

'I sell double-glazing,' I said, thinking the kids would quickly get bored and return to their game.

'Where is it then?' the taller one asked.

'Where's what?'

'Your double-glazing,' said the other.

They both squinted at me, puzzled looks all round.

Hop.

Hop.

'Umm, it's....' I was sinking.

'And where's your car? If you don't live here, you must have driven here?'

'It's at the depot,' I said, anxiously looking up and down the street.

'What? Your car?'

'No, my double-glazing,' I snapped.

I needed to leave. I needed to escape from them. They were asking too many questions.

Just then the door to Number 3 opened, and she came out.

I started to panic.

'Will you two just piss off,' I muttered and started to walk away.

The boys, though, saw straight through me.

'He's after Cleopatra,' they yelled. 'He's stalking Cleopatra!'

My mind was racing.

So, Phil's girl was Bob's Cleopatra, which perhaps explained Phil's behaviour given Bob's obvious approval. I knew if I had any chance of following her, I needed to lose the boys and I risked breaking into a jog.

They were now cackling with laughter.

'PERVERT!' one of them yelled after me.

A door to one of the houses then opened and a large man walked out with the gait of a real-life bailiff.

He had no hair, a thick neck and tattoos befitting a hooligan or D-list celebrity.

'Oi!' he shouted.

I quickened my pace.

'OI, come here…!'

Louder.

My back started to sweat. I needed yards. Metres. I needed to put in some distance between me and the bailiff. He was a big man, but he looked like he moved well on his feet. I half turned, expecting to see him pounding down the street after me.

'PERVERT,' the boys chorused.

But the man was pointing at the boys.

'Oi, you two…. get in here and finish your chores,' he bellowed.

And with that, the boys picked up their ball and disappeared inside. I slowed to a stop and watched them go.

One of them, the taller one who kept asking me all the questions turned and, as the bailiff disappeared into the garage, aimed an obscene gesture at me. Without thinking, I flicked back an obscene gesture of my own.

It was childish, and immediately satisfying.

*

I skipped on and caught up with Cleopatra, keeping a safe distance and followed her down to the train station where we hopped on a fast train heading into town. The carriage was too busy to make contact, and in any case, she was tied up in headphones, so I stood by the door with my collar up and scrolled through the news feed on my phone. I couldn't concentrate though, I was too hot, and I had too much adrenalin still in my system.

When we reached town, she zipped off and I struggled to keep up. Down the escalator, onto the tube, three stops: off.

We came up in a trendy part of town littered with fashion boutiques and coffee shops full of moody looking baristas. It was easier in a crowd and I followed her with increasing confidence. She appeared to be dawdling, though, killing time. She'd go into shops and wander about and then slip out, without buying anything. She never settled, and I couldn't get close enough to strike up a conversation.

I grew frustrated.

She then checked her watch and set off, eventually turning into a restaurant which had floor-to-ceiling glass walls. I saw her speaking to the front of house who smiled and showed her to a table by the window.

Lunch.

I quickly found a bench across the street with an easy line of sight of her table. I sat and waited and watched but nothing happened, and so nipped off to buy a sandwich. The restaurant looked like it indulged its guests. The thick white tablecloths and minimalist décor spoke of tiny portions, expensive wine and a lack of humour.

She was settling in.

When I got back to my bench, a tramp was making

camp. He shuffled about muttering and swearing to himself, moving his big plastic bags and generally making like a dog about to sit down. I managed to claim the end of the bench as my own. The open 2-litre bottle of cider spoke of a man who had lost his way.

I opened my egg sandwich and resumed my watch.

'Jesus Christ!' I muttered.

I couldn't believe it.

'Frank,' the tramp said, holding out a grubby hand.

I saw Cleopatra was now sitting with a man.

'What?' I said, turning to the tramp.

'Frank,' he said.

'What are you on about?' I replied.

'Sorry, I thought you said you were….'

His voice tailed off.

I scoffed and turned back to see Phil talking and Cleopatra leaning in on the table, her chin resting on her hands as she gazed across the table at him. He flayed his arms, and she roared with laughter.

It was all too cosy.

Phil?

What were they doing together?

'I don't understand,' I said out loud.

Too loud.

'Me neither,' said the tramp. 'Not since my wife ran off with my brother.'

He picked up his cider.

As I tried to pull my thoughts together and come to terms with what Phil was doing having lunch with Cleopatra, my phone rang. I looked at the screen and saw it was my lawyer.

'Hello,' I said.

'*You got to know when to hold them,*' he sang tunelessly.

'What?'

'*…know when to fold them, know when to walk away, know when to run…*'

'What do you want?' I said, irritated.

The tramp drank more cider and stroked his stubble.

'They've folded,' he said, 'the bank. They sent a letter saying that your suspension is lifted, and you can go back to work. It worked! We won!'

I bit my lip and mulled the developments.

'Hello?' said the lawyer, 'are you still there?'

I was still there but I wasn't listening.

Phil and Cleopatra were both now standing. They had been joined by another guest. If seeing Cleopatra and Phil joking over aperitifs and breadstick nibbles had been a shock, the sight of the man now embracing them and back slapping and settling down to what had the makings of a long celebratory lunch, left me speechless and dangerously short of breath.

'Hello? Are you alright?' said the lawyer again.

But I didn't hear him. I couldn't speak. I couldn't even move. All I could do, was watch as Gerald flagged down a passing waiter and ordered the table a magnum of pink champagne.

*

'You found him on the balcony?' I said, passing the cider back to Frank.

He nodded.

'Naked?'

'Hmmm.'

I stared out across the road over to the restaurant that had long since closed. It was starting to get dark.

'What did you say to him?' I asked.

'I asked if he was cold and whether he wanted to borrow a jumper or something,' Frank said, his eyes distant, his mind raking over the hot coals of betrayal. 'He was still my little brother.'

'He was shagging your wife?' I said, increasingly souped up at Frank's desperate story.

'I know, perhaps I was in shock or something.'

After seeing Gerald in the restaurant, I had folded into a bit of a tizz. The rage I felt inside was intense, white hot; and I had stood and paced and muttered and swore. I didn't know how, or why, but I knew I had been set up.

And yet, whatever angle I looked at it, I couldn't see why. Gerald's presentation in front of the pallid Tribunal was bad, but in the context of what I saw tucking into a mixed seafood platter to share, it was almost irrelevant.

After I let out a throaty roar, a boiling cocktail of anger and frustration, Frank finally spoke.

'Let it out,' he said, 'let the fire burn.'

His voice was low and coarse, but the words were surprisingly clear. There was real depth to them. He didn't look at me, he just sat on his bench with his head bowed, but I could sense that he had been there.

Eventually I sat down.

'Is your fire still burning?' I finally asked.

'It never stops,' he said and passed me the cider.

We then drank, Frank and me. We finished off his bottle, and I went back to the corner shop and bought two more. And we talked. Man, to man. And he told me about the day he left a client meeting and saw his wife walk into a smart hotel. He followed her in, and just caught sight of her jumping in a lift. He said he sat and watched the lifts and, when a passing waiter asked if he would like a drink, he had started on the whisky sours.

Several hours later, after bribing the housekeeper, he burst into room 177 to surprise his wife who was naked on the bed; her modesty spared only by a bowl of diced fruit. The billowing curtains led him out onto the balcony where he met his brother. Also, naked.

Life for Frank as a successful corporate lawyer had then very quickly fallen apart, and now here he was on a bench, with me, drinking super strength cider.

He hadn't spoken to his wife, or brother, for nearly ten years.

'Nasty piece of work, this Gerald,' he said, after I had told him my own story of pickled woe.

'It appears so,' I replied, picking my words slowly,

still boiling inside from the afternoon's events.

'What are you going to do?'

'I don't know.'

I felt as though I had lost my moorings. It was all a mess. I didn't know what was happening.

Or why.

The lights were also swimming, and Frank sounded increasingly far away.

'Let's go and ask her,' he finally said.

'Ask who?' I said.

'Cleopatra,' he said, 'you know where she lives.' He glanced at his watch. 'It's still early let's go to her house and ask her what she knows.'

I stared at him as he stood up, wondering how he was still going. Frank had been drinking cider all day. Indeed, Frank had been drinking cider for close on a decade.

And so, I let go. I let Frank pack up and I helped him carry his plastic bags to the train station where we managed to get on a train bound for Cleopatra. And as so happens if you've drunk two-and-a-bit litres of mass-produced cider, we were suddenly outside her door in Squirrel Close.

Back at Number 3.

'Come on then,' said Frank, 'are you going to knock or am I going to have to do it for you?'

I sucked in the night air and looked at Frank, all stubble and crumpled fag packets.

I knocked.

There was the sound of feet, and then the rattling of a chain, and the turning of a key.

The door opened.

Cleopatra, wearing leggings, a tight top, and a novelty pair of slippers, jumped and slammed the door shut.

'Sweet mother of God,' he muttered, 'she's a sight.'

I knocked again.

'Go away, or I'll call the police,' she shouted through the letterbox.

It was then that I realised what we must have looked like. Frank hadn't slept inside for months, and I knew my eyes went red and wild when I had been drinking. We must have looked like trouble.

'Listen, I only want to talk,' I said, 'I need to ask you some questions. Please. It's to do with Phil and Gerald.'

Silence.

'Please!' I tried again.

The chain rattled, and the door opened.

Frank groaned.

'What do you want?' she said.

'Listen, I know this looks bad,' I said, nodding my head Frank's way, 'but I just want to ask you some questions, and then we'll go. You see, I work with Gerald.'

She crossed her arms, under her fabulous bosom and leaned on the door frame.

'Frank,' I said, knowing how wide his eyes were

likely to be, 'why don't you go and wait at the bottom of the drive.'

Frank tried to protest, but I pushed him away.

'OK, sorry about Frank. Nice chap. Used to be a lawyer. Fallen on hard times. Anyway, now listen, how do you know Phil?' I asked.

'Phil?' she said.

'Yeah, Phil.'

'Oh, he's a regular at the club I work at,' she said, 'I've sort of got to know him through that.'

'Know him?' I asked, sensing there was more. 'As in socially know him?'

She blushed.

'Are you two dating?' I asked, barely believing my own question.

'Oh, I don't know. I mean it's only been a few weeks. It's not serious or anything…' she tailed off.

'And what about Gerald?' I asked turning to see Frank picking through the bins.

'Gerald?' she said.

'Yeah Gerald.'

'It's funny you said you worked with him.'

'Why is that?' I asked, not seeing anything funny at all.

'I sort of work with him as well.'

'What do you mean?' I managed to ask, my stomach turning.

'Well, I don't really work *with* him. More, I work *for*

him. You see, he's my boss. He owns the club where I work.'

It all went very dark after that.

I don't remember getting home.

CHAPTER III

I sat and stared at Gerald sitting at his desk, laughing, dominating his space with seemingly not a care in the world.

I still couldn't believe what Cleopatra had told me. If seeing her and Phil together was a shock, the sight of Gerald in his crushed lilac jacket and ostentatious cravat was enough to plunge the mind into a dark pit of restless bewilderment.

He owned the strip club? Which meant he was taking clients there to feather his own nest. So why throw me to the wolves? What I had I done to him?

I was in a deep dark pit, emotionally bruised and questioning life's moral framework that I had always taken for granted. I was also aware that, in Gerald's eyes, I was very much seen as expendable.

And now I was back at work. The suspension had been lifted. The steamy team in HR had sent my lawyer a letter with a document for me to sign which essentially said that I promised never to drop Phil in it.

I signed my name with a flourish and a little smiley face.

Inside though, I felt empty.

I needed answers.

When I returned that first day, Gerald had said nothing to me.

He said nothing to me the day after that.

And the day after that, too.

Two weeks passed before he even acknowledged my presence.

'Morning champ,' he said, nonchalantly, easing past one morning with his gym back slung over his shoulder, as if nothing had ever happened. I said nothing and watched him go. I knew my future at the bank was over, but I couldn't not do something about Gerald.

He needed to pay.

That he would end up paying with his life, only came about due to an unexpected conversation with a fellow guest at a friend's wedding.

A wedding, at which, I also happened to meet my wife.

*

It is not unusual to meet a wife at a wedding. Lots of couples first clasp clammy hands in a pew or a sticky reception line up; or first grapple and grope for perfumed undies in a dark cloakroom, lips hot and sweet from the endless trays of cheap Sambuca.

What was unusual was that my wife had taken the opportunity, sometime over the lamb shank, to tell me that I was the most revolting man she had ever met.

'You are quite revolting,' she had said.

She meant it too.

She also appeared unconcerned as to who heard her view on me, and so the whole table had quietly exhaled and shifted from one soft bum cheek to the other.

I had first seen her in the church. She had been talking to a friend near the pulpit, where the camp Vicar would later deliver a thunderous sermon on the challenges of married life, suspicious as he might have been perhaps, of an establishment that still struggled to fully endorse his own carnal hunger.

She was impossibly beautiful.

She had such grace. She had poise, and charm. Her manner was one of vintage sophistication. Gorgeous. And yet she appeared too, to be a contradiction. Her face, when it caught the sun flooding the church, had such innocence. But her laugh! Her laugh was laced with mischief.

I gasped when I heard it.

No, no, it cannot be.

How?

Her beauty, I knew then, was mystical.

I was agog.

Spellbound.

I lost myself in the moment and was unable to avert my eyes.

My troubles evaporated.

It was no longer about Gerald and me; it was now about me and her.

Later, during the prayers, as the Vicar grieved the

moral and sexual squalor of modern society, I gazed across at her and weighed up my chances. They weren't good, and yet I didn't want to give up. I couldn't give up. I needed to believe. I needed to sober up after a loose usher's lunch, and later, after pudding, I needed a tailwind and a good band.

Amen to that.

'You are disgusting, arrogant, infantile, horrendous. Clearly single for good reason,' she had continued, not satisfied, perhaps, that she had fully made her point.

After being dumped by my girlfriend and betrayed at work, I was not in a good place, but my efforts to impress her had seen me brag and boast to the table. I teased and taunted the institution of marriage and ate my starter without using my hands. I had then forced a pregnant woman to do the same.

It was ugly.

And yet, strangely, I let her words wash over me.

The words meant nothing. I was hooked. I was all in. I was also drunk; the flow of champagne too thick to ever have had the chance of sobering up. The table was a blur, but she remained in focus.

My wife and I happened to be on the same table although she was, back then, a long way from being my wife. I didn't even know her name and so when I saw the seating plan, I didn't know. And then she was there, standing by her chair.

Standing next to my chair.

I had mouthed a quiet Alleluia at the camp Vicar who happened to also be on our table. I was going to wink, but held back, reluctant perhaps that a wink might elicit a quiet Alleluia of his own.

'Do you want that?' I had asked sometime later, as she toyed with her chocolate dessert, hoping to re-engage, hoping to move our relationship on.

On, and off the rocks.

And yet, I had leaned in too much. I was aware very late that I was listing; indeed, I was dangerously close to toppling onto her. I had then hung in the air, suspended, and alone. Very much alone. I don't know for how long.

I came to, to silence. The table stared. My wife was leaning back, recoiling from my undignified advance.

The Vicar muttered a soundless prayer.

After the meal I needed air and wandered outside the marquee. The night was crisp, and stars lit up the sky. As they should on such an occasion. I walked across the lawn and sat down heavily on a bench. I could see the figures dancing in the tent as the band leaned into another classic track off the playlist.

I felt lost and alone.

There was a shuffle behind me, and I turned to see the camp Vicar stumble out of the trees and onto the lawn. He stood there swaying and, having seen me on the bench, he came over and sat down.

He then pulled out a hip flask and took a long drink.

'You seem troubled,' he said, quietly, after he had finally swallowed and wiped his mouth on the back of his sleeve.

He passed me the flask.

I took a sip and gasped, smacking my lips and screwing my eyes shut.

It was not like anything I had ever tasted.

I suspect even Frank would have winced.

'Holy water,' the Vicar muttered, 'it takes some getting used to.'

We then both sat, watching the figures and shapes lit up against the wall of the marquee.

The Vicar then pulled out a thin cigarette and lit it with a match.

He flicked the match into the rhododendron bush.

'Have you spoken to God?' he asked.

I shook my head.

Given all that had been going on, it hadn't crossed my mind.

'Talk to me, tell me about it,' he said, leaning back, pulling hard on his cigarette. He then leaned over and put the flask in my hand and made me take another sip.

It tasted no better, but his manner was so caring, his touch so light; without warning the dam began to crack and I started to talk.

I told him everything. I told him about my girlfriend. I told him about my proposal and my subsequent split. I told him about how I couldn't get my money back on the ring as the man in the sharp suit said it was not in the company policy to refund duds. And I told him about Gerald. About the night in the strip club and how I had been hung out to dry.

I started to sob.

I told him about how they were all in on it, but I didn't know how.

Or why.

The Vicar listened but said nothing.

When I finally finished, he took a long drag on his cigarette and then stubbed it out on the bench.

'This Gerald,' he said quietly.

'Yes?' I whispered, stifling another sob.

'This man,' he continued, staring out across the lawn, 'this man…'

His eyes, I noticed in the lights that hung high above the portaloos, had glazed over. And yet his tone, suggested a fire. A passion. I sensed he was being consumed by something else.

'This man,' he said, again, his voice rising slightly.

I wiped my eyes and pulled a hanky out of my pocket.

'He's not one of God's children,' he spat.

And then he turned, and leaned in on me, and grabbed my suit lapel. I caught the thick breath of neat liquor.

'Do you know what?' he asked, jabbing a finger into my chest.

I tried to lean back, but he was just there, in my space, I had nowhere to go.

'Do you know what you need to do?' he said, his

tone lower, his words spitting like pork fat on a grill.

'What?' I asked, not at all ready for his answer.

Not from him.

A holy man.

'You need to kill him,' he whispered.

'What?' I said, thinking I had misheard him.

'Kill him.'

'Kill him?'

'Yes,' he said, 'some lambs need to be slaughtered.'

He had then reached out and put a hand on my knee, which started off reassuring, but he kept it there too long. He then lunged at me with his wet lips. I leaned back, swaying out of the way and he collapsed into my lap.

The voices in the marquee rose, joining the band in a full-throated chorus.

It was all too awkward.

I needed to move and so I mumbled my thanks and got up and returned to the marquee. I was unsettled by the exchange and the Vicar's romantic go at me. The fresh air, and his bizarre suggestion had also sobered me up.

And so, I hit the bar.

Hard.

Later, I had to be pulled out of the drum kit on stage and I woke up in my hotel room fully clothed with the disapproving light of dawn licking the walls.

I had no memory of getting there.

I was immediately seized with the ice-cold fear of the wedding drunk and lay on my bed staring at the ceiling with the words of the Vicar ringing in my ears.

My pockets were also full of cheese.

*

I met my wife again a few months after the wedding, although, she was clearly not yet my wife. Far from it. Indeed, she was about as far away as wives get. She was still possibly a dream. Or delusion, as was proving the case. That she was my wife, might have been uncomfortable news to her, but news, fortunately, she did not yet know.

I met her again at a dinner party.

Whilst the Vicar's ungodly suggestion over how I took care of Gerald's future was a shock, as I played with the idea in my head, I was appalled to discover it was an idea that loitered. It refused to go away. I tried to reason with myself, but the more I saw of Gerald at work, making out as if nothing had happened, the more the Vicar's words gripped my mind.

Kill him?

It was outrageous.

The night I met my wife again I remember was a cold, wet night; bristling with hostility for the reluctant bachelor. Not a night for loping across London's crippled transport network to a maisonette in a far-flung borough, to talk about house prices with contemporaries struggling to make sense of a world of tax, jealousy, and so little holiday. But then, I mulled on the 28 bus, they too might loathe their boss, they too might seethe and spit with deadly rage late at night.

Who knew what would come out of a stolen cigarette on a cramped suburban roof terrace?

Ideas?

Collaboration?

Who knew.

As ever, with travelling across London, I was late.

'I'm so sorry I am late,' I said to the host as I shook his hand.

He had big, strong hands; good hands, I imagined, for strangling humans.

Such was my state of mind.

I left my reluctant host quietly re-arranging the umbrellas in the hall and I moved down the corridor and into the house; a house that was stuffed full of eager guests rubbing shoulders with African artefacts and photos that evoked a more youthful age full of happy-hours and floral bikinis.

I pushed my murderous musings to one side.

'Hi all! So sorry I'm late!' I said, my hands raised in the manner of the guilty husband caught rummaging through the au pair's knicker draw.

The conversations stopped as I was sized up and pigeonholed; like a bull at auction. I regretted wearing an old jersey with moth holes in it, as it could easily have been assumed that I had made no effort at all. A middle-class *faux pas* of quite giddy proportions.

'Do carry on!' I muttered, finally ending the silent stand-off.

I took a gin and tonic off the sideboard and gulped. My host, now loitering by the far bookcase, quietly matched me. He and I would silently get through the ordeal together. I did not recognise any other guests and before any of them could make an introduction I shuffled through and into the kitchen to say hello to my host's wife.

And there she was.

My wife.

Or wife to be.

And the other wife, my host's wife, was also there; not that I cared much for her now. Not now that my heart had started to thump and thud against my chest. I almost didn't recognise my wife; her hair was shorter, and perhaps lighter, although I couldn't be sure. It was, however, most definitely her. She was also wearing a delightfully tight pair of light blue jeans. So tight, I had trouble breathing.

The good news was that she recognised me. The bad news was that her face fell as she did.

'You probably won't remember, but we've met before,' I said, offering a hand, trying as bashful a look as I could muster.

She took it, a little reluctantly, but as I mocked my own sartorial miscue, there was the faintest suggestion of a smile. For me, that was enough. I sensed a glimmer of light and gulped more gin and offered to mash the potatoes sensing that this effort to woo, would need time and patience.

And luck.

And so, I mashed.

As they nattered I listened and mashed. And as I mashed, I gleaned that my wife was still single.

They were stunning words.

As fate would have it, we were once again seated next to each other down at the end of the table, away from the kitchen. We were boxed in and so for my wife, there was no escape. There was no opportunity, even, for her to help get up and clear away the plates.

She was stuck.

I was stuck.

'Where do you fish?'

Opposite me, sandwiching my wife, who was at the head of the table, was a man sent to make me look good. A bore. A man with mottled red cheeks and a nose heading the way of ridicule. And conversation, I was delighted to discover, as dry as stale bread.

'Fish?' I asked.

'Yes, fish,' he said.

My wife looked bored.

'Ponds,' I managed to say; not wanting to appear non-sporting, nor too did I want to misconstrue. 'And you?'

'Speyside,' he said in a haughty manner.

'Rod or net?' I asked, pouring the bore more wine.

'I beg your pardon?' he stammered.

'Rod or net? What do you prefer?'

He stared at me.

'I use a net,' my wife said, joining in. 'Not that sporting, I know, but it is *very* effective.'

Her eyes sparkled.

The bore pushed on. He tried to impress with stories of country houses, aristocratic connections and the suggestion of a vast wealth spirited away in opaque offshore trust structures. There was a vintage sports car, dogs, a Tuscan villa, a tailor in St. James's, velvet brogues and investments in 'property'.

'I have a portfolio of interests,' he said, moving closer in on my wife.

I kicked his shin.

Hard.

'Sorry!' I said, 'so clumsy.'

I grinned.

He didn't.

My wife grinned.

I clenched my fist and punched the air under the table and felt alive for the first time in years.

'Fine,' he said, nodding as I offered another bread roll.

Stale.

Like him.

There was, though, no mention of any actual work.

Sober, I now sensed from my wife's posture, that less was more. I sipped my wine and let him run. I let him jabber and bray and talk himself out. Deep into the mashed potato, there was a leak of a complicated family and a cool, distant father. He slowly started to pop at the seams.

'More red?' I asked pouring him more wine, tipping him over the edge.

He was of no concern to me. He was in the way. He was in between me, and my wife and I needed him out of the way.

Gone.

By pudding his mother's affair was being shared in delicious detail. Come cheese, he was found passed out in the downstairs loo. He had to be bundled into a taxi and sent home.

My wife was then mine.

Alone at the end of the table we mused on the often-unplayable ball that faced those offspring of the emotionally tight but financially endowed upper-middle class. We chuckled. We started to swap stories of childhood. Share snippets. Stolen glances into each other's lives. People started leaving, and yet she lingered. We helped clear up. We were the last two to leave.

At the door, heart thumping, I jumped into the deep black gorge so feared by all men.

'Would you mind if I asked for your number?' I had said, a little breathless.

She said nothing.

I thought I might cry.

As she reached the door, she turned.

'Have you got your phone?' she then asked.

I stared at her. What? My phone? I had asked her

for her phone number. Why would I ask for her number if I didn't have a phone? It didn't make any sense.

Games.

Women, and their games.

'Yes, of course, that's why I asked you for your number?' I said, revealing the dating shrewdness of a four-year-old.

'No, your phone. Give me your phone,' she said.

I fumbled for my phone and gave it to her. The display lit up and I saw her smile as she tapped in some numbers. Awed, I watched as she pressed a final button and I heard her phone buzz in her bag. I felt faint. Lost. And with that she was gone, no kiss, no squeeze of the hand. No nothing.

Gone.

I slumped on the bottom of the stairs, drained, emotionally bruised and a little light-headed at the prospect of a Saturday night dinner date and all it might entail.

*

I had left it a few days before phoning her. A few days wrought with agony and anguish and more uncomfortable dreams about feeding Gerald to pigs or pushing him into baths of acid.

I feared the number she had put in my phone was false. It was a way to fob me off, to escape, to get out of the house. And so, after much lip chewing, I phoned her. I phoned her up feeling clammy and uncomfortable. I got her voicemail so I left a message; a garbled, breathless message wondering if she was busy, suggesting a drink, perhaps supper, or possibly just a coffee. Or not, maybe nothing at all; it depended really, on what she was doing.

I spoke too quickly. I stammered and stalled. I had later thought about looking on the internet to see whether it was possible to somehow delete the message, but I didn't. It was futile, I knew that. Instead, I waited. Minutes felt like hours, hours felt like days. My phone remained stubbornly silent.

I waited some more.

It could have been the next day, or the day after, I wasn't too sure, given my perspective of time had become so warped by the silence, but she called back. No text message – no – a proper phone call, just like the old days. I was in the queue for the dry cleaning and, in my dizzy excitement, I answered her call.

'Hello?' I said.

It came out too loud, like a shout.

'Hello,' she said.

So soft and smoky. So, beautiful.

'Oh, hi!' I said.

'Hi,' she said.

We exchanged news. She had been to lunch with friends. I stuttered and stalled and told her I had been busy doing errands, old fashioned errands. It was a little vague, but I didn't want to tell her I was at the dry cleaner. The dry cleaner was so ordinary it spoke of a shallow puddle of a life and I didn't want her to think about me and shallow puddles.

And yet that, there, was the problem. The dry

cleaner. I had now reached the front of the queue and needed to produce my pink ticket to give to the man who appeared a little miffed, put out even, at me being on the phone. A sensitive soul. I didn't care though, as I was speaking to my wife; although neither he nor she, nor indeed I, at the time, had any idea that she was, in fact, my wife.

It was also hot. So very hot. The big dryers were spinning, round and round, as they do, and there were rows and rows of clothes all covered in clingy plastic wrapping. It was hot and claustrophobic, and I started to prickle with sweat. The queue behind me had now swelled, full of busy people with busy friends and busy things to do.

All so very busy.

'I have it,' I said, fumbling with my wallet.

'Have what?' she said.

'Nothing,' I said.

'You have nothing?' the man asked.

'No, I have it,'

'Have what?' she asked, again.

This wasn't going so well. I frantically emptied my wallet on the counter: credit cards, stamps, receipts, some Canadian dollars, a business card of some faceless man from a pub.

No pink ticket.

'I have the pink ticket,' I said.

'A pink ticket?' she asked sounding a little bemused.

We weren't married. We weren't, more was the pity, boyfriend and girlfriend. We hadn't even gone on date, a date that now, hung in the balance.

'No, no, no. No pink ticket,' I said.

'No pink ticket?' he asked. 'We gave you pink ticket.'

'I know you gave me a pink ticket!' I said, exasperated.

'When did I do that?' she said, equally exasperated.

'You need a pink ticket,' he said.

'I know I need a pink ticket,' I said.

'For what?' she asked.

'No pink ticket, no clothes,' he said.

'I need my clothes,' I said.

'Why are you not wearing any clothes?' she said.

'Yes! I have clothes!' I said.

'No pink ticket, no clothes,' he said.

And so, it went on some more. I became increasingly flustered, with hands rummaging in pockets and bags, busy people behind me watching like elderly relatives watch a disobedient child. I eventually found the ticket and slammed it on the counter and glowered. As the man went to get my shirts, I turned to face the crowd like a feisty mule, a crowd that had become one, united in their thin-lipped judgement of my rag-a-bag performance.

'Perhaps we could go for a drink next week?' I then asked, now strangely confident, my chutzpah fanned by the open hostility of the mob. It was, in a way, wildly liberating.

'Well, yes, that would be great. How about Tuesday?' she said.

POP!

My chutzpah started hissing air.

Tuesday.

The nothing day.

The graveyard shift.

Tuesday night; a night for curating oneself online, plucking it offline, or quietly sobbing into a bottle of cheap Chardonnay from the corner shop, unable to ignore the angry voices shouting at you that you will die alone, surrounded by empty bottles of gin and overdue electricity bills. Tuesday was not designed for dating, it being too early in the week to offer any great hope of romance. Even the wildest imagination could only hope for a brief kiss and a brush of breast outside a tube stop. Tuesday also offered an easy way out for the date that was heading non-stop to Coventry.

'Perfect!' I said and quickly hung up before she could change her mind.

A date! Who cared if it was a Tuesday? A Tuesday was better than a No-day. I picked up my shirts, tipped the surly front of house one full English pound and, strutted out past the mob.

*

'Can I get you a drink?' shouted the barman.

'No thanks, I had better wait,' I had replied, limply raising my tap water. The look on his face was somewhere between pathetic and sad.

Ten minutes passed.

'What would you like to drink?' asked the waitress.

'I'm expecting company,' I had replied, perhaps a little defensively. 'Maybe I'll just look at the menu.'

She passed me a sheet of the day's specials.

I wondered whether we would even bother with the menu? The date had been framed as a drink, not supper. Would supper be too much for a Tuesday date? I mulled the minefield of courtship. The dos and don'ts of the early encounter. It had been a while since I had had a date that called for new pants.

And then, she arrived.

She breezed through the door in a flurry of frosted night air in a vibrant, tight red coat, with rosy cheeks, sporting what looked like a dead stoat wrapped tightly around her neck. I was mesmerised. Such beauty.

The stoat turned out to be a fashionable neck warmer, bestowed to her from her late grandmother. She oozed chic sophistication and her eyes sparkled like the fairy lights that were strung up on the wall behind her. My right knee had started to wobble when I stood up to greet her.

Gin, I had quickly thought, as she slipped out of the red coat, revealing a pair of black trousers that clung to her thighs.

'Two gin and tonics please,' I had panted, barely looking up at the waitress, unable as I was to avert my gaze from my wife. 'And make them doubles.'

When the drinks arrived, the date took on an easy tempo. I asked about her job and her family and discovered a love of the outdoors. I asked questions.

Honest questions. Questions without mirth, or smut. Questions I thought, perhaps, that demonstrated a deep and thoughtful character.

I even quoted Martin Luther King.

'So, what is the best place in the world you have visited?' I then asked, hoping the question demonstrated a life backpacks, excitement and an easy familiarity with exotic lands.

'Ooh, tricky one,' she said. 'I liked Skegness, but it can't beat Scarborough. Yes, Scarborough first, then, Skegness. Then maybe Blackpool. Donkey ride heaven!'

I was caught short. I had not been expecting Scarborough. Or Skegness. Nor indeed, Blackpool. I had, I thought, opened a line of conversation that enabled an opportunity to bond on a deeper level, to swap tales, to fumble and grope for what it was that made the other tick. Yet I did not know her well enough to establish if she was joking. And she delivered it with such a straight face. Not a flicker across the mouth. No flash of the eyes. No nothing.

She toyed with her glass and I thought I saw a hint of smile, but the lights were too dim, and I was a gin and a half to the good. Or bad, depending on where you stood. I couldn't be sure. The silence started to become uncomfortable and I knew I had to say something. A fork in the road lay ahead: Coventry to the left, a mini break in the Cotswolds to the right. And so, I decided to go all in.

'I found Scarborough a little dated,' I said, trying to smile without giving too much away.

I too could be serious. I too could be fun.

'Oh, no. They've done it up. When were you there?'

'A few years back,' I said, relieved that I needn't hold my breath any longer.

'Did you ride the Dragon?' she whispered.

Again, not so much as a flicker of a smile. I'd need to play this one carefully. The Dragon could mean different things, to different people. And I was still not sure if she was joking.

'I didn't, no. It looked too big, too wild a ride,' I whispered back.

'I did,' she said, running a finger around the top of the glass.

Was she being suggestive? What was the Dragon? I thought she might have been flirting. Then I thought she wasn't. Now, the way she ran he finger around her glass, I was convinced she was. Up, down, up, down. I was on my own emotional dragon.

'Did you ride anything else?' I asked.

'In Scarborough, or Blackpool?' she said.

'What happens in Blackpool?'

'A friend once took me up the tower,' she said.

I looked at her closely. Down again. I didn't know what it meant. No one, I imagined, would enjoy being taken up the Blackpool Tower. However nice a friend.

'Did you enjoy it?'

'Just the once,' she said.

'You got taken more than once?' I said in shock and wide-eyed disbelief. I gulped more gin feeling as though I was living part fantasy, part nightmare.

All I knew was that I didn't want it to end.

She paused and then burst out laughing.

'Are you hungry?' she asked picking up the menu. 'Shall we order some food?'

'Ravenous,' I replied.

And I was too, and not just for the menu.

I caught the eye of the waitress and as my wife looked at the menu, I waved my hand at the waitress, beckoning her over. We were ready. We were ready for food. The date I wanted to tell her, was heading non-stop for the Cotswolds.

A mini-break.

With crisp white linen and a late check-out.

I knew, I was convinced, right then, and there, as I sat with glazed eyes and thudding heart that I had finally met my wife.

CHAPTER IV

The atmosphere at work slowly soured, as you might expect. I took to keeping a low profile and avoided Gerald. He occasionally smiled at me, but the smile was thin. Brittle. I chose not to react.

Now outside his circle, looking in, I started to see him for what he was: a nasty, spiteful bully. Vile. A man who relentlessly tormented his hapless minions. He was subtle though, and he was sharp on his HR policies, mindful never to overstep the mark. The bullying was sly, slow and relentless. Drip, by drip, he'd undermine those around him and drain their confidence.

It made me sick.

And angry.

The Vicar was right, I saw that Gerald had to die.

'Some lambs need to be slaughtered'.

There was, though, one man that even Gerald wouldn't touch.

Fox.

A.K.A 'The Fox'.

The Fox was old.

The Fox had been at the bank so long that one client refused to believe he was still an employee, convinced as he was that the Fox had died. He was cerebral and quiet. He spoke to few people and rarely bothered to attend any internal meetings, but when he did, people listened. He sat at the end of a row, his back turned, quietly whispering down the phone to his clients. He had one screen and barely looked at it.

I suspected Gerald longed for news that the Fox had been found dumped in a wheelie bin, naked, with barbed wire wrapped tightly around his throat, but he never spoke of it. Indeed, he never spoke of the Fox, it was if he didn't exist.

He never challenged the Fox, only ever those he had leverage over. Only those who he could control. He was, as many bullies are, both a bully and a coward.

And then there was Blanchard.

Blanchard was a different beast.

Blanchard had wormed his way in from some mid-level bank with a long foreign name, and once he had secured the job he, like many others, bought full bore into the political charade that shaped the perception of dim-witted line managers. He kow-towed to Gerald's whims and wishes and toadied up to those he knew that Gerald favoured.

Yet behind the obsequious façade I saw, in Blanchard, a flawed character with loose, low morals. His eyes were too close together. He fawned. He laughed too easily. He sported a gold chain around his neck that betrayed any sense the man had scruples or loyalty.

He wore sunglasses inside, irrespective of the weather.

A barrier.

Hiding.

His emotions forever checked.

And yet despite his apparent chumminess with Gerald, despite his lapdog tendencies, I sensed something darker in Blanchard. I took to watching him in meetings, where he'd spend his time doodling on his pad, his attention hijacked by hidden thoughts. Dark thoughts. The doodles I saw, were raw - angry even – and brutally crude in their construction, almost childlike. The tense grip and ferocity of each sketch roused in me a surprising thought, and one that, as time ticked by and Gerald's unremitting intimidation ground down the spirit of yet another human soul, was a thought that refused to go away.

In Blanchard, I saw an accomplice.

If I was to murder Gerald, I knew that I'd need an accomplice. To do it alone would be too risky. I would need someone to push under the bus were the plan to fail. I didn't want to go to jail. And Blanchard was perfect.

Murder was, though, a difficult subject to broach on the trading floor and so I waited, patiently, for my opportunity.

*

It came at a drinks party, a colleague's leaving bash. I knew he would be there; I knew the bar was perfect. It was loud and loose, and I planned to word it in a way that could be laughed off if I sensed so much as a whisper of resistance.

I arrived late and took a cold beer from the bucket.

The air was thick with gossip, ties slack. Alcohol had started to stretch the stitching. Despite the relatively early hour, inhibitions had begun to fray. I saw Claire smoking by the window, flagrantly flouting the rules, as was her way, and eased over to join her.

I sat next to Claire on the trading floor. She was a vivacious girl with big blue eyes and a mane of thick blonde hair. She had a rich laugh, and a mischievous sparkle. She played people, letting them know she could be both naughty and nice. She also played the double bass in a wedding band and rode a motorbike to work.

She was a free spirit; a bold, confident woman.

And clients loved her.

There was also a rumour that Claire had once kissed the team that researched the utility sector. All of them. Two men, one woman. Each heavy and hairy, with stained teeth and long nails. They were known as a serious, glum group who spoke in slow, regulated tones. They were not known to smile. Or laugh. And yet Claire had joined a team dinner one time and it, the dinner, so went the rumour, had spun out of control. Tongues had touched. Claire never confirmed or denied the rumour. I asked her once, but she just smiled, and told me that she enjoyed the attention.

Claire also hated Gerald.

She had received a formal warning, one Christmas, for failing to declare a case of wine that she had received from a client. There was a sweep of the post room records and it was picked up and flagged to compliance as having never been declared. Claire claimed she knew nothing about it, having never received any wine. Her own tribunal had given her short shrift and handed down a fine and a formal written warning. Later Claire received an anonymous note from the post room with a copy of the signature of the person who had signed for the delivery.

Gerald.

'You're not allowed to smoke inside,' I said.

'I know. But it makes me feel good,' she replied, blowing smoke in the air.

A rebel.

Always the rebel.

We made idle chit chat as I scanned the bar for Blanchard and I saw him sitting in a booth, deep in conversation with Gerald.

'So, how's the love life?' I asked.

I always asked.

'Busy,' she said.

And it was, it was always busy. She didn't elaborate, and so I changed tack.

'Spoken to anyone?' I asked.

'Yes, the new technology analyst,' she said, drinking more wine. 'Ansgar. Swiss. I think I saw him once at one of my parties,' she said.

Claire had recently told me about the parties she went to in big country houses. They were invitation only. She always went alone. She typically wore rubber. There was fire and ice, and everyone got naked. At one she said she had ended up in the chocolate fountain with an artist from Malmo.

All she could recall was that he had very blue eyes.

I nodded, only half engaged. The chit chat was serving a purpose. I was scoping the scene, getting a feel for the rhythm of the bar. The music. If I was to serve up my chilling platter to Blanchard, I'd need to know how loud to pitch it.

The music was heavy both in beat and tempo.

Perfect.

'Nice guy?' I asked.

I watched as Gerald slipped out of the booth and headed for the bar.

'I'm going to kill him,' she said.

Her words had lost their shape a bit.

'Who? Ansgar?' I asked, turning to look at her, thinking it was a joke.

Only it wasn't a joke. Her face had lost all expression.

'Gerald,' she said.

'Me too,' I said, laughing it away, searching her face for traces of fun.

She grabbed my arm.

'No, I am,' she said, her breath was sweet. And hot. 'I'm going to kill him. I've had enough.'

'When?' I asked.

'At the next full moon,' she whispered.

I laughed some more, but she didn't.

'How?' I asked.

'I don't know.'

'You're crazy.'

'Possibly.'

'You're also drunk.'

'I may be drunk, but what if I'm not crazy?' she said and flashed her eyes.

She then put her finger on her lips.

'Don't tell anyone.'

She then pirouetted away, leaving her words still hanging in the air. She wasn't real. She couldn't be.

Murder?

She wasn't the type.

I watched as she eased herself into a group and put her arm around the lower back of an analyst who had the itchy manner of a man whose experience of naked women had been largely digital.

I had business to attend to and needed to move. My moment, I sensed, had come, and so I pushed Claire's shocking confession aside and eased through the crowded bar, keeping a close watch on Gerald.

'Lovely booth,' I said, as I slipped in opposite Blanchard.

He calmly dropped a calamari ring into his open mouth and chewed, a bit of batter falling onto his lap. He had a smudge of sauce on his chin... I watched Gerald ordering cocktails at the bar.

'He's a good man, Gerald,' I said. And paused. 'You two get on pretty well?'

Blanchard remained silent, still chewing, and so I

continued, inching into the silence. I knew this conversation was one that I would have to own.

'Have you ever thought about doing his job?' Pause. 'Taking his job?' I leaned into the word taking, letting it rise above the background hubbub. 'You'd make for a far better Head of Sales.'

I used my hands. Or one hand. Up and down. Open palmed as if I was presenting him to the Queen.

'And here, Your Majesty, we have Blanchard.'

Yet Blanchard remained silent. He looked bored, but I knew he wasn't. The eyes, I knew the eyes were watching. Behind the ubiquitous sunglasses I knew there were two deep, dark pools of betrayal; pools that were now being stirred by my own spoon of doom.

I leaned in, closer. And paused. The next line would determine whether our futures would be forever bound together.

'I can help you make that happen,' I said, barely loud enough to be heard over the thick din of the bar.

I saw his body stiffen. Over his shoulder I saw Gerald had started to wend his way back, a cocktail in each hand.

'Think about it,' I said and slipped away into the throng.

Gone.

Like a glimmer.

*

'We are constructive on the outlook for gold,' I said, not wholly sure why that happened to be the case.

The report I was looking at was for a gold company which the analyst had thought worth buying. There were a few graphs, and lots of numbers. There was also a bit in bold lettering declaring a positive take on gold.

'I don't like gold,' said my client, in a tone disturbingly like my wife.

There was, I thought, little doubt as to his feelings on gold.

Unlike my wife.

'It's going up,' I said.

'It's not,' he said.

'It is.'

'No, it's not.'

Intellectual tennis.

We eventually decided, in the interests of our own will to live, to agree to disagree. The gold price might go up, or it might go down; time would tell. As the collective will flagged, he reluctantly agreed to take a meeting with the analyst to find out why the gold price might go up, after I reluctantly agreed to take him to a new Japanese restaurant.

I put down the phone and felt weary.

Empty.

It had been another dispiriting exchange.

I looked over at Blanchard talking on the phone, gesticulating, his movements somewhat puppet like. I had left the party shortly after our exchange knowing my work was done. What I needed now, was for my seed to grow.

SOLD SHORT

Take root.

Flower.

Next to Blanchard sat Dominique.

Dominique also worked on the sales desk and was one of those people of indeterminate nationality; the product of international schools with an accent that was unmistakably American, despite her not being American.

At least as far as I was aware.

She could point to Canada on a map. She knew she should not eat potato chips for breakfast. She also knew Mary Poppins wasn't a real person. That those who learn English, choose to do so in an American accent remains something of a mystery. It was though something I had yet to ask Dominique.

Dominique was a dark, moody woman. She was also neurotic and highly strung. She gossiped. She plotted and schemed. In fact, she did very little else. Apart from look moody. She had dark hair, and dark eyes. She wore dark clothes. She was a black hole that drained the space around her of energy.

Dominique was married to Pascal.

Pascal was French and thus also untrustworthy; perhaps because he was French, perhaps because of other reasons, like having a beard, but history suggests, mostly because he was French. Pascal worked in the research department yet appeared to do very little research, instead he chose to spend his days walking around the trading floor with a crumpled coffee cup in hand, looking furtive.

And untrustworthy.

Pascal would have made a wonderful accomplice. He had that nasty, ruthless edge that separated the successful murderer from the convict. His tight beard suggested he was a perfectionist. He also had cunning, and I suspected he might have done it all before. If the police were to dig up his patio, they would find bones. And he was charming. He had that silky-smooth charm of the psychopath.

Pascal was the complete package.

Yet I didn't ask Pascal.

Pascal was too clever.

And French.

I watched Dominique, as she sat at her desk, giving the appearance of work, rat-a-tat-tatting with her long nails on the keyboard, hiding behind the soulless medium of email. I had not heard Dominique call a client all day, yet just this once, I felt sorry for her.

Earlier that day, I was sitting at my desk when Eddy had appeared out of nowhere. He pulled up a chair and sat down next to me. Eddy also worked on the sales desk. He was a good-looking man. Tall. Chiselled. Toned. HR had been left agog in his interview as he extolled stories of bribery and broken-down land rovers in war-torn strips of land they had only ever seen on news bulletins.

Their boxes remained unticked, tongues slack, as their minds slid into rooms of velvet, riding crops and tassels.

It was a lesson for any earnest intern; a lesson perhaps, for us all.

Eddy was sleeping with the girl who worked in the

coffee kiosk. And the girl who worked in the coffee kiosk knew everything, about everyone. I don't know how, but she did. And she would always tell Eddy. And today his eyes were shining. He was the dog who had just been swimming in the lake, he knew, he was not allowed to swim in.

'Have you heard?' he whispered.

He was leaning in on me.

Too close.

A few flecks of spittle hit my face.

'Have I heard what?' I asked.

'Pascal!' he muttered.

'What about Pascal?'

'He's been a naughty boy,' Eddy said, barely able to breathe.

I spun around to see if anyone else was in ear shot. They weren't. Those that were around were on the phone, or busy on email.

'Go on,' I said.

'Do you know that girl who works in the retail team?' he said.

'Which girl?'

'You know! The girl!'

'Eddy, the entire team are girls.'

'I don't know her name. But you know, the ginger one.'

I knew the girl he was talking about, although, I too didn't know her name.

'Well,' he said, 'I heard that Pascal's been having a go. You know…'

He failed to finish his sentence. He whistled. His eyes were as wide and eager as an eighteen-year-old on the suggestion of popping into a Bangkok strip club, for lunch.

His eyes said it all.

I didn't think of Dominique then, but I did now. She may have had the charm of a wasp, but she didn't deserve that. No woman deserved that.

Blanchard then got up to leave and pulled his jacket off the back of his chair. He was sporting a bright blue suit, so tight I swear I could hear him squeak. He sauntered out, walking back in his heels, lapels loose, his gut out. As ever, he sported an open collar – no tie – and so the light occasionally caught his gold chain. He looked shiny. Cheap and shiny.

Disposable.

Yes, Blanchard was, indeed, my man.

Not Pascal.

Not with morals like that.

*

Whilst I had made little progress in deciding how it was that Gerald would die, I was soon given the perfect opportunity to groom my accomplice, my side-kick; the man who, I hoped, would be the one heading to prison, on our behalf, should the sirens ever wail down upon us.

As luck would have it, Blanchard and I were put to work on the same IPO.

An 'Initial Public Offering'.

An IPO was when a company would decide to list on the stock exchange, to sell shares in the business to outside interests, to investors who were desperate to make a return, perhaps having previously been sold several other IPOs that didn't. Such deals were our bread and butter, and for the bankers who packaged them up and flicked memos our way full of angry capital letters, they were the jam and peanut butter too.

Blanchard and I were burdened with being 'team leaders', a high-profile role that offered an easy scapegoat for management should the deal be too bitter a taste for the client. Gerald had put us together to coral, schmooze and beat our colleagues into submission, to ensure that each client had been press-ganged, cajoled, or bribed into taking a meeting with the febrile analyst who supposedly knew what the company did.

You see, there were other banks also tasked with the chore of prising money out of the sinewy fingers of their diffident clients. It was just their clients were also our clients and, in the sweaty undignified scrap to win their order, it was necessary that they see our man, not their man, or, indeed, their woman.

I did, though, know that our man was, indeed, a man.

Not a woman.

At least during the week.

This meant that Blanchard and I would go for coffee most days. Ostensibly to talk through how the deal was going and yet the meetings, on my leaning, readily took on a different course.

A darker course.

We talked.

More specifically I asked questions, and Blanchard talked.

He told me about his clients, his house, his TV, his car. He talked about exotic holidays and fancy festivals and the bars of private clubs littered with the leathery faces of washed-up celebrities. He talked of padding around country retreats sipping carrot juice in oversized, fluffy white dressing gowns. He talked a lot and I prodded and poked and quietly sipped my coffee. I wanted us to build a rapport.

'Another?' I'd ask.

'Go on.'

'Skinny?'

He'd nod, and I'd order another couple of lattes. Always a skinny one for Blanchard for he was watching his weight. As he should be. Carrot juice was a good idea, I told him, given his build and lack of any obvious metabolism. I smiled and nodded a lot. I wanted Blanchard to be comfortable, relax, to open himself up. To trust me. We rarely bothered talking about the IPO, but occasionally I'd use it to prise open my unsavoury can of death.

'Gerald wants this deal to price,' I said, one time, sensing my moment.

'I know. He's under pressure,' Blanchard replied, gazing longingly at the carrot cake on the counter.

'From who?' I probed, knowing full well.

'Pascal,' he said.

Pascal had been popping up a lot in meetings of late, standing quietly by the door, listening, watching. He would sometimes ask inane, pedantic questions, each one specifically aimed at undermining Gerald. And he was relentless.

I suggested that Pascal had muscled himself in on the deal as he saw it as an opportunity to further his own march on a corner office and a longer job title.

'He wants the Head of Research job,' I said, looking up as our lattes arrived.

Blanchard busied himself by adding three sachets of sugar.

Skinny no more.

'I know,' he said.

It was a good sign.

Blanchard, I knew, had his ear on the latest political manoeuvrings of the office. He knew who wanted which seats. And where. He knew because he was also busy making manoeuvrings of his own. He too wanted more. More money. More power. Always more.

'Did you hear about the remuneration meeting?' I asked.

Blanchard shook his head, slowly. He liked to think that he knew everything.

'Gerald let 10% of our bonus pool go. Pascal argued it should go to research and Gerald let him have it.'

Stirring.

Always stirring.

'Why?' Blanchard asked, his voice barely above a whisper.

Disbelieving.

He himself had then started to slowly hiss like an espresso machine.

I didn't answer.

I let him hiss.

The reason was, I didn't know. I had made it up. I was not party to the remuneration committee's idle greasing of each other's bare buttocks. Blanchard, though, did not know that I had made it up. And in any case, his mind was a-whirr, now steaming at the injustice of potentially being cut out of the bonus pool. The banker's worst nightmare.

The bonus was a basic right.

I let the silence enjoy itself. I sat back and let his emotions grip him. He needed to feel anger for what I had to say next and with Blanchard mouthing words that refused to come out of his mouth, I struck.

'He needs to go,' I said, emphatically, picking my moment.

Blanchard stopped, and stared.

'What do you mean, go?' he asked.

'I mean go,' I said, meeting his eye.

The words were cool and detached. I held his gaze, my face impassive, ghostlike, devoid of any feeling; or as much as was possible in a well-appointed coffee shop.

Blanchard said nothing.

'Gerald goes. You take his job,' I said, laying it out for him. 'He got paid a million pounds last year.'

'Two million,' Blanchard said quickly. 'He got two yards last year.'

That I knew, but I wanted him to say it. I wanted him to taste the words and let the number cavort around his head. Two million pounds was a lot of carrot juice.

'How?' he asked, his brow furrowed, cogs grinding.

'Conventionally, we would stage a coup. We would sew up the team and deliver a vote of no confidence. We oust him and present you as his successor, just like they do in Africa. But that takes time, and I wouldn't trust anyone to stick with us. There is a risk we'd get hung out to dry.'

Blanchard nodded.

'Yes, too risky,' he added for good measure, before adding another sugar.

'The other option is … he dies.'

The noise, the hissing of the coffee machine, offered the perfect backdrop to my obscene suggestion.

Silence.

'Cappuccino with chocolate sprinkle?' yelled the barista filling the gaping void in our conversation.

'As in dead?' Blanchard whispered.

'As in dead,' I said.

'Like Terry Wogan?'

I nodded.

Solemn.

Serious.

I couldn't see his face as he was now looking down, stirring his coffee once more and so it was difficult to know his reaction. But I needed to see it. I was very much out on a limb. He slowly looked up and I saw in him, not excitement as I had hoped, but traces of fear.

'You'd do that?' he asked.

'Yes, he needs to go,' I said, now feeling, morally, a little exposed. 'Of course, I would. Anyone would. He's a bully!'

My words though, were hesitant, I couldn't grasp his line of questioning. Blanchard didn't seem the judgemental type. Not when there was two million pounds at stake.

'Dead, as in kill him?' he asked.

'Yes.'

'When?'

'Well, that depends. We'd need to plan something. You can't just bump someone off like that,' I said, snapping my fingers.

'How?'

'Again, we'd have to plan something.'

I grew irritated. Did the man have no imagination? I started to wonder if I had picked the right running mate. But I needed to tread carefully. I needed him now. I needed him more than he needed me.

'There are many ways to kill a man,' I said, softly,

hoping the words cut through the steamy ambience of the coffee shop.

Dangerous words.

As they should be.

He gulped his coffee and then wiped his mouth with his hand, his face giving away nothing. He had black hair and thick eyebrows. His eyes, close as they were, and, on the face of it, deliciously devious, were also sunk quite far back into his head.

They were difficult eyes to read.

It was all so dark.

So right.

And yet now, I needed some of that darkness to poison his mind.

Slowly.

Drip.

Drip.

Drip.

I sighed.

It was turning out to be more difficult than I thought it would be. Two million pounds? I thought it would have easily been enough to set Blanchard off. To buy his loyalty. And yet I was, now, like the inexperienced flasher, dangerously exposed. I had undone my gown and shown him mine. But he still had his gown done up. Which meant he had me. And if he stayed covered up, I was vulnerable.

'Will there be blood?' he asked.

'I don't know! There might be,' I said.

'I don't like blood,' he said.

All I could do was nod. Slowly. This was not where I thought the conversation would go. I wanted anger. Hate. I wanted Blanchard to froth a little himself. I needed him to be consumed by a darker force.

I changed tack.

'If you're not up for it, just say,' I said, taking a risk, leaning back in my seat. 'I know a few others who want his job.'

Blanchard sat back in his chair, thinking, weighing up his options, mirroring my own defensive body language.

'He has a villa in Provence,' I added, throwing a scrap Blanchard's way, hoping that he would assume that he too could have a villa in Provence.

'Provence?' he said.

'Provence,' I replied, not quite sure what he meant. Surely, he knew where Provence was. 'It's in France.'

He shrugged.

I was losing.

I was struggling to sell my plan and I was now out of lattes. Three in one sitting would have been too many. I would have overplayed my hand and Blanchard would have then realised how desperate I was. And then, as I had all but given up, as I was starting to think about damage limitation, perhaps even having to shove Blanchard under a bus on the way back to the office, he sat forward and held out his hand. The prospect of someone else taking Gerald's job had done it.

Envy.

Jealousy.

Greed.

The standard weakness of any man.

More so a banking man.

'I'm in,' he said.

His gown, finally, fell open.

I shook his hand and looked him in the eye.

The safest place.

'I'll do whatever it takes,' he said. 'Only no blood, I don't want any of his blood on me.'

I nodded, wondering whether I had just made a terrible mistake.

CHAPTER V

I lay back in the sunshine, feeling the warmth on my face. It was magnificent. The sun. The hot rays. The vitamin D. The sky was so blue it was mesmerising. As it should be for a summer's day; a day for a picnic with your wife, although she was, as we well know, not yet my wife.

'Have you put some sun cream on?' she asked.

'No,' I said, my eyes closed.

'You should.'

'I know I should,' I said, inclined to do nothing of the sort.

'You'll get skin cancer and die,' she said.

'At least I'll die with a tan.'

She threw me a tube and as I creamed my face, I realised how far we had come. She was now nagging me, which surely meant we were now an item. A real boyfriend and girlfriend.

The first date had gone well. And so, we went on another. We went to a comedy club, and then walked, down the river, through the park, and up past old deserted warehouses ending up in a late-night Turkish restaurant that had plastic chairs, strip lighting, and a TV showing typically chaotic scenes from Istanbul.

The food had been delicious. We talked and talked. And laughed some more.

I didn't want it to end.

But it did.

With a kiss.

We had then gone on another date, and another. We went to the Theatre and saw an awful play. We walked along the Southbank, we sipped coffees in flower markets and watched a desperately depressing film on a wet Sunday night.

'Did you enjoy that?' I had asked, as we waited in the rain for a taxi.

'Not really,' she said.

The film was about a man who killed his wife because he loved her so much he couldn't bear to see her suffer.

'Maybe we go bowling next time,' I suggested.

'Maybe,' she said.

And now we were in the park. On a picnic. In the sun. On a date, one Sunday, as I had originally intended.

'My parents are down next weekend,' my wife then said, somewhat idly. Idle but deliberate, so very deliberate.

'I wondered whether you would you like to join us for lunch?'

She continued to busy herself with the picnic.

The parents.

I imagined the vice-like handshake of her father.

The gaze. The awkwardness. A meeting when so many words go unspoken. It was, though, an interesting question she had asked. Interesting as we hadn't had the discussion on our relationship status. I hadn't asked her to be my girlfriend, nor she me. As ever, though, it would have been nice to know where everyone stood. What to tell one's car insurance people come renewal time.

Had one's *status* changed?

There is a period of dating when it's just dating. It then becomes something that is a bit more than dating. What follows is a period of exclusive dating. I once had a louche go at open dating, as in dating more than one girl at once, but it wasn't for me. It was exhausting and expensive and I ended up resenting them both. And women in general. I went cold for a couple of months afterwards.

Cold and lonely as it turned out.

My wife and I, though, we were through with the exclusive dating saga. We were possibly no longer even dating at all given she had now asked me to meet her parents. This surely meant, that we were now an item, a real boyfriend and girlfriend.

'They want to meet you,' she said.

And thunder clapped the skies. It had happened: my father-in-law knew that I existed. I, his foe, his nemesis. No longer imagined, now real. I saw him pacing his garage muttering vile and venomous threats. Time and her ticking hands were all that stood between us, and now, it appeared, the meeting was nigh.

'Lovely,' I said, 'shall I book the Fox and Hounds?'

SOLD SHORT

*

'You're going to have to meet them on your own. I won't make it. My train has been cancelled. I am so sorry.'

I was walking towards the Fox and Hounds and now, I had a problem.

A very real problem.

My wife was stuck at some train station I had never heard of, and we were due to meet her parents for lunch. Her parents, my wife had told me, were ten minutes away from the Fox and Hounds and she had no way of knowing when she was going to get there. I thought about running, turning tail, throwing my phone into a skip, and hiding out in a snooker hall all afternoon. Joining all the other pallid, clammy men who were also running and hiding; there being no other reason to be passing a sunny afternoon in a dimly lit snooker hall.

Yet I couldn't do it. I knew that. I needed to face the parents, with or without my wife. And so, as I arrived at the pub, I pushed open the door and walked straight to the bar. If I had ten minutes, I had better make the most of it. My future depended on it.

'The largest gin and tonic you have, please.'

My phone rang.

'Are you there yet?' my wife asked.

'I am,' I replied.

'Are my parents?'

'No, they are not,' I said.

I tried to think of something funny to say, but I

couldn't. There was nothing funny about lunch with the in-laws. I could also tell from her voice she was stressed, and so I said nothing and took a sip of my gin. The pub was a traditional English pub. There were no TVs. There was no music. There were newspapers and scotch eggs. In winter, they had a log fire, with smokeless logs in line with the council's eco-stringent laws. It was quiet. For men in cords and tweed coats, the Fox and Hounds served the same purpose as a snooker hall.

Escape.

'Call me when they arrive,' she said and hung up abruptly.

I finished my gin.

And waited.

I ordered another one.

Outside I saw an elderly couple walk slowly past. It was unclear whether this was because they were lost, or just old. They stopped and conferred over something, it could have been a phone or more likely, given their vintage, a map of London that was struggling to keep up with the capital's voracious developers. I watched, my heart thudding a little harder, wondering if this was them: my in-laws.

I felt my buttocks tighten.

'It's behind you,' I wanted to yell like they do from the cheap seats at the pantomime.

How could they miss it? They were right outside the pub. A sign of a big red fox and a pack of rabid hounds was hanging not more than a metre from where they were standing. Yet the occasion was no pantomime. I phoned my wife.

'I think they're here,' I said, 'they're outside, literally outside. But they are standing, looking at their map. I think they are lost.'

'Oh,' she said, 'that's odd, they've been there before, several times, they know where it is.'

As she said that, the elderly couple outside walked off. She, leading, he, trailing in her wake. A fate that awaits all men, bar bachelors and homosexuals.

'Panic over, it's not them. I assume your Dad doesn't have thick white hair?' I asked

'No, he doesn't,' she said.

'Bald, is he?'

Silence.

'So, what are you wearing?' I added, courtesy of the gin. What hindsight might call brave, and a little foolish.

'What did you say?'

'What are you wearing, you know, what panties have you got on? That is if you are *wearing* any panties? I don't mind.'

My tongue was thick. I felt a fuzzy and warm.

Reckless.

'Call me when they are there.'

She hung up.

I chuckled to myself, a quiet, satisfied laugh; a laugh of man who had the buffer of at least two of London Transport's turgid travel zones between he and his wife.

I was disturbed by a quiet cough behind me.

'I think you know our daughter?' said a clipped, home counties voice.

It was like bone china.

I spun around and there they were. My in-laws. She, posing the question; he, hands in pockets looking distant and threatening.

Moody.

'Why yes, umm, HELLO! It is so nice to meet you,' I said, stumbling off the stool, a little light-headed, instantly regretting putting away half an hour's gin, in ten minutes.

We all shook hands and my father-in-law tried to crush my hand and grind my knuckles together like a playground bully. I was expecting it though, and with what strength my withered corporate arms could manage, I fought back and held firm. Our eyes they locked, and time stopped.

He had heard.

I knew it.

He was bald too, bald as an eagle, although as I turned to catch the barman's eye, I sensed it was a comment that he had immediately forgotten; a question that had ended up lost, deep in the nettles of his mind followed as it had been, by my gentle enquiry into his daughter's choice of knicker. It was, given the circumstances, not the best of starts.

'Now, what can I get you to drink?' I asked, rubbing my knuckles.

I ordered her a white wine and the bully half a

bitter. As we waited, I stole a glance at him. He had the look of a wizened Gestapo officer. Flinty and uncompromising.

Merciless.

'And would you like another *large* gin and tonic?' the barman asked.

I saw my in-laws exchanged a look.

'Lovely,' I said, quietly cursing his tone.

'I'll bring them over,' he said, enjoying my obvious discomfort.

Australian, no question about it.

The table, then, had beckoned, but before it beckoned my phone buzzed. The news was not good news. My wife was still stuck on the same platform and the trains had been cancelled.

All of them.

And so, we sat down. And smiled. Thin smiles. The conversation lurched uneasily from topic to topic. It was clumsy and awkward. I feared, too, the near pint of gin that the barman had put on the table, dwarfing the Gestapo's half pint of bitter, had hardened their resolve and they quickly confirmed that I worked for a greasy, culturally rotten bank, which essentially made me morally destitute and a long way from the son-in-law of their dreams.

I did not mention my plans to murder my boss.

'My soup's cold,' the Gestapo said, when the starters had eventually arrived.

His wife, my mother-in-law, although she didn't know that she was my mother-in-law, tried to make light of it, cooing and tutting. I suggested sending it back and made a play of attracting the barman's attention, but I was hushed down.

'We don't like to complain,' my mother-in-law said.

The Gestapo quietly buttered his roll.

'Bankers,' he muttered under his breath.

I decided then, to focus on the mother-in-law, believing the Gestapo was a lost cause. I gave her everything I had, so much so that by pudding, I had her laughing, giggling even; indeed, I spotted her twirling her hair a little. Saying goodbye, my mother-in-law held my hand as she kissed my cheek like she would her favourite son-in-law.

She smiled.

The Gestapo, though, lurked nearby and as we shook hands, he thanked me for lunch, I knew he had questions. Many questions. I knew that he would have liked to have spent the afternoon in his garage and, having tied me to a wooden chair with the garden hose, ask those questions with his pliers and drills and barbed wire all within easy reach. But that wasn't going to happen, not now, not today; not with my mother-in-law watching on, beaming like she had just been told she had won a fortnight at Butlins. I waved them off, confident that I had done enough to make sure we would meet again, but not so confident the Gestapo would be as pleased to see me.

I knew, as he did, that the Gestapo had unpleasant ways of making men talk.

*

'What have you two been doing?' Gerald yelled.

He was mad, fuming, He was on his feet, pacing his office, his fists clenched. I looked over at Blanchard, who was slumped in a chair, his face impassive. His thoughts, I hoped, were wicked thoughts, perhaps carefully considering gruesome ways to fashion the end of Gerald.

'If this deal doesn't go well, you two are finished,' Gerald spat.

I too was sat, in a chair. Blanchard and I were both sat, like two little schoolboys, and Gerald was standing. Gerald couldn't sit, as he was too angry.

The problem, Gerald told us, was that he had been out to lunch with Phil. Sordid Phil. Phil was, as I knew, a big client. A man who oversaw his own sprawling, bloated organisation, itself too, racked with anxiety and self-doubt. Phil was a client with deep pockets, a man with coffers stuffed to the brim with the savings of thousands of pensioners and when it came to the deal, he was a man who mattered.

Gerald said that, after they had sat down, he had slipped into an easy sales patter and had mentioned the deal over the prawn cocktail starters. He had talked about the opportunity. He had talked about the growth prospects and exciting pipeline of new drugs. He winked and dropped his voice and whispered of the confident tone of management when talking 'off the record' about the impeding approval of a potential 'blockbuster' drug. Dollars. Millions and millions of dollars. The timing of the float was, he said, as Phil balanced a large prawn on his delicate fork, 'ripe'.

Phil though, had sipped his wine and nodded and said that he was aware of the deal as he had just seen an analyst from another bank. A rival bank. A passing waitress had asked if the starters were satisfactory and Phil had smiled.

But Gerald had not.

Gerald couldn't talk, as his mind was running wild. If Phil had taken a meeting with this other bank and had decided to funnel some of the pensioners money into the deal, then his order would then be placed through that bank, not our bank.

The fee would be paid, but not to us.

Gerald, on his return, had immediately summoned us to his office and without preamble or small talk demanded to know why Phil had not seen our analyst.

'He didn't even know we were on the ticket!' he had yelled. 'Why didn't he know? Has anyone spoken to him?'

He thumped his desk and then paced up and down.

Up and down.

'I called his secretary and left a message,' Blanchard said, the tone of his voice delightfully indifferent.

A murderer in the making.

As Gerald started to steam once more, hosing us with more expletives, I quietly marvelled at our situation. The three of us. Gerald yelling and Blanchard and I just sitting, conspiring, quietly plotting Gerald's own miserable death. The deal didn't matter, only Blanchard and I knew that.

'And you!' Gerald yelled, looking at me, 'what have you done?'

I waited for him to suck in some air.

'I'm not sure if this deal is a good one,' I said, quietly, staring out of the window.

I wanted to see push him. To see how mad he would get.

'I have been hearing things about the patents. They were incorrectly filed or something,' I said, my words clipped and deliberate, 'I've been told the patents are worthless.'

Silence.

As he stared into space there was a commotion on the trading floor, a brief collective murmur. A voice shouted, although the noise subsided as quickly as it arrived. I glanced at the clock.

1.30 p.m.

Payrolls.

Once a month the US government published how many jobs they thought had been added to the economy. The number, despite later revisions, was often held up as a barometer of broader economic health and despite it always being announced on a Friday, it courted a good deal of interest. The murmur suggested a number different to what the economists thought, as the number so often was. The earnest, I knew, would use it as a reason to call a client. The majority wouldn't bother.

I looked up at Gerald thinking perhaps he had not heard me. Perhaps he too was mulling the missed forecast of employment data, only I was wrong. He had gone quite pale, almost white, and his lips started to move but no words came out.

Blanchard started to look a little uncomfortable.

I tried not to grin.

And then he erupted. Never have I seen a man so angry. It was as if years of pent up anguish had finally been torched, the fuse lit by my comments. Brave, honest comments. Loose comments. Perhaps it was all too much. The truth. A mouldy principle long forgotten.

I don't know.

In any case it didn't matter. He lost control. The fury was remarkable, quite astonishing, and never had I seen a man's teeth so close. A girl, yes, but not a man. His teeth I saw, as he shouted inches from my face, were so small. I would have thought a man would have had bigger teeth but up close they looked not much bigger than a child's teeth. His breath too, was also strangely odourless and not at all what I would have expected from such a vile man.

I don't know how long the rant lasted, as I lost interest.

I knew the deal, like Gerald, was dead.

It was only a matter of time.

*

The deal, though, like Gerald, wasn't dead yet.

The timetable of any IPO was a frantic two-week run of marketing during which the management of the company would also come in and present to the sales team. The sales team would then know more than they did and would be better able to persuade their clients to buy the deal and the orders would flow.

Or so the theory went.

The management team were due in for lunch and I, as deal captain, needed to ensure the sales team turned up. I spotted the Fox reading the obituaries, which he did every day. Perhaps it is what happens when you get old, when mortality becomes a bit more relevant, when youths are indolent and feckless and when knees ache days before the TV weatherman warns of heavy overnight snow.

If the Fox was reading the obituaries, though, it meant that he had finished his morning calls and so I sidled over.

'Please come to the management meeting,' I said following a polite, attention seeking cough.

He didn't move.

'There will be sandwiches,' I offered.

The Fox stopped reading and looked up.

'What kind?' he asked.

'What kind of what?'

'What kind of sandwiches?' the Fox muttered.

'Does it matter?'

'Yes.'

'I don't know. Normal ones. Cheese, ham. Maybe some tuna.'

'I don't like tuna.'

'Well don't have any!'

Frustration started to simmer but I needed to be careful. After our meeting with Gerald, Blanchard and I were under pressure. Gerald had whispered that the powerful people were watching the deal and we needed to up our game.

It was a threat.

He had gone on to suggest that our interest in the bonus pool was vulnerable. This had irked Blanchard, as he knew it would. Blanchard loved the bonus pool, almost as much as he loved carrot cake.

I let the tuna comment go.

'What does the company do?' the Fox asked, still reading about the rich life of a well-known Hungarian composer.

A life of sound.

'Drugs,' I said.

He looked up.

'Tricky business drugs,' he said. 'It's all comes down to the pipeline.'

'I know,' I said. 'It's full. The pipeline has lots of potential. They have drugs waiting approval for all sorts of things.'

I hated myself for lying, but I needed the Fox at the meeting. He asked good questions.

'Patents?'

'Yes, they have patents,' I said, which was factually true, they did, they just weren't very strong patents.

The Fox finished the obituaries and folded the paper in a neat square leaving the crossword exposed, his intentions clear.

'I'll come,' he said, 'but I don't like drug companies. Nor do my clients. And I don't like tuna sandwiches.'

It didn't matter. That the Fox would come was enough. He could sit at the back and do his crossword, I didn't care. What I needed was bums, as there were a lot of seats.

'3 p.m.,' I said, 'don't be late!'

*

The meeting was a disaster.

I packed the room with a tasteful mix of experience and youth, the back seats filled with a stray group of idle interns I had found huddled near the vending machines talking in hushed tones about how it wasn't at all like Hollywood.

Gerald sat at the front, his knees jiggling, staring at space. I sat near the door, and was content as I could have been, given the circumstances. The room was full. My job was done.

There was a small raised platform with a desk, behind which the management team would sit. We were all in rows, in front of the platform. The room was slightly bigger than your average suburban garden. The windows didn't open, and the stale fug of boredom hung in the air. To the side, were the sandwiches. A glorious array of nibbles. Indeed, everything a man, or woman, or, as was the goal of HR's steamy policy, everything a gender-neutral could want.

We chewed.

And waited.

And then the management team had arrived accompanied by a blur of dark suits.

The suits belonged to the banking team. The

ruthless set of alpha males who lay awake at night, tossing and turning, minds racing, wondering how many more deals they would need to do, to have a profile in the financial pages of the weekend press.

The bankers sourced and nurtured the deals and we then had to sell them.

The suits shuffled in at the back, all square jawed, all men. One woman. To a man, and woman, they were intense. Terrifying. Their eyes scanning the room for any signs of weakness, any signs of distraction. They demanded intensity. Satisfied there were enough bums on seats to ensure no awkward chit-chat with management in the return lift down, they then pulled out their phones and start scrolling.

There were other deals.

More deals.

The treadmill never stopped.

The meeting started badly.

The management had a presentation with them, a presentation they hoped to display on the two large flat screen TVs that hung on the wall behind them. Only they couldn't get it up. An IT man was summoned, a man with the long ponytail and pallid skin expected of a man who spent his days fiddling with leads.

Steve.

I knew Steve, only because Steve unlocked my terminal when I forgot my password. Steve busied himself with cables. He muttered. He got on his hands and knees. He disappeared and returned with a different lead. His expression never changed. All the while, management smiled, thin smiles. They adjusted their ties. They sipped water. A sweaty junior banker offered them a tuna sandwich each, but they declined.

Having let his shirt casually ride up his back to reveal to the sales team a cleft of bare buttock, Steve eventually got the presentation up on the screen, and started to tidy up his leads.

And yet he took so long.

So deliberate he was, winding each lead up and tying them together with little wire fasteners that he got the bankers hopping from brogue to brogue. They shot each other dirty looks. They forgot to breathe. My back started to sweat. And then Steve was gone, with a smirk, and management flicked into sales mode.

'We are thrilled to be here today, to tell you our story,' said the Chief Executive, a man with a deep tan and too much jewellery for someone raising money.

Next to him was his Chief Financial Officer. His CFO. His numbers man. The CFO didn't look like he lived quite as well.

'As you will know from your analyst,' the CEO continued, raising his hand to don a typically oily platitude to the man who had furnished the deal with an alarmingly optimistic report, 'we have an exciting pipeline of drugs, and a strategy to ensure we are the number one player in our sector.'

The CFO shuffled his notes.

'Let me start...' began the CEO.

'Can you tell us about your patents?' said a voice.

I knew that voice.

The Fox.

I turned and saw him sat at the back. He was sitting with his legs crossed and his crossword balanced on his knee. He wore horn-rimmed reading glasses and looked very clever.

'Perhaps I can first tell you about…' said the CEO.

'Patents,' said the Fox, taking off his glasses. 'Perhaps first, you can tell us about your patents?'

The bankers stopped looking at their phones.

'Trouble,' whispered Claire, who was sitting next to me.

The door opened, and Pascal quietly slipped in. The temperature dropped further. More trouble. The CEO shot his numbers man a look and nodded. It was his time to shine. The CEO was big picture, strategy, he didn't do the detail.

'Yes, of course,' the CFO said. 'What would you like to know?'

'This trial you did. The one where the results showed your drug somehow worked. Where was it done?' the Fox asked.

'It was done over the course of two years, using a sample size that fell within the approval of the regulator,' said the CFO.

'No, *where* was it done?' the Fox asked.

The CFO looked at the CEO and both blinked. The interns stopped eating the free crisps. Even the callow youth had noticed the souring mood. The CEO slowly nodded at his CFO.

'We outsourced the trial,' the CFO continued, 'as

you know we are a lean business. Our strategy is to develop the science, and then bring that science to market through the most efficient channels. The companies we use, we trust; we let them deliver results. We don't get too involved.'

'That's interesting,' said the Fox, 'but you haven't answered my question. *Where* was the trial done?'

Pascal smiled as he helped himself to a small plate of olives, he seemed to know what was coming.

'I'll tell you where the trial was done,' said the Fox. 'Puerto Rico.'

The analyst gasped, and the bankers murmured.

'I've been there!' whispered Claire.

'Puerto Rico?' said the CFO, searching the back of the room for help. This was not what they expected.

Throats were cleared.

'Yes, Puerto Rico,' continued the Fox, 'which I believe, is good for spotting certain migratory birds, but is not an approved jurisdiction of the Federal Drug Administration.' He then paused. 'Which makes the data from the trial inadmissible. Which means your patent has been incorrectly filed.'

And with that Fox put his glasses back on and returned to his crossword. Pascal spat out an olive stone onto his plate and the beard glistened.

I wondered whether he had set the Fox up to cobble the deal. It was in his character. And he too was clever. And yet I wasn't sure why he would want the deal to fail. The fee, after the bankers had taken their cut, would still drip into the bonus pool.

And yet I suspected he was playing bigger games.

The management team battled on. They plodded through their presentation trying to pretend nothing had happened. They stuck to their script. They asked if anyone had any questions, but no one did. Despite their dogged efforts, the stench never left the room and I felt increasingly queasy. If the deal ran into trouble because of the Fox's intervention, heads would roll. And as we all shuffled out, I saw Gerald talking to a banker, a man so senior I had only ever seen a photo him on the bank's intranet site. I had long assumed he wasn't a real person.

And the banker didn't look unhappy, nor too, Gerald.

By the time the meeting had finished, and I got back to my desk, it was getting late. It was also a Friday and so I decided to slip away, to disappear. I told Claire I had a meeting in the West End should anyone ask, and I logged out and headed home.

I also needed to pack and prepare; for I had a big weekend in front of me, away from the souring IPO and away from Gerald.

*

My weekend involved my in-laws.

They had invited my wife and I to stay, in a quite thrilling development to our fast maturing relationship. We drove up early on the Saturday morning. I was tired after a long week at work, but I was also excited, albeit a little on edge. The Gestapo on his home turf was a massive proposition.

As we parked the car I gazed over at his shed and I

wondered whether my screams would carry to the house and stood and stared and I pursed my lips trying not to imagine the pain.

'Are you ok?' my wife asked.

'What? Yes, fine,' I said, although I feared my voice tailed off.

I noticed the house was upwind.

'Welcome, come in, come in,' my mother-in-law said, as I followed my wife through the back door. 'How was the traffic?'

'Fine!' I said, 'no problems at all.'

I grinned. There was little to be gained by going into any more detail. The Gestapo stood silently by the cooker, eyeing me up with surly suspicion. So too, I noticed, the dogs.

There were two dogs; both small and bull-doggy. They came running up to me and started to sniff my legs. I smiled and tried to shoo them away, but they were relentless. They wouldn't stop. They started to whimper, and so I shooed with a bit more vigour. I was though, given the circumstances, careful to shoo with a smile. And so, the dogs kept sniffing and I kept shooing. I had to put my bag down and use two hands.

My wife didn't seem to notice.

'Bitches,' I quietly muttered.

Or not, given their names: Bruno and Boris.

'Stop it dogs, leave him alone,' my mother-in-law eventually said. 'Bruno, *stop it!*'

But did they stop? No, they did not. Both Bruno and Boris kept sniffing.

'Drink?' My mother-in-law finally said, perhaps to make things better.

'Oh, yes please,' I said, a little too quickly.

'G&T?' she asked with a suggestive smile.

'Go on then,' I said.

I muttered a quiet Alleluia and slowly tightened my grip of Bruno's collar. The Gestapo slipped off to his shed, presumably to fetch the gin, or the tonic. Or both. Or perhaps to stab another dart into the grainy photo of me that he had found on the internet and had pinned to the back of the door. Perhaps too, another nip of whisky and the calming fondle of a chisel.

'Come through, come through,' my mother-in-law said, 'come and sit by the fire.'

She insisted on taking my bag.

'Here, let me help, Mummy,' my wife said, and they disappeared upstairs, exchanging news.

I ambled into the sitting room where a log fire crackled and spat, and stood by the fire rubbing my hands, savouring the silence, savouring the simplicity of a log fire. And yet, as I stood, I had that troubled sense I was being watched. I felt eyes boring into my back. I spun around half-expecting to see the Gestapo ghosting over the deep red Iranian rug, bull rushing me; a hot poker levelled at my exposed midriff.

Instead of the Gestapo, I saw a massive moose.

Behind the door, bolted to the blood red walls, laughing over the drawing room, was a moose's head of quite staggering proportions. Its eyes! They were terrifying; eyes that hid the pain of a sudden death. The crack of shot, the moment. Lost. Gone forever.

So too the dreams, perhaps, of having little moose.

There was then the soft sound of a footfall in the doorway and I looked up to see the Gestapo.

'Wonderful moose,' I said.

'It's an elk,' said the Gestapo.

'Indeed,' I said, 'a wonderful elk.'

Silence.

'Do you?' he said.

'Do I?'

'Shoot.'

'Elk?'

'Shoot. Pheasant, grouse, geese, game. I could go on.'

I laughed.

'Of course!' I said, 'I mean no, no. No, I don't.'

Silence.

Crack.

Pop.

He walked over and handed me a gin. I took a sip. It tasted like tonic. He stood next to me and we both gazed up at the elk.

'So, did you take her down?' I asked.

'Him, yes I shot *him*. He has antlers,' the Gestapo said, his tone dismissive.

Of course: antlers.

The conversation then quickly ran aground. When I heard my wife and mother-in-law coming down the stairs, I finally stopped holding my breath. I let the air whistle out through my teeth and, wanting something to do, I moved to take a seat next to the fire. As I sat down, they came in and I saw the look on my wife's face drop.

'What are you doing?' my wife asked, her eyes wide, desperate, pleading even.

'What?' I asked, innocently, unaware – like many a son-in-law before me – of the situation.

'What are you doing sitting there?'

'Where? The chair?'

'Yes. That's Daddy's chair!'

I looked up at him, but his face offered me nothing. It was blank. At the time, I thought, perhaps even a little indifferent. Somewhat serene. My wife told me later that I had misread him. The last man to sit in his chair was his dead brother; before he was dead.

'Don't be silly, dear,' said my mother-in-law breaking the silence, 'he can sit anywhere. Now I better go and check on lunch.'

Don't go. Don't go. I looked up at my wife. Please don't go. Don't leave me.

The elk gazed down.

'You too, my friend, you too,' he laughed, throaty. Were he alive, spittle would have flecked the floral print sofa.

His beady eyes blazed.

'Plenty of space up here my friend. I give you 12 hours.'

SOLD SHORT

*

I woke up freezing.

The summer duvet was just too thin. And too short. It was a child's duvet. But then I was in a child's bed, up in the attic, in rooms you find in large houses that had once been filled with laughter and dens and midnight feasts. Rooms that were, back then, fully engaged with the central heating system.

Not now though.

The attic was now a wasteland. Cold. Bereft of life. Boxes and boxes. Boxes everywhere, full of stuff and clutter deemed too stale for charity, too personal for the car boot sale, where vultures circled in fingerless gloves even as you parked the car.

I still felt mortified at what I had done, horrified, I couldn't believe I was capable of such an act. At the time, though, I had felt like it had been my only option.

After lunch, the Gestapo had asked if I would be able to help him in the garden. My wife smiled and nodded and grinned.

'That would be fun!' she said.

More nodding.

I sensed that I needed to say yes.

'Of course!' I said, my enthusiasm, I knew, a little too sugary.

There was an old tack room behind the garage that had fallen into disrepair and was in danger of collapsing. It had no roof and the exposed brick walls were old and unstable.

'Be careful of that wall,' the Gestapo had said, 'I

don't think it is structurally sound. Ted is coming on Monday to take it down.'

He gave me a spade with instructions to dig a trench next to the tack room. He didn't explain why. And I didn't ask.

I got digging.

And digging.

And digging.

'I'm off to get some tiles from the warehouse,' he announced after half an hour.

At last I thought, finally I had a chance to rest. I had been digging non-stop and my back was beginning to ache. I knew I couldn't stop with him there. I couldn't show any weakness. I threw the spade down and put my hands on my hips, leaning back, arching, looking up at the sky. I then tried to stand up and touch my toes in one motion. Smooth. Like I used to be able to do. And yet I did it too quickly and the blood rushed into my head. I felt dizzy. I lost my balance and, as I stumbled, I put out a hand to stop myself falling.

And I pushed the wall.

As it turned out, the wall was indeed, unstable.

It collapsed.

And, to my horror, as the wall collapsed, I saw Bruno, with his back to the wall. He was sitting, watching Boris sniff and slobber his way through the compost heap at the bottom of the garden. Or perhaps thinking about chum. Or perhaps he was thinking why he and Boris so enjoyed licking their own balls. I didn't know what he was thinking, but what I did know was that Bruno did not see the wall and he was crushed.

Dead.

I stood and stared. Panic had then quickly set in. I started to dig through the rubble with my hands. Desperate. Frantic. My mind a mess. I knew that I needed to get rid of the body. No one must ever know. If the Gestapo knew that I had killed his dog, I'd never get to marry my wife.

My eyes desperately scanned the garden. Perhaps I could bury him, but digging a grave would take too long. The compost heap was too obvious. There was no pond, no well, no watery grave. And then I saw it. I knew that it was, ethically off-side, but I did it anyway. I had no choice.

With Boris watching on, I stuffed Bruno's bloody body into the old oil tank.

When the Gestapo returned, I explained that the wall had just crumbled. I shrugged my shoulders. I suggested that the digging might have weakened the foundations. What I didn't tell him was that I had pushed the wall and it had killed Bruno.

'And where's Bruno?' he asked.

Boris barked.

'I don't know,' I said. 'I haven't seen him. I thought you had taken him to the shops?'

The Gestapo chewed his lip and said nothing.

We had then all spent the next few hours looking for Bruno, but to no avail. Eventually the search had been called off and we had returned to the house. The Gestapo was agitated and upset. I felt bad, but then I couldn't tell him the truth. If he knew that I had killed his dog, I would be finished, and I would never see my wife again. And that was something I couldn't let happen.

After a stiff and silent supper everyone had gone to bed and I was exiled to the attic.

An attic that I knew, was now haunted by Bruno's soul.

CHAPTER VI

The following week, the atmosphere at work deteriorated. Gerald was under ever more pressure, and like many, he responded by lashing out. Fur flew. The deal staggered on, but it was losing momentum. The Fox's intervention during the sales meeting had cast a shadow over the whole thing and, despite the bankers' best efforts with spit and polish, the rot had set in. The whispering started and once the whispering starts, on any deal, it was only a matter of time.

Gerald took to sending Blanchard and me emails, warning us of grave consequences if the deal was to fail. I dug deep and harassed clients and colleagues, but I knew it was futile. The deal was finished. And yet as the atmosphere at work turned ever more toxic, my domestic prospects took a sharp turn for the better. Midweek, after another frenetic day at work flogging the phones for the ailing IPO, I took my wife out for supper.

'I think my father likes you,' she said, as we waited to order.

'He does?' I gasped, the words not sounding real.

'Yes, he does. You should have seen him with my other boyfriends.'

I wondered if Bruno's body was the only body in the oil tank. I couldn't believe it, though. I was thrilled. It was music to my ears.

'And have you found a new flatmate?' I asked, my eyes grazing the menu.

As a question it was naïve, so very naïve.

'No, have you?' she asked, staring straight back at me, her elbows ominously moving on to the table.

'No, not yet. I think I might stay where I am for a while,' I had said, playing with the pepper pot.

My flatmate too had moved out. Moved out, to move in with his girlfriend. Time, we know, waits for no man.

'What? With a spare room?' she had said, her tone noticeably sharper.

'Maybe. I haven't thought about it to be honest. Moving flat seems like such a hassle.'

'Two medium rare steaks?' gravelled the delightfully impatient waitress.

'*Bien sur,*' I had muttered, serving my own schoolboy French with a skittish smile.

She grunted and put the plates down with the grace of a gruff French waitress which, indeed, she was.

'Perhaps some tomato sauce too, when you get a moment?' I asked, my tone possibly a little apologetic for a paying customer.

'How about I move in?' she said.

My wife, not the waitress.

And she said it just like that. Straight up. No

beating around the bush. No waiting, even, for the tomato sauce. I was led to believe the subject of moving in together had many couples diving into the clutches of eager eyed relationship counsellors and, in extreme cases, causing some couples to split. It was a big one, given all it entailed. Yet did my pulse judder? Did I sweat? Did my life flash before my eyes?

No.

'That sounds great,' I said, as the waitress delivered the tomato sauce.

It just came out. I didn't think about it. My lips were already moving. It was natural. Why would I not want to live with my wife? If I lived alone, stray cats would move in. The light bulbs would pop, one by one, slowly, over the course of many months, plunging the house into darkness. It would be cold. The plants would wither and die. The bathroom would smell. The cleaner would quit, professionally disillusioned. I would never entertain. My circle of friends would get smaller, day by day, month by month, until I only saw a clutch of school friends who too lived with cats and broken boilers. Occasionally I'd be asked to lunch by happy couples who lived in warm, tastefully furnished town houses, with funky coloured cushions and dauphinoise potatoes in the oven. I'd be the last to leave, drunk. And sad. So very sad.

Why would I want that? Why would anyone want that?

'Oh,' she said.

I grinned.

I was ecstatic as at my age, I knew, that if we were

going to live together, we were going to get married.

*

I let my soul go. I let it soar. I let my emotions froth and frolic about the vast expanse of Handel's vivid imagination as *The Queen of Sheba* exploded out of the organ. As I always imagined it would. I stood, trussed up and tingling with anticipation at the front, by the altar, with my back to the packed congregation and closed my eyes.

I had indeed proposed to my wife and she had said yes.

She had moved in very soon after our steak dinner. She bought funky coloured cushions. She moved all my photos around. She invited friends over for midweek suppers, and it was strange, as the weeks and months passed, my mood changed. The darkness gave way, to something brighter. The prospect of a different life, a better life. The shoddy drug deal got pulled in the end and there was nothing Blanchard and I could do about it. The Fox had smoked the truth out of the story and it never recovered. Once deals like that start hissing air, they never stop.

And yet there wasn't any immediate fall out. All that happened was that Gerald ignored me. There was no violence, there was no nothing. It was if I didn't exist. I didn't know what he was planning, and yet, I found that I didn't care. After living with my wife for several months, I had other matters on my mind. More serious matters.

A proposal.

I had started to entertain a proposal.

The problem I had was that I knew I needed to ask the Gestapo for his daughter's hand in marriage, which was a terrifying prospect for the Gestapo remained an enigma to me. I didn't know the man. I also worried that he might think I was still too new and that we hadn't been together long enough.

I fretted and vexed and wondered if I should wait. The weeks leaked by, and then something snapped. I woke up one weekend when my wife was in Amsterdam on a friend's hen do, wide-eyed at the sight of another man's penis, and I decided just to get in the car and go and ask him.

I arrived at his house, unannounced, high on caffeine, just after lunch. Looking back, I should have perhaps put a little more thought into it, perhaps, even, phoned ahead. I didn't. Instead I charged out of the car scuffing my shoes on the gravel and rang the doorbell. My mother-in-law had answered the door, drying her hands on a tea towel, appearing wholly indifferent to my frothy, souped-up appearance.

She smiled, as she always did.

'Do come in,' she said, 'how was the traffic?'

Her manner was calm, expectant even. Warm. Welcoming. It was if she knew. But then the mother-in-law, not just my mother-in-law, but the whole lot of them, they all have special powers. They know. They know before you know. And that day, when I rang the doorbell and stood outside her kitchen, hopping from foot to foot, she knew.

'Tea?' she asked.

I nodded. She knew I did, she knew that too.

The Gestapo had been out running errands and so, I waited. I had another cup of tea. That I needed to speak specifically to the Gestapo appeared not to affect my mother-in-law in any way. She pottered. She even produced a newspaper and I went and sat in the summer house and read the classified adverts to calm myself down. The sun beamed through the window. It was warm and after a long drive and the adrenalin subsiding, I soon fell asleep.

And then I woke with a start.

There staring at me through the window was the Gestapo, his face, as you might expect, half in shadow. I sat up, groggy and confused as he barged in and sat down on the sofa next to me. Silence, as I always feared, enveloped us. I coughed and enquired as to his errands, and yet he just grunted, lost as he appeared to be, in his own thoughts. He was even more distant than normal, cut adrift. He was but a ghost, a man looking for something, words, anything.

And yet all I got, was silence.

'The thing is…' I said, desperately wanting to get it over with, but my thoughts then evaporated to be replaced by, nothing.

I heard Boris bark.

And then, breaking his own stay of silence, he just said it:

'Yes.'

I stared at him, my mind scrambling. Thoughts came at me too quickly. I couldn't process them. So many thoughts. Yes, to what? I hadn't even asked a question. Not yet anyway.

'I'm sorry?' I said.

'My answer is, yes,' he said, his eyes as flinty as an aunt after too much sherry.

I licked dry lips. How did he know I was going to ask him a question? Looking back, it was, perhaps, obvious; stark even, given the context of my mad dash to his well-upholstered doormat.

'I love her,' I said.

The words just popped out of my mouth, as they often do under pressure. Abide by the truth.

'I know,' he said. 'As do I.'

And that was that. We sat there, the two of us, on the old garden sofa, looking out across the lawn, watching the birds nibble on his nuts, both reflecting on our love of the same woman. He was tense though. I could feel it. I could feel it in the air. This was the moment that he had been dreading ever since his little girl had first left home. The moment he knew that he finally had to let go. And did he even have a choice? My asking was largely ceremonial. He knew it, I knew it. The love chapel on Sunset Boulevard possibly beckoned, were he to chase me down the drive with a spade.

No invitation.

No photos.

After a while, I don't know how long, he got up and left and I watched him go and vowed to get to know the man, however long it took. He had trusted me with his daughter. Did I deserve his trust? With Bruno floating in his oil tank, possibly not, but I hoped in time I could earn it. I wanted him to know that his daughter would be cherished and loved and kept safe in a world cheapened by the slow disintegration of traditional family values. I wanted to tell him that his daughter meant more to me than life itself.

She was my life.

I didn't, though, nor did I ever ask him the actual question I came to ask. What I did do was drive straight back to London.

And I had felt alive.

I had felt gloriously alive.

*

I stood at the altar and turned and watched as my mother-in-law was escorted to the front, resplendent in pink and orange.

I smiled.

She smiled.

The church was packed, full of family and friends and friends of family. So many smiling people. The sun flooded the pews, picking out the verdant flowers and blistering display of colourful hats. It was perfect. And yet, as my mother-in-law approached the front instead of sitting down on the pew as per the dress rehearsal, she slipped her chaperone and advanced to meet me.

It appeared that sometimes the script was inadequate.

I moved forward to greet her, my beaming smile masking my nervous state of mind, and stooped to kiss her cheek. And as she kissed my cheek, she whispered something in my ear. A sentence. A thunderbolt.

'I know you killed Bruno,' she whispered, her words so soft, not even the Vicar could here. 'I saw you push the wall.'

My body stiffened. Another witness. Another problem. And then she smiled and kissed my other cheek.

'Your secret's safe with me,' she said and squeezed my hands which she was now holding.

The congregation smiled and exhaled, happy to see that the mother-in-law was happy as she turned to take her pew. I was convinced I was dreaming, hallucinating. It wasn't real. Nothing was real. Voices started up in my head and I heard a dog bark. I pinched myself hard on the wrist, turning my skin white and bit my lip. I looked up to see the Vicar gazing down, watching my act of brutal self-harm with his kind, Godly eyes.

'It'll be ok,' he said with soft reassurance, 'marriage is a beautiful institution.'

He smiled.

I swallowed what would have been a quite shocking confession and then the church bells tore into their opening salvo lifting the congregation to their feet, announcing the long-anticipated arrival of my wife. I closed my eyes and sighed. It was real, it was all real. And I turned to see the sight that I had so longed to see and drew sharply on the holy air as I watched my wife walk slowly up the aisle on the arm of the Gestapo; a Gestapo, I was thrilled to see, whose stone-cold eyes were now welling up with tears.

I turned to face the Vicar and, with the back of my hand, wiped away a small tear of my own.

*

Marriage.

Everything had changed, but then nothing had changed.

'We need salt for the dishwasher!' my wife had shouted as I left the house one morning shortly after returning from honeymoon.

We had honeymooned in Scotland. My wife had been brave and stoic when I had told her where we were going. It rained.

'This is fun,' she had said, as we ate chocolate digestives in a municipal car park after our ferry to the islands was cancelled.

The rain lashed the window and I had wondered whether there was appetite for another game of backgammon. It's easy to get on when it's thirty degrees and you're sharing a plate of iced melon as your feet dangle in the Indian ocean. It's a bit harder when your options for the day involve Radio 4, getting wet, or more backgammon. Humour. Find solace in humour, I told her as I rolled the dice. As with marriage, you might say. Humour and shepherd's pie.

No dice.

Yet those early months were glorious. I found an inner peace, a happiness. I was married and, as the Vicar had implied during his blistering sermon, this was it. It was for life and there was no going back. No changing of minds, or beds, and this suited me fine. Her parents even came to stay, and when they arrived, I welcomed them with the enthusiasm of a summer intern, fussing over my mother-in-law, carrying bags, fetching drinks.

'Any news of Bruno?' I asked the Gestapo quietly, as we shared a whisky on the sofa, our knees too close to properly relax.

He looked sad and shook his head and I reached forward to pass him the bowl of tortilla chips.

'Sorry to hear that.'

Later when they were out at their gala dinner, I snuck into their room and turned off their radiator. It made me feel good, happy even, happy that I was now the one in control.

My happy state did not last.

The following morning, I was in the laundry room, folding laundry, when without footfall or discreet cough I looked up and she was there, my mother-in-law, just standing in the doorway, watching me. The naked bulb of the room left the atmosphere bare and exposed. I mumbled a greeting, unsure of where our relationship now stood. We had not spoken properly since the church, since she told me that she knew that I had killed Bruno. I smiled back and continued to launder. And yet, she just stood there, leaning on the doorway, her arms folded.

'How was your dinner?' I asked.

Silence.

'I always knew you were the one,' she finally said.

I smiled, feeling both warm and a little nostalgic.

'From the moment I saw you. I knew,' she continued.

I didn't know what to say. I felt a glow in my belly.

'You had it. Unlike any of her other boyfriends.'

'Well, I...' I began.

But she quickly cut me off.

'The banker,' she cooed. 'As soon as she told me what you did, I knew. I have read what you people are capable of.'

I slowed my folding and the stifled air of the windowless laundry room caught my throat.

'Well, I knew too,' I said, still smiling, 'I knew on our first date. She was the girl for me. I am a lucky man.'

I looked up hoping to see a smile. But I didn't. Instead, I saw amusement.

'Not my daughter,' she said. 'The dogs!'

I stopped.

Bruno.

From the depths of the Gestapo's oil tank, he continued to fiddle with my life.

'I knew you were the one to finally get rid of Bruno,' she said.

I stared back at her.

'From the first moment you walked into our house, I knew. It was the way you shooed. The way your smile masked your true feelings. And the way you twisted his collar.'

I didn't know what to say.

'I knew then, you were a keeper,' she said, her voice lower.

I felt a little hollow.

'All her previous boyfriends never had it in them,' she whispered, 'all of them, soft public schoolboys. They had to go. Every one of them. And the last one, the barrister.... he kept CATS!'

I stared back at her.

'CATS!' she mouthed.

She then laughed.

Shrill.

Piercing.

And then she was down, and up, and down, weaving between the tea towels and damp socks. Down and then up again, right in front of me, so close I had to shuffle back, almost knocking the basket of washing off the table.

'The thing I want to know,' she said, quietly, leaning in on me, leaning in so close I could smell her perm. 'The thing I want to know,' she continued, this time in a whisper. 'What did you do with the body?'

I gazed back at her, emotionally at sea, and tried to make something of it.

'It was an accident,' I said, 'the wall just crumbled. I had no choice.'

I tried to put some moral distance in between me and my actions.

'I know,' she said, softly. 'But where's the body?'

'The oil tank,' I whispered.

She gasped.

I pursed my lips and then shook my head.

We both then stood and stared. Our relationship, I knew, was now different. New. Fresh. We would have to start again. Our dreadful secret would now be the bedrock of our future bond.

'What's wrong with them?' I asked. 'The dogs. Why don't you like them?'

She picked up a wet sock and held it, gazing into space, for a long time.

'They lie on my cushions,' she said, quietly.

I mumbled something, hoping it came across as sympathetic. She then reached out and squeezed my arm and was about to say something, but my wife then appeared in the doorway.

'What are you two up to?' she asked, her voice light and happy.

As always.

'Just talking!' my mother-in-law said, smiling, quickly picking up a pair of my damp undies and carefully putting them on the rack. 'And helping your husband do the laundry!'

'Oh thanks!' my wife said. 'I told you I married the right man, Mother.'

'Oh, I know, my love,' she cooed, 'I know, you most definitely did.'

Marriage might have brought me a happiness I never knew was possible, but it also changed other relationships too.

'Many hands make light work,' I said, and then turned and winked at my mother-in-law.

Our awful secret, I sensed, would remain just that.

A secret.

*

Life slowly found a natural rhythm, a routine; small things peppering our days. Trivial, but safe.

Normal.

'We need chicken thighs and loo roll,' my wife would text me.

And I'd sit at my screens at work, wondering whether she had found my smutty poem I had left propped up against the jam. A ditty that I had scribbled on the lid of the cereal packet as I had waited for the kettle to boil that morning. Romance: poems, chicken thighs and loo roll.

Perfect.

Blanchard and I continued to meet, to plot and scheme, but I lost some zest. I lost my intensity. I still wanted Gerald dead, but I was no longer consumed by it. My anger, subsided. My life was now richer, it had direction, it had real meaning.

In time I also slowly started to become concerned about Blanchard. My early fears of a chaotic accomplice were starting to bite. He was impulsive, and shockingly indiscreet. He had taken to sending me links to newspaper reports of various murders. The body of his email would often carry nothing other than an exclamation mark. Often in a very large font size, and frequently in red.

'Too messy,' he'd write.

'What was he thinking!' he'd comment, circling pieces of text.

And yet when we sat in coffee shops plotting and scheming, he, chewing on whole cakes of carrot cake, he was quick to balk at my suggestions. 'Too violent,' he'd gasp. 'Not sure about that,' he'd mutter, and I'd sit and steam and stew. And he would chew and chew, his mouth slightly open, crumbs falling, bouncing off his ample gut.

And then I started to fear that he knew. I started to worry that he knew I needed him, that I couldn't do it alone. Paranoia stepped in, loitering in the shadows of my mind, delighting at the havoc it could wreak on my feeble plans to make the world a better place by ridding it of Gerald.

As the months slipped by, I then started to worry that Blanchard was playing me. Using me as bait. Setting me up for a sting. I started to worry it was I who would be taken away in cuffs and humiliated in the press after an anonymous leak. I was convinced there was little going on behind the eyes with Blanchard, and yet, his eyeballs were set so deep in his hairy head, I couldn't be sure. I saw nothing, but that's not to say there was nothing.

And so, we talked and talked.

And Gerald continued to bully.

And then I had come home one night, as I was prone to do, and she was there. My wife. She followed me from the kitchen to bedroom and then back to the kitchen. She was chatty, although there was nothing unusual in that.

Women, I had discovered, liked to chat. About this and that. Some might accuse them of talking about things that didn't matter a great deal in the epic struggle to see society on its backside. A struggle that would see you declared a success by moving into a house with enough garden for summer games of croquet. In any case, I didn't mind. I liked to hear her news, her voice. I listened. I had even learnt, over time, to share my own.

'I had a beef sandwich for lunch,' I had said, knowing that sometimes, anything was better than nothing.

'I am pregnant,' she had replied.

The words cannoned around my head.

A baby.

I stopped doing what I was doing. The implications were immense.

I was, though, thrilled, and excited and as the months slipped by, Blanchard and I met less and less. He still emailed me clippings, but my focus was elsewhere thrust, as I was, into a world I knew so little about. I had seen friends become pregnant. I had seen pregnant women at work, in the street. I had seen them at drinks parties and at conferences. I had even seen a pregnant woman on a beach and had marvelled at the marbled veins of her tummy. But I knew nothing of a pregnant woman behind closed doors, behind the makeup and polite small talk. I knew nothing of morning sickness or swollen hands.

The months passed. Months and months. The sickness abated but the body was under siege. It had been taken over. My wife smiled. Yet it was a tired smile. I'd rub her feet and make her tea, but I couldn't share it. I couldn't share the disturbing feeling of physical change. Her eyes became watery. We signed up to an NCT class to meet other pregnant people. We started skipping social events and my wife got big.

And then came the names.

'What about Hubert?' my wife had said. 'Or Roco, I quite like Roco.' She added them to the growing list on her phone.

I wanted to throw Bruno into the ring but didn't. I knew it would have been too much for the Gestapo. It was all still too raw.

And then my wife's waters had broken in the middle of the night. One night, bang on time. She sat in a hot bath and waited until dawn to wake me. No words were exchanged as none were necessary: we were on.

I packed an overnight bag with miniatures of whisky and clean socks, and we shuffled down to the car, pausing in the lobby of our block of flats as another contraction passed. I swallowed my rising panic and yet, like a highly trained combat marine, I slipped into a trance. My NCT training took over. I could have driven to the hospital with my eyes closed, so well I knew the route and when we arrived the midwives rushed out to meet us and took control, cooing and clucking, offering hot towels and a sense of immediate safety.

And I stepped back into the shadows of the birthing room and sucked on a loose miniature, composing myself for what lay ahead.

The birth of my first child.

CHAPTER VII

The birth was a blur.

There were midwives and the liberal use of the gas and air by all concerned. Eventually though, after what felt like a lot of moaning, a baby appeared. He was blue and slippery and then as I welled with pride, with a flat voice, as if she was announcing the delayed 7.12 from Clapham Junction, the midwife announced she would be back in a minute but was just off to get him breathing.

Gulp.

With our boy gone, silence fell across the room.

It was odd, eerie even. So much had happened but now there was a void. A chasm. A gaping sense of nothingness and a horrid pang of worry. Out of the shadows a smaller midwife, with an impish face, quietly broke the silence.

'We're now going to deliver the placenta,' she announced.

There were no trumpets.

And with that she produced a very large syringe.

'Where is he?' my wife asked, clearly not as asleep as I thought she was.

'Have some water,' I said, passing her a cup.

She sat up, slowly.

'He's gone for some checks,' I said and quickly smiled. My role now was to protect and reassure. 'Normal stuff, nothing to worry about.'

It was all I could say.

'I want to see him,' she said.

I nodded, knowing it was the least she deserved.

'I know, me too,' I said, 'he'll be back very soon.'

And it turned out he was. The midwife appeared, holding him, wrapped up in a fluffy towel. Ten toes. Two ears. Willy. Job done.

'Nothing to worry about,' she cooed, passing him over.

I stared at him. My boy. To be frank, not quite as beautiful as I had hoped. Still, he was breathing, and that was what mattered. We weighed him, took the obligatory photos and then the midwives were gone. We were alone, a family for the first time. I looked at the clock, and saw it was almost 4 a.m. We wrapped him up and put him in a tray next to the bed.

'I love you,' I said to my wife, but she was already fast asleep.

I sat down in a chair next to his trolley, watching, thinking about the world and the life that had just started. And as I thought, I started to feel anxious. The world was not in a good place.

It was a world that was punch-drunk. A world hot with jealousy and religious conflict. Disease remained rife, so too, corruption, war, and terror. Society was broken. The system was riddled with conflicted corporate interests and government policies that paid lip service to hollow eyed electorates; embittered, marginalised, and increasingly cut adrift. Communities were lost and divided, crushed by the bitterness and bewilderment of a life that had failed to keep up its side of the bargain.

Sea levels, too, were rising.

I stared into the darkness and, as the adrenalin subsided, my emotional state deteriorated. The high was gone. Now it was me, and my boy. I was now a father, a role model, and a teacher. The person he would turn to, to explain all the hate. To answer his whys, to unpick the reasons for all the bombs and mass shootings and seals wrapped in plastic. It would be my words that would attempt to contextualise the cynicism of a system corrupted by so much greed and self-interest.

And why all the debt?

I would need answers, I knew I'd need answers. Sleep became impossible. There was too much to think about. I stood up to stretch and pace the room. My time had come. I needed to protect him, to shelter him. To offer a hand when he tripped, a shoulder and a sherbet dip, when he wept. I stopped and peered at his little face in the gloom. Such innocence. My breathing became quick and shallow and as I stood up over his cot tears started to roll down my cheeks. I looked down and my fists were clenched. I was clinging on.

And then, I stopped.

Gerald.

It was obvious. He was it. He was society: greed

on legs.

A bully.

A sheep that needed to be slaughtered.

And an old fire roared back to life in my belly and I knew then, what had to be done.

For society.

For my boy.

*

I had to go back to work.

Living in a domestic bubble, days and hours consumed as they were by a fierce focus on keeping your baby alive, it is easy to lose touch with the world. But it had to end. Someone had to pay for all the nappies. I also had a murder to plan. I didn't want my boy to grow up in a society that let bullies win.

I got up early and caught the train into work and as the stations whistled past, I looked around the carriage at the other commuters. Some were asleep, others were reading newspapers carrying headlines of more senseless terror attacks. The rest were on their phones, scrolling, scrolling, scrolling. Always scrolling.

Killing time.

I eased through the revolving doors of the bank and nodded soberly to the security guard. As I stood on the escalator, I saw Gerald walk in and glide past the same security man, his eyes down, glued to his own phone, flicking on emails that had little relevance other than to busy his own petty existence in middle-management.

And then I felt old feelings start to boil. Disgust.

Hatred. I wondered idly whether I could push him off the walkway, down into the atrium to meet his death on the very mock marble that he scuttled over each, and every, day. It would be a suitably gruesome end and it would make a delicious story for the tabloids. The sub-editors would have difficulty breathing as the facts poured in on the tape.

I arrived at the second floor and looked over the edge. It didn't look quite high enough. It was also a conspicuous spot, and yet I imagined many a colleague would slip past, their eyes glazed and unseeing. Some I suspect, those whose lack of a bonus had left their spouse rampaging around the house with a hockey stick as they cowered in the cellar, would even lend a shoulder to help heave Gerald's buttocks over the edge.

'He's back!' I felt slap on my back.

I turned.

Eddy.

A colleague that I didn't want to kill.

'Morning Eddy,' I said.

We walked across the trading floor together and I sat down at my desk and tried to remember my password.

Modern life, a life of passwords.

As I tapped, Gerald eased up behind me and I caught a whiff of the familiar, pungent cologne.

My instinct was to grab his fleshy jowls and batter his head on my idle keyboard, but I didn't. My plans for murdering Gerald were still smouldering ideas, rough sketches. Snatched scenes in idle moments.

They still had no substance.

'There's a deal to sell,' he muttered as he passed.

No greeting.

No congratulations.

I said nothing and grabbed a pad and set course for the conference room that was fast filling up with colleagues.

All hungry for details.

All hungry for fees.

*

I put down the phone.

It had been a dispiriting morning of harassing clients, sweet-talking them, calling them up with news that money was piled on the table, stacked up like warm donuts, and they, the client, just had to reach out with their sticky fingers and help themselves. There was, I had tried to quietly infer, a greedy man in all of us.

My mother-in-law had also left several messages to call her back which was another worry. I looked over at Blanchard as he worked himself up.

'I don't know if that is true. I don't care. I'm hanging up now…. What?… Well you're gay too!' he shouted.

And then he hung up.

I sighed.

The team was on edge. With our budget looking like it was going to be missed there were murmurings of a jobs cull. A rationalisation. Livelihoods would be lost. So too hopes and dreams of bespoke walnut kitchens. The senior management team were also on a drive to validate our value as they wanted to weed out the weak. To cut costs. And they wanted to find out what value we all added.

It was a question of great discomfort for many, hidden as we all were in a sprawling, bloated corporate melee where individuals were identified, not by name, but by desk number.

And Gerald, as ever, was their messenger.

That morning, after the meeting, he had announced a new system of docking calls; clocking interactions with clients. Measuring who said what, to whom, and for how long. He said that we would be ranked each week and those at the bottom would be given warnings. The tide, we all knew, was going out.

He announced his initiative with a quiet zeal, his jaw fixed, his eyes intense and a little watery both at the same time. He could have been on the moors scanning the horizon for grouse. Or some other luminary of the RSPB sticker book.

I scrolled down my screen of morning touchpoints. I'd hit a lot of voicemail recordings which was, on reflection, deeply depressing. What job involved speaking solely to voicemail? A message which you knew would never be played. A message destined to never charm an ear. Deleted, as it would be, into the black hole of cyber space. As if it never happened. Even in a call centre people phoned you. That they then shouted, was not important. It was an interaction. It was human.

Still, voicemail counted as a hit, a touch point

providing, that was, the message was longer than thirty seconds. Thirty seconds and it counted as a point. I clutched to that truth and had warbled and chuntered my way through the thirty second barrier. It was like a hostage negotiation. Keep them on the line, keep talking.

Only with less at stake.

And no one on the line.

Gerald had also been different of late. He had morphed into something else. Something even more hideous. With year-end nigh, he knew that the bonus pool was being finalised and how much was in it. And so, he had started to quietly manipulate people, to play them off against each other. He'd whisper little whisperings in ears, in coffee queues. He'd call people into meeting rooms, so that everyone could see, but not hear. He'd put his arm around shoulders. He'd tease. He'd jest.

Others he blanked.

'Things may ripen soon,' he'd murmur in the lift, and then move on leaving in his wake a sense of unease.

And hope, hope that he knew would soon be crushed, by him.

His games split the team. Some would say they knew, that they had been given the wink whilst those that had not would then ask themselves why, allowing insecurities to flower, so too, hate.

For Gerald.

It was obvious he had no one's interests to hand but his own and, despite his meaningless seat in middle management, he revelled in it: seeing others suffer. Bankers, stewing in their own juices, terrified at the prospect of no bonus. If no bonus, what did it all mean?

The atmosphere on the trading floor grew ever more toxic.

*

Lunch had beckoned, and I headed outside, down some alleys and cobbled streets to a small café I knew. A steamy café, one where you ordered not by dish, but by number.

'Number 5, love?' the lady asked as I sat down.

I nodded.

Always a number 5.

I took a newspaper off the rack and, idly flicked through it, as I waited. Sleaze, anger, celebrity angst and boobs. Bar the latter, perhaps, it made for a depressing read which was no good for my mood. I was soon closing in on the classified adverts when an article caught my eye.

'DEATH AT LA POOL PARTY.'

I read the article.

Chip Makowski, 23 years old from Littlehampton, Missouri, had died. Chip had drowned at a pool party in Los Angeles. The report said that he had drowned in the jacuzzi and no one had noticed. The pool party had been too good, full of half-naked revellers, dancing, snorting cocaine off each other's tummies. They were all witnesses, but the police had reported there were no witnesses. No one could remember a thing. High as they were, no one even remembered seeing Chip, or being in the jacuzzi with him. He had just died. Drowned. Sometime between midnight and 1 a.m., according to the coroner.

A tragic death.

Or was it? Yes, it was tragic for Chip, but what if not all revellers were high. Or drunk. What say, one reveller was even sober. What then?

'Number 5?' called the lady.

I sat stock still. This was it. This was how we would do it.

'Number 5?'

A copycat kill.

I sat back in my chair and considered the possibility, and it all started to fall into place. The Christmas Party. I sat back, my brow furrowed, my mind a whir. We could juice Gerald up during the Christmas party and then late on, when eyes had glazed, and hands were wandering, desperately groping for exposed flesh, we could spirit him out and into a taxi and make our way to a lido. Or an open lake. Or better still a featureless city centre hotel equipped as they all are with tranquil pools and steam rooms. We could throw some drugs into the mix. We could buy in some topless call girls and then watch as lust and Gerald's own hedonistic leaning led him to his final resting place. The jacuzzi. His life slipping away as his lungs slowly filled with bubbly water, the sober hands around his neck simply too strong.

It had everything; all I could have ever wanted.

Everything.

It had nudity and hookers and drugs, all set against

the faceless transitional backdrop of a corporate hotel chain. The sordid morals of a soiled slice of society would be laid bare under the breathless gaze of an impatient media. We maybe even had an analyst at the bank who covered the hotel company with a buy recommendation. There were cakes and then there were cakes and cherries.

And cream.

Perfection.

I pulled out my phone and emailed Blanchard. I told him to meet me in the sauna later. I didn't say why, but he'd know. And then I tucked into a number 5, my spirits soaring. Bacon, beans, sausage; poached egg.

And hash browns.

For once, all impossibly delicious.

*

After lunch, I skipped back into work. Now that I had a plan, I felt energised.

The lifts were broken, and so I walked down past the post room and took the back stairs up to the trading floor and, as I capered up the steps, I turned a corner and almost tripped over Claire. She was sitting on the stairs, on her own, her knees tight to her chest, a clump of tissues in her hand. She had been crying. A lot. Her eyes were red and puffy. Her hair was a mess.

I sat down on the step next to her.

'Bad day?' I asked.

'They're all bad,' she said.

'Let me guess, Gerald?'

She rolled her eyes.

'I think he's really after me now, I know it. He's trying to get me out.'

I scoffed.

'He can't! You know that?'

'I know,' she said with a wry smile.

And he couldn't either, Claire was untouchable. She knew it. Everyone knew it. Gerald hated Claire because Claire mattered more to the bank than he did. Claire mattered because someone had told HR that she had kissed the utilities team. All of them. That it had never been confirmed by Claire, or the utilities team, was irrelevant. HR couldn't take the risk.

Claire was a woman, and there was no way the bank could lose a woman; any woman. There were simply too many men. The ratios were all wrong. Claire was also, given the gender balance of the utilities team, potentially, a lesbian. Or bi. Or possibly even something else. Perhaps Claire didn't even identify with gender. Perhaps she was neither she, nor he; just it.

All so fashionable, so 'youth'.

Claire was, in diversity terms, pure gold.

And so, Gerald quietly fumed. He found it intolerable that a junior member of his own team was beyond his reach. Beyond his control. There was no way he could fire her. If he had even tried, he knew there was a risk that he might well find himself outside by the delivery bay, holding a stapler and phone charger with his spare suit stuffed into a bin liner.

He could, potentially, even end up in court. HR may not have made any money for the bank, but as they sat and whiled away afternoons playing pass the parcel with a chocolate orange, eyes shiny with excitement, everyone knew, even Gerald, that nothing happened without their buy-in.

Claire's job was safe.

She sniffed.

'It'll be ok,' I said, 'maybe someone will push him off the roof at the summer BBQ.'

I stopped short. I said it in jest, but I caught her eye and was reminded of what she had said in the bar. The full moon. She too had coals that smouldered. I don't know why I said it, I wasn't thinking. She, though, was clearly now pondering the same thing, perhaps trying to remember exactly what it was that she had said.

As we sat and indulged our thoughts, and eyed each other up, groping for where the boundary to our friendship lay, there was the sound of heavy footsteps labouring up the steps. I looked up and there stood the Fox. He remained where he was. Motionless. His sharp eyes took everything in.

'Do you need to book a stair for lunch?' he asked, with a suggestion of a smile.

'We were just plotting the downfall of the entire senior management team,' I said. 'Claire thinks we skewer them for insider dealing, I say we gun them down in the lobby.'

I laughed.

Silence.

'I'd go with the lobby,' pondered the Fox, 'insider dealing is too hard to prove, and you need to make sure. Shooting them would also be more satisfying.'

He chuckled and sat down on the stair below us and offered us up a chip from his sad polystyrene box. I took one and watched him eat and noticed he had strong hands, with thick rough fingers that had little nicks on them. They were hands that worked the land. Capable hands.

'Gerald?' he asked, dabbing a lone chip in some tomato sauce.

Claire nodded.

'Who else?' she said.

The Foxed chewed, looking at nothing.

'I've known him a long time,' he said. 'He's a difficult man, and an outsider. It's something he's been fighting all his life. He's always been an outsider.'

I took a few more chips.

Interesting.

'And ever since he started here, he's always been political. He's always been ruthless and will stop at nothing to get more money, more power. He's a nasty piece of work.'

He laughed, a sort of light chuckle, and continued to stare into space.

Thinking.

Weighing something up.

'Funny you should mention it. We tried to kill him once,' he said, chuckling some more.

I sat and stared at him, and then looked at Claire. She shot me a look that I couldn't read.

'As in kill, kill?' asked Claire. 'As in dead?'

'Yes! Ghastly man. We had it all planned too,' he said.

'How?' I asked, feigning shock and disbelief, trying to hide my obvious interest. 'What happened?'

It was on reflection, a quite startling statement. Extraordinary. And in the stairwell, too. Stairwells and their musty secrets. The Fox saw an analyst coming down the stairs and waited. What he had to say was not something for passing ears.

'It was on a grouse shoot with clients. What was his name? Lobbers, that's it, I forget his real name, anyway Lobbers had organised this day's shooting for our clients.'

'Tweed?' I asked.

'Yes, lots. Now the context was that Lobbers had almost gone to jail because of Gerald.'

'Why?' Claire asked.

'Lobbers had overheard an analyst in the lift, talking about a small oil company that had found some oil. And so, Lobbers bought some shares in this company for his personal account. Quite a lot of shares.' He took another chip and chewed. 'Anyway, it turned out they had indeed found oil. Millions of barrels of oil and the shares doubled overnight.'

'That's illegal,' Claire muttered.

'Yes, but back then the rules weren't really rules. They were never enforced. Lots of people did it.

Lobbers bought everyone on the desk a bottle of champagne with his profits. All except Gerald. He didn't like Gerald and the feeling was mutual. They were going for the same promotion.'

'I like the sound of Lobbers,' Claire said, taking another chip.

Chips.

Balm to the soul.

I smiled.

It was strange, the tension had eased. The shock of the Fox announcing that he too had once been part of a plot, not just to oust, but to kill Gerald, had dissipated. It was if we had all found kindred spirits to whom death was, in some instances, clearly unavoidable.

The Fox continued.

'Anyway, Gerald sneaked on Lobbers to compliance, who called in the fraud squad from the financial regulator. They pulled off all his phone records. They found calls to his broker the day before the announcement. They pinned him. Lobbers was arrested, and it went all the way to the high court.'

'Did Lobbers know it was Gerald who ratted on him?' I asked.

'He guessed as much. Anyway, he got off. The court threw his case out on the first day. It turned out the police had not followed the right procedure and the phone records were inadmissible. Without the phone records, there was no real evidence. It had a certain stench to it: the timing, the fact the company was a client of the bank, the fact that Lobbers knew nothing about oil companies. But there was no actual evidence.'

'Lobbers walked free?' Claire said.

'Yes, but it cost him. His legal fees were bigger than the profit he made on the trade.'

'And so, he decided to kill Gerald?' I asked, ignoring the remaining chips.

We were beyond chips.

'Yes, Lobbers was incensed. We went out to celebrate his victory. Messy. Very drunken. At some point, he got up a head of steam and said he was going to kill Gerald. Someone else offered to help. I thought it was all a joke, so I said I was in too. Only it wasn't a joke. He was serious.'

I fixed the Fox with a look. He, like Claire, didn't seem the sort.

'What happened?' said Claire, impatiently.

'It was a disaster. The plan was to shoot him. Make it look like an accident. The shoot was an official client event and so Lobbers made sure Gerald came too.'

'With a client?' I asked.

The Fox nodded.

Claire grimaced, 'Poor chap.'

He continued.

'Lobbers had tipped the game keeper. A rough, murky man who, I suspected, would have done it himself for a bottle of cheap whisky. Anyway, it was a misty day, as they so often are on the moor and we were all strung out. The game keeper had pushed Gerald out on to the flank, he was the last in the line. And the next man in?'

'Lobbers,' I said, grinning, quietly marvelling at the playbook.

So clean.

'What went wrong?' Claire asked.

'Lobbers missed. He shot Charles.'

'Charles?' I said.

'Yes, Charles. Poor thing.'

'Who was Charles?' Claire asked.

'Gerald's dog,' he said. 'Lobbers was always a terrible shot.'

I whistled through my teeth.

So close.

'What sort of a person calls their dog Charles?' Claire whispered.

'Gerald,' he said.

He too, grimaced and I idly wondered whether Boris was trained to go on a shoot. We all then sat, quietly contemplating dogs and death. Each lost to their own thoughts of how close they came, or would perhaps come, to murder.

'What happened to Lobbers?' I eventually asked.

'Dead,' the Fox said. 'Brain tumour. About six months later.'

I shook my head.

The sad irony of life.

*

The afternoon dragged by.

I was bubbling as my plan, the more I thought about it, was perfect, and I couldn't wait to tell Blanchard. At the appointed hour I walked into the gym with my kit bag casually slung over my shoulder. Knowing I was not there to pump iron or plod remorselessly on a treadmill had an immediate effect on my behaviour. I felt guilty and conspicuous. I imagined the police poring over the CCTV footage for clues. Did I stand out? Was my gait any different? I shuffled in past the desk with my head down and headed straight for the changing room.

It was sad that we needed a gym in the basement. The sedentary nature of modern living, coupled with food processed within an inch of its life, meant we were all destined to die obese in our own beds. The fire brigade would have to remove us with a winch through the bedroom window. It would be reported in the local paper that it had taken three fire engines and twelve firemen several hours to remove the body. It would be reported as a waste of taxpayers' money.

As it would be.

I knew that I needed to cross train, or row, or do something to get the heart rate elevated above its resting rate.

Or perhaps plot a murder.

Indeed.

The locker room was empty, as I had hoped it would be. Few had the freedom to be absent from their desks yet, as salesmen, we were constantly absent; out visiting clients, out spreading the gospel. It afforded the perfect smokescreen. That we were away from our desks was nothing out of the ordinary. I changed quickly, avoiding the glare of a naked German whose face was the only bit of him that I recognised. I knew he worked in exotic derivatives, a line of business that meant absolutely nothing to me. He had intense blue eyes and tight, curly brown hair. He had also raised one leg on to the bench and was towelling his *wurst* with alarming aggression. All the while, he just stared straight at me.

Disturbing.

Most disturbing.

No wonder we all went to war.

I did the British thing and avoided eye contact, pursing the lips as if preoccupied with matters of etiquette, pomp, and sticky puddings. His actions were disturbing but investment banks, I had realised, attracted personalities from across the behavioural spectrum.

I donned some board shorts and skipped across the verruca strewn floor and opened the door to the sauna and stepped in. It was empty. It was also cool, and so I picked up the bucket of water and poured it over the stones, which sizzled and spat, and sat down on the bench waiting for the heat to hit.

I checked the time.

4.03 p.m.

I had told Blanchard to arrive at 4.05 p.m. I thought it important, for some reason, not to arrive together. I heard the door to the changing room open and feet pad across the floor and I started to sweat. I could hear shuffling and the occasional grunt, but not much more.

The sauna door then opened and there was Blanchard in possibly the tightest pair of Speedos ever made. They were at least two sizes too small. It was obscene. His tackle bulged in the body-hugging polyester and his fabulous gut fell over the top of his briefs. Hair adorned his belly, climbing up to cover his chest. His gold chain remained in place. It was, more so than usual, a breath-taking sight, quite horrendous, yet mesmerising at the same time. He shut the door and stood in the doorway.

'Hello, Sailor!' he said, his hands resting on his hips with unnecessary derring-do. It was an entrance befitting of a camp Christmas pantomime.

'Ah, Blanchard,' was all I could muster.

'We need more water,' he promptly said.

He disappeared with the bucket and returned a minute or two later, water spilling out of the top. He then poured half of it on the stones. The heat rose, and it quickly became unbearable. I feared I would struggle to think straight given I was barely able to breathe. Blanchard sat down heavily and, oblivious to the heat, proceeded to tell me about one of his clients who was having an affair with a junior colleague.

When he finished, I eased the conversation around to Gerald.

'I have a plan,' I said.

'You do?' he said. 'Blood?'

'No blood.'

'Poison?'

'Drowning.'

'Interesting.'

'Yes, possibly in a jacuzzi, the night of the office party.'

He scratched his belly as I told him my rough plan. Getting Gerald into the hotel. The drugs. The hookers.

'It might even be fun,' I added with a rueful smile.

He sat in silence; half hidden in the corner. It was frustrating, I couldn't read his expression, I couldn't see his reaction. I rolled the dice.

'Of course, if you have changed your mind, you can back out. Now's the time to say.'

'No, no, I'm in,' he said, his voice light and somewhat casual, 'it sounds like a good plan.'

I ploughed on, a little uneasy over his tone. He sounded careless. Flaky. Which, I had always feared, he was.

'I've been doing a bit of research,' I said, 'the Marriot Hotel is an easy walk from the restaurant.'

'I know the Marriot,' he muttered, 'I often meet clients there. Big lobby.'

'Yes, it's perfect. It also has a spa downstairs. With a jacuzzi.'

'So, all we need to do is get him down to the spa and into the jacuzzi?' Blanchard said.

'Yes,' I added, 'and then drown him.'

It needed to be said. The thing with death is that you can't ignore it, you need to talk about it, get it out in the open.

'And then what?' Blanchard asked.

I looked at him, unsure my accomplice was asking the right sort of questions.

'We leave. We get out,' I said, impatiently.

'We'll also need to take out the CCTV,' I said.

Silence.

Death.

It still hung in the air. There, but not there. As ever, ignored.

'And are you OK to drown him?' I finally asked, sweat dripping from my brow.

The question had to be asked but as he sat just staring at the floor I wondered if I had been too direct. Perhaps the question was too rich, perhaps the edges had been too sharp.

'Do you know Gerald once had a dog called Charles?' he said.

This, of course, I did know, although I didn't know why Blanchard also knew.

'No,' I said.

I needed to know where he was going with it.

'He did,' Blanchard said, and then he stopped and paused. 'I heard that he shot him.'

'Who? Gerald? Gerald shot Charles?' I asked.

'That's what I heard.'

'By accident?' I asked.

'No. For pleasure,' he spat. 'On his patio.'

I sat back and whistled through my teeth. Perhaps Blanchard was a dog lover, perhaps that was what fuelled his fire. God bless the Chinese whisper.

'Jesus Christ,' I said.

'Yes. The man is a monster.'

More silence.

I poured some water on the stones to turn up the heat as he had yet to answer my question. I didn't know if I should ask it again. There was no doubt he had heard me. The conversation then lurched further off topic.

'I drowned some puppies once,' Blanchard said, his gaze fixed on the hot stones.

'You did?' I asked.

There was not much more to say. Perhaps Blanchard didn't love dogs after all. He was, I was slowly finding, full of surprises.

'Yes. My aunt's dog had a litter. There were too many. She needed to get rid of some, and so I drowned them.'

I stared at him, unsure where to take the conversation.

'How did it make you feel?' I finally asked, a little part of me worried about my accomplice's mental state.

'Excited,' he said.

I shifted on the bench as it was not the answer I had expected.

'Of course,' I said. 'Standard reaction.'

Although it was, of course, far from standard. It was a very long way from standard. I wondered how old he had been as his hands held the puppies down under water, and what emotional scars he had been trying to itch. He looked at me, his eyes now glistening with sweat and anticipation.

'Yes, I'm OK drowning Gerald. Just no blood. There can't be any blood.'

I nodded.

'Good, so that's sorted then,' I said, now distinctly uncomfortable. 'I'll make sure the CCTV has been knocked out.'

The plan, I knew, was a loose one. It had been hastily conceived and there were many moving parts. Perhaps, too many, but then at least we now had our roles sorted. Blanchard was clearly a man that I didn't know and yet, the puppy story, were it true, gave me confidence that he would see it through. He had been there before, watching as life slipped away, eyes glazed as hands slowly squeezed.

Experience mattered.

The door then opened and a man I had never seen before walked in with a towel around his waist. He looked us both in the eye, and then picked up the bucket and poured the remaining water over the stones. He then removed his towel and reclined, naked, across the bottom bench.

I looked across at Blanchard.

'German,' he mouthed.

Another one.

Did they not do any work?

*

It was still dark outside as Blanchard had insisted on getting there early, before the lanes got busy. He had emailed me after our meeting in the sauna and said that he wanted to practice. To have a dry run. He said that he had been thinking and, whilst he had drowned some puppies, he had never drowned a man, and so he wanted to see what it was like. He wanted to get his moves straight and figure out the best method. He wanted, he said, to size things up.

And, importantly, find out how hard he needed to squeeze.

It was an unappealing prospect, filling the role of Gerald in such a chilling rehearsal, but it wasn't one that I could say no to. We were now a team. If our plan was to succeed, Blanchard needed to be comfortable, he needed confidence and, if that meant creeping out of the house before dawn and travelling across London to a distant lido, so be it.

I got changed and slipped out onto the open pool area. It was bigger than I thought, the lido. Much bigger. The stones were cold, and a nasty wind nipped off the water. I had initially objected to such an early morning dip, but Blanchard had insisted. It had to be the lido and it had to be early morning.

As I walked down the cold paving stones, I saw him in the water, bobbing, with only his head visible; his dark head, quietly bobbing in the dark water. I scanned the lido for any other early morning bathers, but it appeared there were none.

We were alone.

I eased myself down the steps in the shallow end.

It wasn't the hour, nor indeed the occasion, for a belly flop. We had a murder to rehearse. The water was surprisingly warm, and I quickly swam over to where Blanchard bobbed, in the middle of the lido.

'Morning Blanchard,' I said, my feet trying to touch the floor.

And yet they couldn't find it, Blanchard had positioned himself too deep and I had to tread water.

'Morning,' he said, his face wet, glistening in the feeble light of dawn.

'So how do you want to do this?' I asked, getting right to the point.

'I've been doing some reading,' he said. 'And the best way, appears to be strangulation.'

The word sounded sinister, which it was, more so in the dark, in the middle of a deserted lido. Blanchard, also, made it sound particularly sinister.

'Should we not do it in the shallow end?' I asked, beginning to feel a little out of breath. Treading water was surprisingly hard work.

'Sure,' Blanchard said, 'whatever suits.'

He then dipped under the water and swam off. He took big powerful strokes and moved well in the water for such a big man. His movements were almost graceful, in sharp contrast to his travels on dry land. I followed, slower and distinctly less graceful.

I had never been comfortable in open water.

As I reached Blanchard, I noticed it was getting a bit lighter. I was looking up at the sky and so I didn't notice him come at me.

But he did.

He suddenly came at me with his hands raised. His stiff cold fingers went straight for my throat. We fell back into the water with a splash. I tried to push him off, I tried to move away. But he was quick. And strong. Surprisingly strong. I managed to knock his hand away and get to my feet, but he was quickly back on me. His flesh was cold and hairy, and I struggled to get a grip. And then I was down, down under water. His hands closed in around my throat, dragging me lower. I tried to prise his fingers away, I tried to push him, I kicked and writhed. But I was weak. I was tired from all the treading water.

The air was being forced out of me. I tried to keep it in, but I couldn't. He was too strong. I continued to fight and tried to gouge his eyes, like they suggest you do to a crocodile, but he just pushed me down and turned his face away. And then, as I had all but given up, as I began to take leave of my senses and scenes from my childhood had started to play out in slow-motion, he abruptly let go. I stood up, and sucked in the air, feeling my neck. I coughed and coughed, and water stung my eyes. I was livid. My throat was on fire. I wanted to yell at him, but I didn't have enough air in my lungs.

'Are you two lovers?' a voice then asked.

It was an old voice. It was also close, and hoarse. One of those voices that let the end of each sentence fade a little. I spun around and there was a small man in a swimming cap and goggles. His face was craggy and old. The cold light of dawn was particularly unforgiving.

'What?' I said, still spluttering, still in shock.

I wiped away some blood from a small scratch on my chin. Blanchard had eased back into the water, only his head still visible.

'Are you two lovers?' the man said.

'Lovers?' I asked.

'Yes.'

'What? No!' I said, struggling to understand, 'no, we're not lovers.'

'It's ok if you are,' he said softly.

I looked at Blanchard, who remained bobbing in the shadows with a glazed look on his face.

'We're not lovers,' I said, 'we're work colleagues.'

'Oh, I see,' said the man.

'Why do you think we're lovers?' I asked.

'George and I used to do that.'

'Do what?' I asked.

'Grapple,' he said, raising his now feeble arms.

'Grapple?'

'Yes.'

'Why?'

'George found it exciting.'

I stared at him, not knowing what to say.

'Sexual,' he added, wistfully.

The man gazed across the water; his face sad.

'I do miss him,' he said, gently.

He then reset his goggles and swam off. I watched him go and shook my head and then spun around to face Blanchard, anger bubbling back, rising through my scorched throat. I was confused, unlike George.

'What the hell were you doing?' I shouted.

Blanchard bobbed.

'You hurt my neck!'

'Surprise,' said Blanchard.

'What?'

'Surprise. I also read the best attacks contain an element of surprise.'

My neck was red and raw. There was more blood. Little nicks from Blanchard's long nails.

'Did you have to squeeze so hard?' I asked.

But Blanchard didn't answer. He just bobbed. Looking. Looking at me, quietly kneading his own deadly thoughts.

Silent.

'We're going to be late for work,' I said, still angry, but realising I wasn't going to get an answer.

Part of me was also worried he might come at me again.

'I'll see you in the office.'

I swam off, not knowing what to feel. Blanchard surprised me. I had long worried that he didn't have it in him, but now, I knew. In the lido, I saw a violence in Blanchard that I had never seen before and for the purposes of our grotesque plan, it was good news.

Very good news, indeed.

CHAPTER VIII

I looked at my screens to check what was happening in the market. It was down, the screens were bathed in red. When the stocks went up, the screens went green. When they went down, they went red. Today, red; apt given it was the day of the Christmas party and all it entailed.

Death.

With my calls for the morning done, I headed out to get a coffee and run through the plan one more time. On my return I pushed through the imposing revolving doors and I bumped straight into Gerald.

'Sorry,' I said, 'Not looking where I was going.'

It was the first time we had spoken in weeks.

He looked tired, a little pale, even.

'Are you ok?' I asked, despite myself. It was almost instinctive; perhaps simply human nature.

Concern.

I clearly didn't care for the man, but he looked white.

Very white.

'No, not really. I feel awful,' he said.

He looked awful.

'Yes, you don't look well.'

'I'm going home. I'm not sure I'll be able to make it to the party tonight.'

I cursed under my breath. It could be the best decision he ever made.

'That's a shame,' I said, 'it should be great fun.'

My words though were hollow. It would be anything but fun. For him. And I. And Blanchard. A torrid night for all.

'Yes, a shame. I'll see how I go.'

I watched him shuffle out of the door and walk off to the tube stop, his head down, leaning into the wind, and hoped he got better.

For obvious reasons.

I took to the elevators, heading up to the second floor my thoughts a torrent of drugs and bubbles and the look on Gerald's face as Blanchard stared into his eyes, hands tight around his neck.

I walked onto the trading floor to see that the desk was all but deserted. Such was the time of year, there was little incentive to wring the tape for any remaining commission. The year was done. Why work when you could lunch? I sat down at my desk, my screens blank, so too my mind.

'Not out for lunch?'

I spun around.

The Fox.

'Not today,' I said.

I tried to think of something witty to say, but nothing came to mind and so, I grinned. It was all I could do.

'Your mother-in-law called,' he said.

'She did?' I asked, as casual as I could make it.

'Yes,' he said, 'she left a message.'

He handed me a small post-it note. I glanced down at it and swallowed hard. In his neat writing, he had written: *central heating?*

I grunted.

'Cold time of year,' I said, a little lamely.

It was an odd message, but I couldn't think what it meant. My mind was too frayed. There was too much going on.

'Thanks,' I said and threw the note in the bin.

And yet the Fox continued to sit, and watch, slowly spinning on the chair, this way and that. Side to side. His eyes never left me. There was no one else within earshot. The floor was quiet, eerily quiet, and I started to feel vulnerable.

'You seem to have become somewhat chummy with Blanchard recently?' he finally asked, although I wasn't sure if it was a statement or a question. 'I wouldn't have put you two together. Different taste in shoes,' he added, cryptically.

Blanchard did, indeed, have an awful array of shoes. Brown. Square toed.

Frightening, both morally and socially.

This, though, was dangerous ground. The Fox was a stoat as wily as my wife's neck warmer, the difference being, the Fox was alive. Old, but very much alive.

'Yes, it's odd,' I said, buying myself time, 'I think there's more to Blanchard than meets the eye. I got to know him a bit doing the IPO.'

The Fox drummed his fingers under his chin.

'I'd say you two are planning something,' he said.

Fact.

The statement was unexpected. I stalled some more, turning to log on to my computer, yet I could still feel his eyes on me. He was a crafty man, Fox. And I couldn't grasp his angle. I had no footing.

It was most uncomfortable.

'Like what?' I asked, as innocently as I could.

'At a guess, I'd say it has something to do with Gerald,' he said, his voice barely above a whisper.

I spun around and eyed him up.

And he eyed me.

Silence.

Too much silence.

'I wouldn't trust Blanchard,' he said. 'And not just because of his shoes.'

'Why would I need to trust him?' I asked, probing, testing him out. I wanted to see what he knew, but he just stared back at me. His phone then started ringing.

'If you play with fire, expect to get your fingers burnt,' he whispered.

I was about to say something, I don't know what, I hadn't thought of anything, when he pushed himself up off the chair and sidled off to answer it. I watched him go. The question I needed to know, was how much he knew and what was with the cryptic message on Blanchard? I sensed he was fishing, casting some bait, but something didn't feel right. It had been an uneasy exchange, more so as I knew what the man was capable of. He too had been drawn to violence.

I knew I needed to be careful.

The afternoon dragged by, not helped by my state of mind. To avoid the Fox, I tried to keep as busy as was possible which, so close to Christmas when clients were so thin on the ground, was a challenge. Even the most distasteful client was out for lunch, invited by a broker desperate for an authentic name to fill out on the expense ticket. At five to four, I picked up my gym bag and with the Fox buried, as always, in the obituaries of the newspaper, I slipped away and took the back stairs down to the gym.

The gym, as you might expect, was also empty and I quickly stripped off.

3.59 p.m.

Sauna time.

As I waited in the sauna, I replayed the conversation with the Fox. It was odd, the tone of his voice didn't chime with the words. I thought he'd have been more hostile, more aggressive. Yet he wasn't. His words were warm. Almost caring. Perhaps he wanted in? It was clear he didn't like Gerald, but for Fox, why bother when he was so close to collecting his pension?

Perhaps it was a warning.

He was right, though, I couldn't trust Blanchard, and yet I also needed Blanchard, our fate was now the same. There was no backing out now. I looked at the clock on the wall: 4.08 p.m. Where was he?

I poured more water on the stones and shut my eyes. It had been a long day. I felt tired. I tried to push all thoughts aside and think of nothing. Space. White space. I tried to let it all go and drift into that detached state of consciousness that comes just before sleep, but I couldn't, not with murder on the mind. Peace was a state that remained beyond reach. I was edgy and nervous and apprehensive. I knew that if the plan slipped, or took a different course, I knew that I would be asked the question. Did I have it in me? Could I be the one to force the air out of Gerald's lungs?

As I confronted the shocking reality of what might lie ahead, I knew in my heart that I could. We all can. We all have it in us. The reason I knew this, indeed, drew confidence from it, was that one recent weekend I too had tasted rage.

White hot rage.

It had been a get-together; a happy, sugary meet up of babies and eager parents, all wet lipped for gummy bears and tight talk on school fees. I forget where. A tasteful townhouse with an open plan living area and lots of chrome and cream furniture. The heating could be controlled from the supermarket via the web. The garden lawn was laid with fake turf.

All so vogue.

I, however, had been inside, watching my boy play with a train. He sat and held it, staring at the wheels, turning it in his hands, dropping it, picking it up. I had been talking to a man. A man in jeans and a tight pink cashmere cardigan who also laid claim to one of the babies in the room. There had been babies everywhere, so too trains. Other parents hung around the edges of the room, all talking and smiling and nodding. All looking over each other's shoulders. I had been talking to this man, but I too hadn't been listening.

I was looking over his shoulder, watching my boy play with his train. It gave me such pleasure. He had looked so happy, so, content, it made me happy, despite my murderous state of mind.

And then this other boy had walked over and grabbed my boy's train. My immediate reaction was mature. I reasoned that this bigger boy had clearly been brought up badly. It wasn't his fault. He was probably neglected, raised by a bored, foreign-looking nanny. He was possibly just confused. He would, later, when he was even bigger, start torturing the cat. He would sink into obesity. His self-esteem would collapse. Expulsion from school would be somewhat inevitable and it wasn't even his fault.

Blame would lie with society.

A culture that had warped his parents lives and riddled their minds with deep-seated insecurities about their own self-worth and financial grade. A system that drove them both to work 12-hour days leaving them quietly suffocating in guilt at missing another bath time.

All for a better life.

'The market is fully priced,' the man had purred,

the words slipping out of the corner of his mouth.

'What?' I had asked, not listening.

'I've been liquidating,' he said.

'Food?' I asked, turning to face him.

'Stocks,' he said.

I think I might have grunted.

The little bully, then, clearly not satisfied with taking the train, put a sticky hand on my boy's chest and shoved him over in an act of grotesque, gratuitous violence. He had then walked off with the train.

And hell had burned in my eyes.

I was barely able to hold myself together. I rushed over to pick my boy up and soothe him, my eyes scanning the floor for the bully. A woman came up and offered to hold him. She knew, she could tell. I had business to attend to.

It was then that I had turned and hunted down the child and had found him in the playroom, standing alone by the window, still holding my boy's train. I fought with the urge to push the boy over and press his face into the deep carpet and whisper in his little ear, that if he ever came near my boy again I'd throw him, and his teddy bear, into a canal.

I wanted him to taste fear.

Instead, I grabbed his arm and prised the train out of his soft, feeble fingers.

'Get lost,' I said, glowering.

It was shocking.

Later, driving home, I was still mulling my actions,

still trying to rationalise the anger that I had felt towards a small boy. I had felt a little foolish, embarrassed even, and yet at the same time I was quietly exhilarated that I was able to feel such anger.

Rage even.

It was electrifying in the context of a life lived in the musty air of the English middle class. Electrifying and quite thrilling and, I was intrigued to realise, unusually moreish. For the first time, I realised what pure love can make a man do in protecting his child. Where does he draw the line?

As it turned out, there was no line, and it dawned on me, as we waited in the torpid, early evening traffic, that there is a rage in all of us, and that we are all capable of violence.

Which meant, if pushed, we are all capable of murder.

*

'We expect a rotation out of the growth cohort into value which, relative to growth, trades at two standard deviations below its historical average.'

I stared at the paper I was reading from, feeling deeply uncomfortable. Speaking to clients did that.

'Value!' my client scoffed, 'Value traps. All of them! Where is the earnings growth?'

He was stiff and aggressive, and I feared I had touched a nerve. I imagined he was cleaning spittle from his handset. Perhaps taking another nip of whisky from the open bottle. His office, like mine, deserted. Party season. I touched my reindeer horns, largely as a means of reassurance.

Blanchard had not turned up.

I had waited for half an hour in the sauna but then left. He was a no show. I checked my phone but there was no message and I feared the worst. Drunk. Slumped on a park bench somewhere, clutching the leg of a deep-fried chicken in each hand.

Unconscious.

Useless.

I had been about to leave for the office party when my phone rang. It was late, the market had closed, and the pubs were packed. I was only at my desk as I had made it halfway down the escalator and realised I had forgotten my reindeer horns, which I had gone back to pick up and was now wearing.

The client was a prickly sort. He rarely spoke to me. Instead, our relationship had developed over email, which was strange, but of the age. He and I punching out short, bitty, sentences to each other. Occasionally I'd send a longer email with proper adjectives highlighting to him the full body of research our anxious, catty cacophony of research analysts had written; an email which, as far as I was aware, he had never read. I often tried to phone him, but all I got was his voicemail. I hit his voicemail with depressing frequency.

'Please leave a message after the tone…'

Modern life.

Indifferent.

Cold.

The work place had changed.

Gone were the rich, fleshy relationships of the pre-tech age. There was no longer any personal connection. I could not remember the last client I had hugged with any meaning. It was more sterile, there was more distance. We were too often left groping in the dark, unable to read cues or understand what it was that our clients feared.

The reason being, we didn't know them anymore.

I sat down in my chair. I was tired. I was also apprehensive about murdering Gerald.

'You're wrong,' my client said.

It was difficult not to agree. I had been reading from a stray piece of paper I had found on my desk.

'I've got to go,' I said and hung up.

I texted my wife.

'All well? Hope you have a good night. Off to party.'

I wondered if I should tell her about the murder. The ill-conceived plan to drown Gerald. Run it by her, like any husband might with a big decision. It was a big call. Were we to be caught, it would be she who would have to explain to our boy what had happened.

I sat and toyed with my phone and looked at the clock. I needed to get to the party, yet something held me back. I stood up and gazed across the empty trading floor. I didn't want to go. I knew it was starting something that might not end well, something that might change my life.

Change my wife's life.

My boy's life.

Did I really want that?

My real grown up life had only just started and now I had a family to support. Yes, the world was a mess, but there was hope. There was the UN. And Greenpeace. We could register for an allotment and grow vegetables.

My fire flickered.

We should pull out, I thought.

Abort.

It was a bad idea. A very bad idea. It was crazy, killing Gerald in a hot tub.

I'd still go to the party, but I'd tell Blanchard it was off. It was the right thing to do and I immediately felt better.

I went downstairs and hailed a cab and yet, as we waited at some traffic lights, my mind boomeranged back onto Gerald, as if on its own accord. I thought of all the unhappiness he caused. All the tears. The man was a tyrant. A man consumed by his own need for power.

And control.

And money.

I thought of Claire, her face swollen from all the tears. The smudged mascara. The misery. The deep loathing of Monday mornings. The hanging dread of going to work, walking back into such a venomous world; a world all of Gerald's own making. I thought of all the people who had come, keen and eager, only to leave disillusioned. Their confidence crushed.

All because of Gerald.

And I thought of what he had done to me.

Maybe he deserved it? Maybe it was just his time?

I watched the throng of shoppers flood their way towards the Christmas lights, all in search of gifts for friends and family, and I felt an unfamiliar power charge my core. I felt a surge of love for my fellow man, my fellow woman. Good people.

We should do it, we had to do it, we had to go through with it. We had to make a stand against him and his god-awful bullying; against all bullying. We should do it for humanity.

For my boy.

Plan A.

Death by bubbles.

Some lambs need to be slaughtered.

The Vicar was right.

I stared out of the window as we crossed the river and my phone vibrated in my hand. I looked down to see a message from Blanchard. The message was of an emoji of a bomb and a knife. Nothing else. I stared at the screen and felt a nasty turn in the pit of my stomach. Blanchard had been out at a long lunch. He had missed our appointment in the sauna and was now likely demolishing cocktails amidst the reckless mood of a year-end Christmas party. I feared that the evening was not going to go to plan. A or B, if indeed there was time to write a Plan B.

Which there wasn't.

As it turned out, I had never been more right in my life.

CHAPTER IX

I tipped the cab driver as I felt bad that I had not talked to him. Poor man stuck as he was in traffic all day long, only the radio for company. A conversation would have been nice for him. But not tonight, not from me.

Not with murder on the mind.

As ever, for a venue that had muscled its way onto the London scene, there was a reception committee by the door. All mitts and beanies and day-aged stubble. The mood was hostile. I reported to the girl that I was on the guest list, but she just looked at me, with thin lips, her brow furrowed. The thick set bouncers swayed from foot to foot, expressions absent, fists primed. I stared back at them. The girl checked her clipboard, spoke to someone on a walkie talking and finally nodded at the goon who reluctantly opened the door.

I moved in and surveyed the scene.

Various little groups had formed, as they do at such functions. Like moths, drawn to lights. Faces they knew. It was still too early for alcohol to numb the nerves, too early to let the guard down, to properly let go. There was, though, an undercurrent of energy. It was year-end, and the lid could finally come off the steam cooker.

I saw the Fox leaning on the bar on his own and squeezed my way through the crowd to join him. I still needed to try and tease from him what he knew. If indeed, he knew anything about our plan. I suspected paranoia at play, but I still needed to know.

'You're late,' he said with a smile as we shook hands. We'd never shake hands in the office, but we did in the bar.

'There are still clients to talk to. Commission to be made,' I grinned, or as far as I could grin given my state of mind. I could not see Blanchard, nor for that matter, Gerald.

'Has Gerald made it?' I asked, turning to wave at the barman.

I knew from our earlier conversation this was swampy ground. The Fox paused. His eyebrow rose as he sipped his whisky and I held my breath.

'Yes, he has,' he finally said. 'Why do you ask?'

The eyebrow was still up but I had been prepared for his question. I knew it would come.

'Oh, I saw him this afternoon,' I said, 'he told me he was going home as he didn't feel well. Said he wasn't sure he was going to be able to make it.'

The eyebrow gave back some ground and I breathed.

'What can I get you?' I asked. 'Is that whisky?'

'And soda,' he said. 'And make sure it's the 12-year old Balvenie,' he added. 'none of that nasty cheap stuff.'

I sighed and pulled out more money.

Across the bar I could see Dominique, half in shadow, brooding, seemingly bereft of any festive spirit. I pitied the poor soul having to sit next to her and turned to the Fox and handed him his drink, bracing myself for a further grilling. I was saved by Emma, the team secretary and party hostess, who appeared, wearing her own set of reindeer horns, and told us we had to sit down to supper.

As I turned to go, the Fox grabbed my arm.

'Here, take this,' he said, holding out his hand.

He was holding a small business card. I took it and slipped it into my pocket. The Fox then stepped in, close enough so he could speak into my ear.

'If things don't go to plan, call the number. He can help.'

He then squeezed my elbow and walked off to find his seat for supper. I pulled the card out of my pocket. All it had on it was a phone number. No name, no nothing, just a phone number. I put it back in my pocket trying to work out what had just happened. What did it mean?

'You need to sit down!'

I turned to see Emma: horns, breasts, glitter. Visually she was a lot to take in.

'Yes, yes of course,' I said, my mind still scrambling, struggling, unable to see truths in the dark lighting.

I found my seat and cursed quietly. It appeared I was to be the poor soul sitting next to Dominique.

'Good evening, Dominique,' I said as she arrived, emerging, as ever, from the shadows.

'Hello,' she said, her voice dark and a little husky,

I searched her eyes for any humour, for any spark. Nothing. She was, as always, wearing black. All over. Her dark hair was scraped back. She wore heavy eyeshadow and too much make up. All so dark, all so depressing. We sat down to a long silence and she started to suck up what little festive spirit I had.

'You, Dominique, appear to be the meat in our sandwich,' said Eddy who, like Dominique, had appeared from nowhere.

He laughed, as he was prone to do.

I smiled.

Dominique didn't.

Eddy, sat down, and started talking to Dominique. Her face suggested she was not so enamoured at being the filling in our tight sandwich. Too late. It was shaping up to be a long night, a long night for all of us. All except Gerald, whose night, indeed whose life, should end, shortly before midnight.

Tick tock, tick tock.

The bar area started to clear and as everyone sat down an uncomfortable sight met my eyes. Outside there was a smoking area. I hadn't seen it when I had walked in as there were too many people. But now they were all seated, I could see it. And I could see Gerald, puffing on a small cigar talking to Blanchard.

Blanchard had his arms outstretched, like he was telling a story that involved a bird of prey. He was not wearing a jacket, despite the cold, and was sporting a tight black roll neck top only ever seen socially in ski resorts. I couldn't see his face, but I could see Gerald's.

He was laughing.

Why would Gerald be laughing?

'Have you any plans for Christmas?'

I couldn't decide what it meant. Had Blanchard changed his mind? What had he told Gerald? Were they in cahoots? Was I now in danger? Trust. The Fox was right, Blanchard and I had so little trust.

'Have you any plans for Christmas?'

'I'm sorry?' I said.

'Have you any plans for Christmas?' Dominique asked.

I turned to face her.

'I do yes. If I make it through tonight.'

*

'I felt so stupid and ashamed, finding out like that.'

I looked at Dominique and nodded. It was all I could do. There were some occasions where words, any words, just don't fit. They're the wrong shape. On such occasions, it was important not to force them.

'It must be tough,' I said.

I was sitting, bent over with my elbows on my knees. It was a serious pose that was befitting of the conversation.

After the plates had been cleared, Eddy had disappeared. When Dominique had returned from the loo, I saw that her eyes were puffy. She had sat down and all but finished her glass of wine. She had seemed unsettled, distracted even. Tense.

'Are you ok?' I had asked.

She nodded, but I could tell she was a long way from OK. She was nervous. Anxious. Taunted from the shadows, riddled with shame. Pascal's affair was common knowledge. Colleagues feigned pity, desperate to know how she was holding up.

Humiliated.

And so, we talked.

It was bitty at first and as I prodded and probed, she avoided eye contact. And yet I persisted, lobbing easy offerings her way: holidays, hopes, haircuts. The order didn't matter. She got comfortable. And she continued to drink and as the wine took effect, she let go and bared her soul.

She told me about her childhood. She told me that her father had worked in the oil industry, and so they had moved around a lot. From country to country. She had lived in Russia, Kurdistan, and several war-torn African countries I wasn't sure still existed. The family had finally settled in Houston, Texas, where she had gone to University. In her second year at University her parents had split up. The American Dream.

'Affair?' I asked.

She nodded.

'Yes, it hit me hard,' she said. 'I had a sister in New York, and another in Hong Kong, so they weren't around, and I had to pick up the pieces.'

'How did your mother cope?' I asked.

Dominique looked sad.

More sad than normal.

'She didn't. She was crushed. She never recovered.'

She told me that her father had joined the Country Club; a showy place where the oil executives would sit on the patio and swap tales of spudded wells and strippers. Her mother hated the Country Club and never went. She didn't play golf and she didn't play tennis. And the other wives made no effort to include her.

'She was too foreign for Houston,' Dominique said.

Anyone not from Houston, I thought, was probably too foreign for Houston.

'Let me guess, the affair started at the Country Club?' I said.

She nodded.

'It was all so predictable. She was the ex-wife of another member. Daddy wasn't her first. Anyway, it was messy. As you might expect.'

I grimaced and tried to convey an expression of compassion. No easy matter given how juicy the conversation had turned.

'What did your mother do?' I asked.

'She left. She went back home. As far as I know, they have not spoken since.'

She stopped a passing waiter and asked for another glass of wine. Talking helps, so too wine. The scars were rough, and she needed help.

'Daddy and I moved in with her. She lived in a huge house courtesy of her divorce. She had two daughters my own age.'

'Tricky,' I offered.

'They hated Daddy. And hated me. They hated everything. The world. They were out of control. Drink. Drugs. Boyfriends. Lots of boyfriends. And they controlled their mother. She carried too much guilt. She tried to buy them off. All she had was money. And they used her.'

'Was he the first lover to move in with her?' I asked.

She nodded.

'Difficult,' I added.

I tried to imagine breakfasts. I assumed they were played out in silence. If indeed, they breakfasted together. Or breakfasted at all. There didn't sound like there was much demand for pancakes and maple syrup.

'I couldn't stand it. I had to move out.'

'No kidding. Where did you go?' I asked.

'I moved in with a friend of mine from college. She was so sweet. We had done some volunteering together, working in a local school. Her Dad would come and pick us up. They'd sometimes invite me back for supper. I got to know them. She had an older brother. They were such a nice family.'

'Good people?' I said.

She nodded.

'Christian people. I started to go to Church with them on Sundays. I felt safe with them.'

'Stability,' I muttered.

'They knew how awful it was or me, and then one day my friend asked if I would like to move in with them. They had an annexe flat which was empty.'

'How wonderful,' I said.

'Yes, to start off with.'

She shifted in her seat.

'Why, what happened?'

'It was on a camping trip. I knew it was wrong, but I was so lonely. And he made me feel so special.'

'You slept with her brother?' I asked, slowly, unsure of where the story was going.

She shook her head.

'The father,' she said.

'The Christian?' I asked, a little breathless.

She nodded.

'How?'

'It just happened,' she said, staring at the table.

So many questions.

'How long did it last?' I finally asked.

'It went on for about six months. He'd climb through my window after supper. It felt wrong, doing what we were doing with his family next door, but it was too good to stop. I felt wanted.'

'But it did stop?'

'Yes. He gave me a ring. He said it was special, so I shouldn't really wear it which was fine as I didn't really wear rings. I put it on a necklace which I wore. He said he liked knowing it was always close to my heart.'

'He said that?'

She nodded.

'Pathetic,' I murmured, shaking my head.

Men.

'I'm guessing the wife found out?'

Dominique nodded.

'Yes. She saw the ring on my dresser. Normally I put it away, but I had forgotten. It was her ring. Can you believe that? He gave me one of her rings. She accused me of stealing it. I remember it so clearly. It was down in the pool house. We were on our own, and she just lost it.'

'What did you do?'

'I told her the truth. I was many things, but I wasn't a thief. I would never steal from her. She had been so kind to me.'

'And so, you told her about the affair?

'Yes, it just came out. I was a mess. Sobbing and crying.'

'What did she do?' I asked, trying not to pant.

'She hugged me.'

'No way?'

'Yes, she came and sat me down and hugged me as I cried. She told me it was ok. That these things happen. She stroked my hair.'

'Incredible,' I said. 'How Christian. And so, she forgave you?'

Dominique paused. I sensed there was more to come and yet, I was unprepared for what followed.

'We had just been swimming, so we were in our bikinis,' she said, and paused, leaving the words just hanging there. Waiting to be picked off and fondled.

Like her.

'Sweet Mother of God,' I muttered.

Surely not. No way. Things like that don't happen in real life.

'It was strange. I don't know why. She was so soft. And kind. And she smelled of peach. I don't know how. It just, sort of, happened.'

'You kissed the mother?'

I needed confirmation.

'Yes,' she said.

The schoolboy in me started to shake, uncontrollably, with excitement.

'Did you sleep with her too?' I finally manage to ask.

She nodded.

I swallowed hard, not sure if it was appropriate to ask for more detail. I looked around. People were laughing. Drinking. Enjoying themselves. If only they knew.

'How did it end?' I asked.

'It got complicated. There were too many lies. I had to move out.'

I nodded, barely able to imagine the lies that would have been needed.

'I had to get some control back,' she said.

We both stared at the table, both thinking very different thoughts. She wasn't an attractive lady but, in this instance, that wasn't the point.

'So how did you end up in London?' I eventually asked, after the waiter had cleared the plates.

'Pascal,' she said. 'I moved to Paris after graduating. I needed to get away. I wanted to get into fashion and so did all sorts of menial jobs for various fashion houses. It wasn't what I thought it would be.'

'Not enough glamour?'

'Not any glamour. It was a horrible world. It was all about who you knew. It was mean. And bitchy. And the people were awful. They were all shallow and materialistic.'

'And so, you thought you'd try banking?' I asked, unsure if there was much of a difference.

Part of me still regretted letting the story drift away from the scene in the pool house, and I wondered whether I could wrestle it back, but Dominique had moved on.

'Yes,' she said. 'A friend's boyfriend worked for a bank and we were out one night, and he was saying his bank was hiring and that they would hire anyone. Literally anyone. And so, I applied. And they did. They hired me. I told them that I knew nothing about finance, but they said it didn't matter.'

'Few do,' I said. 'And that's where you met Pascal?'

She nodded.

'He worked in research. We met at a drinks event for clients. He was so charming.'

Charming and deadly.

'You know, I also really liked his beard,' she said.

'I bet your father had a beard,' I mumbled to myself.

'My father had a beard just like it,' she said.

Bullseye.

I thought about making a comment, but nothing suitable came to mind. She said that they had had an intense, passionate courtship. A whirlwind. There was a different European city every weekend: Barcelona, Vienna, London, Venice. They stayed in the best hotels. They ate in the top restaurants.

And Dominique fell in love.

They were married within a year.

'Pascal then got a job in London, and so we moved here,' she said.

'What did you do?'

'Nothing at first. We found a house in Notting Hill, and I explored London. It was wonderful. A new city. A new life.'

Perfect.

'And then this job came up and Pascal suggested I apply. I had done a similar job in Paris, so I had some experience.'

A new job. A new life. And all had been perfect until the day when Dominique had been taking some time in the loo and had heard two interns talking about Pascal's affair.

'You know the stupid thing,' she said, her eyes

welling up again, 'you know what I was most upset about?'

I grimaced. Part grimace, party encouragement. I didn't know what was coming next but whatever it was I wanted to hear it.

'What really upset me was finding out like that. From gossip in the ladies' loo.'

She had a point. Even an email would have been slightly better. Perhaps soften the blow a bit.

I patted her knee. It felt right, she needed reassurance, she needed a friend. I had always thought Dominique was, well, icy. She had always been so unfriendly. At work, there was nothing there, her guard was always up; she kept everything and everyone at a distance. A safe distance. And yet now I knew why. I saw her for who she was. A broken woman, angry at her family, angry at her husband. Angry at the world. I saw behind her sad, panda-like eyes and felt her pain.

We sat in, what felt to me like the compatible silence of friendship, quietly sifting the coals of our conversation.

'It's all very quiet down here! Who's died?'

Silence no more.

I looked up.

Blanchard.

*

Blanchard's black polo neck top was not suitable for dinner. It was just simply too tight. He was, though, sober, which came as a pleasant surprise given his animated antics outside with Gerald.

He winked at me as he sat down.

'Boring you rigid, is he?' Blanchard asked.

Dominique, laughed. A soft laugh. Dare I say it, a light laugh; a laugh that suggested our conversation had helped ease her emotional load.

'No, it was I who was boring him,' she said.

Blanchard cocked his head a little. It was a minor move but one that I noticed. He was, perhaps, not such a social rhino as first thought. There was some more mindless pitter-patter, before Dominique stood up and said she was going outside to have a cigarette. We both smiled as she left and watched her go. She was wearing what would be described, outside of a London it-bar, as pyjamas.

Each to their own.

'Where were you this afternoon?' I asked sharply, after she had gone.

'I needed some kit,' he said, smoothing his hands over his tight, black polo neck. 'I have some gloves too.'

'Gloves? What kind of gloves?' I asked.

'Black ones. Black leather. I can't have any blood on me.'

'There won't be any blood,' I said, looking around, checking no one was within ear shot. 'We're drowning him, not smashing his head in.'

'I know,' he said. 'But I also don't want to touch his wet skin. It makes me feel, I don't know.... A bit peculiar.'

He pursed his lips at me as he sat back. His face caught the neon lighting from outside of the window and, in his tight, black outfit, he looked menacing. And somewhat ludicrous. The whole thing, I knew was ludicrous, but we were in too deep. I didn't tell him about my late wobble. My doubts. They were my own. I needed Blanchard to have a clear head.

'Whatever,' I said. 'How's Gerald? I saw you talking to him outside.'

'Yes, he's better. I suggested that he and I go to the Marriot later. To get away from all of this.' He waved dismissively at the party. 'He said he was up for it, which means he's feeling better.'

'That's good.'

'Yes. There is a slight problem though.'

'What?'

'He's not drinking.'

'That's not good,' I said.

It was a blow. We ideally needed him drunk. Very drunk. Still, it wasn't a deal breaker.

'We'll just need to drug him,' I said.

'With what?' he asked.

'Leave it with me. I'll make some calls.'

It was a problem though. I didn't know where to source some drugs. Or indeed what drugs to get him. I had a friend who was a vet, but she lived too far out of town. I pushed the problem to one side. There were more pressing issues.

'And are you sure you can take him?' I said quietly.

Blanchard nodded, stretching his fingers.

'Take who?' Dominique asked, appearing from nowhere.

Not as quiet as I had thought.

'Take you,' Blanchard said, quickly, a slightly smutty edge to his tone.

I looked at him, surprised at his ability to think so quickly on his feet, and a little queasy in the event of it, indeed, being some sort of limp innuendo.

'Where?' asked Dominique, seemingly taking up the dance, her panda eyes now glazed with wine.

I coughed, not knowing what Blanchard was likely to say, feeling as though I was in the middle of an unlikely mating ritual.

'The Marriott,' he said out of nowhere.

I couldn't believe it. What was he doing? We had explicitly spoken about the need to slip away, just the three of us. Just us: Blanchard, Gerald, and myself. And now, it appeared, so too Dominique.

'I love the Marriott,' she said, smiling at Blanchard. 'They do the best Sex on the Beach.'

I was agog.

It was a ritual.

They were flirting.

I brooded through pudding. I was unable to talk to Blanchard as Eddy had reappeared and sat down next to me, slurring his speech. Drunk. Blanchard and Dominique were on the other side of the table and the house music had been dialled up a notch. Sin beckoned, flesh too. Around the bar eager lips moved closer as etiquette started to fray.

I saw Claire outside having a cigarette, and so I went outside to join her. I needed some air.

'Having fun?' I asked.

She looked distracted.

'Everything ok?' I tried asking again.

She pulled hard on her cigarette and continued to gaze at the ground.

'It didn't happen,' she said, quietly. 'He was supposed to have a fit. His throat. His throat was supposed to swell up.'

I stared at her. And then looked around. We were on some decking, away from the main throng of smokers. I satisfied myself we were out of ear shot and sat down next to her.

'What the hell are you talking about?' I asked.

'Gerald,' she said.

'Gerald?'

'He was supposed to die.'

'Die? When?'

'Lunchtime.'

She shot me a look that would have iced any man's balls.

'What do you mean? He was supposed to die?'

'Prawns,' she said.

'Prawns?'

I shook my head. I wasn't in the mood for games.

There was too much on my mind.

'The full moon,' she then said, her face pale and indistinct. I looked up into the sky and saw the moon, imperious and pure as it gazed down through the City's polluted air. Down on people plotting and scheming their way to a better life. Like Claire, and Blanchard.

And me.

I remembered passing Gerald in the lobby, looking pale and sweaty. I shook my head. Was it connected? I was slow to pick up the thread.

'You fed Gerald prawns?' I asked, not knowing how it made any sense.

It was preposterous.

'I did,' she said.

'How?'

'A sandwich.'

Claire feeding Gerald prawns sounded bizarre, but in a sandwich, it made a bit more sense. Gerald would often have someone fetch him a sandwich, as he sat and glowered at his screens, shouting at stock prices. A man possessed.

'Why?' I whispered.

She looked over my shoulder, checking no one had grazed into ear shot. No one had. They were all too busy sucking on their nicotine. Oblivious. Their own health, too, a long way from their addled minds.

'I overheard him on the phone talking about his allergies,' she said. 'He has severe allergies. I never knew it. I swear he said he couldn't eat prawns. I'm sure he said that his throat would swell up and he'd suffocate if he ate them.'

'Perfect,' I muttered.

'I know, it was perfect. The canteen would have been to blame. It was so clean. Death by prawn and a thousand-island sauce. It was almost poetic.'

'Only it turns out that he isn't allergic to prawns?' I said.

'No.'

'You should have tried nuts,' I said. 'I bet he's allergic to nuts.'

'I know,' she said, her voice drifting, lost to dark thoughts, and what might have been. Hindsight. Much like picking stocks, it's all so much easier with hindsight.

'Anyway, what are you and Blanchard up to?' she asked, fixing me with an intense stare, turning the conversation around.

I turned to look at her.

'What do you mean?' I asked, trying to stall, trying, as always, to buy myself some time.

'You know what I mean. I know you two are planning something,' she said.

First the Fox, now Claire. Her words caught me off guard. I took a deep breath, sucking in the night air. I knew that I could trust her, she hated Gerald more than anyone, but now was not the time to let her in on our filthy plan. If it could, indeed, be called a plan. The fewer people knew about the night's agenda the better.

'I'm not sure what you mean,' I said.

It was weak.

She knew.

And I knew she knew.

Her eyes narrowed, and she reminded me of my wife. Women have a sixth sense for the truth. There is no point lying, no point trying to run. They will hunt you down and find you. When they want the truth, your option is basically to tell them. Come clean. It was, I knew, even then, my only option.

'We're going to kill him tonight,' I whispered, 'in the Marriott jacuzzi. We're going to make it look like an accident, an overdose or something. Blanchard is going to drown him.'

Silence.

She pulled hard on her cigarette.

'I knew it!' she said, 'Yes, I knew you were up to no good. Why didn't you tell me? You know I want him dead?'

'I thought you were joking,' I said, a little lamely. I felt bad. I should have told her. She would have made a far better accomplice than Blanchard.

'Is Blanchard up to it?' she asked, quickly.

'Yes, I think so.'

'He better be,' she said.

She stood up and flicked her cigarette into the fake herbaceous border.

'Tell me the plan.'

I chewed my bottom lip, wondering how much I

should tell her.

'We're going to get Gerald to the Marriot after supper. Into the bar. Drinks, drugs, hookers. Then Blanchard is going to suggest a jacuzzi. Get him down to his smalls. And then drown him. I'm going to source the drugs, to drug him. And cut the CCTV.'

She said nothing.

'It might work.'

'Might?'

'Yes, although you'll need to do all of that by 11 p.m.?'

'11pm? It's the hotel spa! It never closes, it's part of the hotel That's the whole point!'

She looked at me as if I had never planned a murder.

'The spa at the Marriot is run by another company that rents the space off the Marriott. It is a separate business. It has nothing to do with the hotel. It all gets locked up at 11 p.m.'

I stared at the floor. This really was bad news. It had never even crossed my mind.

I looked at my watch.

9.23 p.m.

*

I fiddled with the packet, but my hands were so sweaty I couldn't get them out.

'Anything else, sir?' the barman asked.

'No, that's it, that's fine. Thank you.'

We had managed to get Gerald to the Marriott. As it turned out, Blanchard and Dominique had managed to get Gerald to the Marriott, as Claire and I had gone on ahead. I had pulled Blanchard aside and told him the news that the spa shut at 11 p.m. and that I had to go. I hadn't told him that Claire was now also part of our murderous gang, as he didn't need the distraction. Dominique was proving to be enough of a distraction on her own. I noticed the top button of her blouse had come loose. It was unclear whether it had done so on its own accord.

Gerald, Blanchard, and Dominique were now sitting behind me, waiting for their drinks, which I had just ordered from a barman who was American. And eager. A man who had grown up in a tipping culture.

'You guys looking for fun?' he asked, his tone, somehow, both grubby and chummy, all at once.

'What was that?' I said, without looking up.

He put his elbows on the bar and leaned over. He was uncomfortably close. I stopped fiddling with the packet of pills.

'Let me know if you want girls,' he said and nodded at two glamourous, pussy cat-dolls who had perched themselves on the end of the bar sipping, one might imagine, pure Sex on the Beach.

On the house.

I smiled, thinly.

'Thanks.'

One of the pussy-cat dolls looked up and she smiled too. It was a beautiful smile, both white and false at the same time. So effortless, so professional.

They were perfect and just what we needed. I smiled back, or as best I could under the circumstances. I still needed to get the pills into Gerald's drink and now I had unwelcome attention.

'Maybe later,' I told the barman, who nodded and went back to speak to his girls and cut more lemon.

I finally managed to get the pills out and I shoved the packet back in my pocket.

As Claire and I had walked over to the Marriott I had told her about the plan, about drunken and disorderly goings on in the spa; goings on that would hopefully allow Blanchard an opportunity, in and amongst the champagne and bubbles and nakedness, to hold Gerald under water long enough to fill his lungs with water. Only Gerald wasn't drinking.

'What drugs have you got?' Claire had immediately asked.

'None' I said, 'I don't have any. I was going to ask the concierge. I know they usually have the means.'

'I have some,' she had said, rummaging around in her bag; one of those big bags that women carry about, irrespective of whether they have a weekend away planned or not. It was huge. A budget airline would not have been pleased. She pulled out a packet.

'They're for period pain. Pain killers. I get bad period pain, so I am prescribed these extra-strong painkillers. I don't know what's in them but a few of these could take down a rhino.'

I looked at the packet and grunted, unsure of the topic of period pain. I shoved the pills in my pocket. They would have to do.

When we arrived, Claire had said that she'd go and sort out the CCTV and had disappeared. I hadn't seen her since. I sat and scoped out the bar for a bit and walked around the lobby looking for fire exits. I asked the reception desk how long it would take to order a taxi. Normal stuff. What any accomplice might do. And then they had arrived: Gerald, Blanchard, and Dominique. They had swept in, joking, and laughing. Dominique was clinging to Blanchard's arm. They looked like bankers who had come straight from a champagne-fuelled party.

Which, of course, they were.

I had made a move to greet them, but I was beaten to it by the concierge who had leapt up and scampered over the thick rug with remarkable speed and grace for a man in brogues.

'Mr Gerald, Mr Gerald. It is so good to see you again!' he had said in a thick accent.

'Pietro,' was all Gerald mustered, shaking the man's limp hand.

He was friendly but stand off-ish, for Pietro had the familiarity and manner of a man who knew what skeletons lay gathering dust in his cupboard. Pietro knew things that Gerald was reluctant to share openly with work colleagues. With anyone. I had glanced up at the clock on the wall as I eased over.

9.46 p.m.

'Hey, you made it!' I said, slapping Blanchard on the back. 'It looks like you've fallen into the wrong crowd boss!'

My voice sounded tinny. It didn't sound like me. I

felt detached, as if I was watching myself play out some morbid drama. Which I was. He grinned and reached out to shake my hand. He was clearly feeling better. For now, he was feeling better. That would possibly change as Blanchard's gloved hands closed in around his neck.

'Let me get you some drinks,' Pietro said to me.

'No, no, don't worry, I'll get them,' I had replied firmly.

Pietro backed off.

Claire had suggested I slip four pills into his drink, but four seemed too much. They were big pills and four might kill him and so we had settled on three. But now as I stood at the bar grinding the pills in my hand, trying not to let any of the powder fall onto the floor, I thought maybe I should play it safe and do four.

I didn't.

I stuck with three and when the barman wasn't looking I quickly picked up Gerald's drink and dusted the powder into it. He had ordered some sort of long cocktail with a fizzy mixer and the powder quickly dissolved. That he had ordered an alcoholic cocktail was the first positive news we had had all night.

I saw Blanchard sitting at the table with his leather gloves on, unsure what to make of it. Or him. He seemed relaxed though, perhaps too relaxed given that Dominique appeared to have her hand on his thigh.

'Get these down you,' I said, putting the drinks on the table.

I feared I was too aggressive, but Gerald barely blinked and picked up his cocktail and took a long sip.

'I needed that,' he said, smacking his lips.

I pushed the paranoia aside and we chatted. About this and that. I noticed the pussy cat-dolls squirming in their seats, letting their skirts ride up tanned thighs.

'We should get them over,' I said, lightly kicking Gerald's foot under the table and nodding in their fleshy direction.

He grinned.

'And more pop,' he said, his eyes fixated on the dolls.

I nodded and got up.

'You two ok for drinks?' I asked Blanchard and Dominique as I left.

'Same again,' said Blanchard, circling a gloved finger in the air.

Dominique giggled.

The barman had been well schooled, as you'd expect in the Marriot, and he was already on it, mixing and shaking his shaker with a busy expression; busy, but cool. I smiled suggestively at the pussy cat-dolls. Or as suggestively as I could, as I stood at the bar fingering Claire's packet of period pills in my pocket. Maybe four was right. We couldn't take any risks and Gerald appeared to be wearing the first three well.

When the barman returned with the drinks, I told him to suggest to the dolls they come and join us, and I flicked another broken up pill into Gerald's glass. Dominique moved closer in on Blanchard as the dolls made their approach. They were nothing but professional and, sussing what was what, with uncanny female intuition, pulled up two chairs either side of Gerald.

10.01 p.m.

I caught Blanchard's eye and tapped my watch. He nodded.

He had surprised me. He might have looked ridiculous in his black polo neck and leather gloves, but he appeared calm and in control and, crucially, he wasn't drunk. Yes, he had been drinking but it was measured and precise. It was most unlike Blanchard.

Another round of drinks came and went.

And another.

The pussy cat-dolls were soon competing to sit on Gerald's lap. Gerald, though, was beginning to look a little weary. His eyes had glazed over, and his speech had become laboured. I worried that four pills had been too much for him. Four pills and several pungent cocktails. Three, four, maybe five?

I had lost count.

I sensed, though, that we needed to move. We couldn't let him pass out in the bar and yet Blanchard was on it. He stood up and leaned over the table and whispered something to Gerald and the dolls. They looked at each other and nodded. And then they all got up and left. Dominique too. Trailing behind them as they all snaked their way across the lobby towards the lift for the spa.

And it was on.

Just like that.

I, as per the plan, stayed in the lobby. The eyes and

ears. I was also responsible for taking out the CCTV. All Blanchard had to focus on was the actual murder. He seemed happy with the arrangement, and so we had left it at that. He, after all, was in line to pick up Gerald's substantial pay packet.

I glanced at my phone.

10.46 p.m.

I needed a drink to calm my nerves.

The barman made no comment that I had remained in the bar on my own, and I offered no explanation. I left an outsized tip to ensure he might struggle to recall the events of the evening where he ever asked. He knew the game. I took my beer and sat at a quiet, corner table and crunched my way through the complimentary bowl of salty pretzels.

I had not seen Claire, but she had texted to say the cable had been cut.

10.54 p.m.

I sat and watched the lift, my mind strangely blank, given our rotten plan.

10.59 p.m.

The bar had thinned out, but it was still busy, peppered with the easy hum of conversation. Frank Sinatra floated above the occasional soft pop of champagne cork; year-end targets no longer relevant.

'Fly me to the moon, let me play among the stars... Let me see what spring is like on, Jupiter and Mars...'

And then it happened.

The scream.

The ambience was shattered.

Heads popped up from velvet booths as an ear-piercing scream is prone to prompt.

There was the clatter of a champagne flute falling to the floor.

The bar looked over to the lift, as one. And there was Dominique. She was, as the barman would later tell the police, 100% hysterical.

She was also covered in blood.

*

There was blood, everywhere.

There was so much blood it looked like there had been a massacre.

On seeing Dominique, I had hustled through the bar and skirted the lobby. She was flapping and yelling and so I didn't stop to ask her what had happened. A wide-eyed bell-hop was also closing in on her, given her screaming was putting off the continental custom that had just arrived, hot off the Eurostar, in search of Harrods and young royals.

I skipped down the steps of the fire exit and into the spa.

It was quiet.

So, very quiet.

I knew I wouldn't have long.

The reception of the spa was dimly lit, and the air was thick with the scent of lavender. Generous portions of potpourri lay waiting on side tables; bowls of temptation sitting idle for the hungry hand of the rasping American tourist unable, in the indistinct lighting, to discern the difference between air freshener and corn chips.

I edged through to the pool where I assumed the jacuzzi might have been put by the architects, keen as they would have been to create the holistic treatment area of their brief, and it was there that I stopped.

The blood.

It was everywhere.

The body was slumped over the steps leading up to the jacuzzi, a jacuzzi that bubbled with glib indifference to the tragic events that had clearly just taken place.

I couldn't believe what I was seeing.

This wasn't the plan.

I felt panic rising in my throat. My chest tightened. The walls started to close in on me, and the air, that hot and humid air of the indoor aquatic environment, made it difficult to breathe.

I looked at the body.

The tight briefs.

The blood.

And the black gloves.

Blanchard.

I checked his pulse, trying as best I could not to step in the blood and, holding a pose that in different circumstances would have scored well in a game of Twister, I held my breath. There was something. It was weak, but there was a pulse. He was, though, very unconscious. I peered at his face, so peaceful, bar all the blood; blood that was now matting his thick black hair.

'What happened?' I muttered, not expecting much of an answer.

That he had a pulse was a relief. He was not dead. I wasn't Blanchard's biggest fan, but he didn't deserve to die like this. Gerald deserved to die, hence all the trouble, but not Blanchard. As I stood up to slip out a dim-lit fire escape, and perhaps vault down onto the roof of a car parked in an alley, I stopped.

Where was Gerald?

I knew that I needed to remove myself. I needed to disappear. I had a career.

A wife.

A son.

And yet, I also needed answers.

On inspection, the changing rooms were quiet. I stood and stared at a pile of damp towels piled up in the corner and assumed that he had gone. He must have slipped quietly out of some side door knowing the police would also be wanting answers. I was about to turn and run, when I saw the sign to the massage rooms.

My pulse quickened.

Where else?

The sign pointed down another dimly lit corridor and I was about to investigate when I heard a door bang, and the sound of distress. A voice cut through the soft whir and hum of the water cooler. The voice was abrasive; the words too. There then came heavy breathing and I jumped into a thick patch of fake ferns by the lifts and dipped down in the dark. Footsteps hurried down the corridor, stumbling, quick, and a man emerged; his shirt loose, his jacket creased and crumpled on his arm. He carried his shoes and expression of guilt.

Pure guilt.

And it was a face that I recognised.

'Pietro,' I whispered.

As he waited for the lift, he slipped on his shoes and tidied himself up, cursing all the time. The jacket went on. So too the tie. And then he disappeared into the open lift, distracted. Hot. Unaware of the carnage that lay bleeding on the tiles of his jacuzzi.

I climbed out of my leafy hiding spot and turned to sweep the massage rooms and, as I turned, I ran straight into Claire.

We both jumped.

And cursed.

'What the hell?' I muttered.

'What the hell to you too!' she whispered.

I quickly took in her equally dishevelled appearance, her hair, the smudged lipstick. And her rosy cheeks.

'No,' I said, 'no way. The bellhop?'

'He's a concierge!' she said. 'And he's cute. In a swarthy, foreign sort of way.'

'How?' I asked. 'You know what, I don't want to

know. We need to get out of here.'

'Why?'

'Blanchard!'

'What about Blanchard?'

'Go and look in the jacuzzi. See for yourself. We need to get out. Have you seen Gerald?' I asked.

But she had gone.

I followed my nose down the darkened corridor and pushed open the door to another small waiting area. More subdued lighting. More bowls of potpourri. There were four frosted doors and I quickly checked the first three.

Empty.

I pushed open the fourth door and turned in one movement, assuming it too would be empty, and there he was. He was lying on the masseuse's table in his undies, his trousers crumpled on the floor.

He was also fast asleep.

I knew we needed to get him out, we couldn't leave him there. What with a bloody, semi-naked Blanchard slumped on the steps of the jacuzzi, there would be too many questions once the police figured out the connection.

'Is he alive?' Claire whispered, peering through the door.

'Yes,' I said.

'Bollocks.'

'Help me! We need to get him up. We need to leave.'

'With him?'

'Yes. We can't leave him here,' I said. 'Here, grab his legs.'

She tried to argue but I was already pulling Gerald off the table and we manhandled him down the corridor and out into the main reception area.

'Which way?' Claire asked, breathing heavily.

I stood, weighing up our options.

'The stairs,' I said.

The lift then whirred into life and I saw the down arrow on the display above the door flash red. They were coming.

'The door!' I whispered, grabbing a better grip of Gerald under his arms. Claire ran over and pushed it open. The lift slowed its whirr.

Company.

The arrow flashed.

I dragged Gerald across the floor and we fell through the door as the lift pinged open and a team of paramedics rushed out, followed by Pietro, barking directions.

Gerald groaned.

I watched, through the small glass window in the door, as they all rushed through to the tranquil pool area of the hotel's website. I whistled through my teeth. It appeared Blanchard would live.

Claire and I picked up Gerald and dragged him down the dark corridor. There were no stairs, as I had hoped, just another door.

Through we went.

We found ourselves in a large room, with big machines that spun and whirred. It was hot. Not as hot as an indoor aquatic area, but still hot, hot like you get in the tight company of large machines. It was also dark. I sniffed and caught the familiar scent of washing powder.

'We're in the laundry,' I muttered.

'Which way?' Claire asked.

I peered into the darkness.

'This way,' I said, on nothing more than a hunch.

Time was against us and we needed to disappear. And yet it was so dark and hot. At each turn, there were more machines; machines that continued to whir and hum and spin. Too soon we were lost. All I could see were shelves of linen, and boxes and boxes of washing powder. As we stood there, mulling yet again our next move, we heard a door click open.

We stopped and listened.

The door closed and there followed, footsteps; clear, clipped footsteps. The footsteps of a man who knew exactly where he was heading. I dragged Gerald behind the world's largest tumble drier and we waited in the shadows. The steps got louder, and, despite the hypnotic hubbub of the spinning machines, I could tell they were heading our way.

Gerald groaned, and I slapped my hand across his mouth and closed my eyes. I thought about my boy, fast asleep at home, oblivious to my increasingly sticky situation. I told myself I had done nothing wrong. I had broken no laws.

The footsteps were now close – tap, tap, tap, tap – and they were heading straight for us. Clipped and efficient. I could barely breathe.

And then they stopped.

The game was up.

'Come, we go. This way. You go out back through delivery bay.'

The voice was decisive and calm, and the accent strangely familiar.

I opened my eyes.

Pietro.

'God bless your horny, foreign backside,' I muttered.

He offered no explanation of why he thought it necessary to check behind the tumble driers, instead he guided us out through the spinning sheets and pillowcases, through another couple of fire doors and out onto a quiet street via the delivery bay.

We were at the back of the hotel.

I didn't know what to say, my head was still spinning.

'Now go', he said.

'Thank you,' Claire whispered. 'Thank you.'

'Yes,' I said. 'Thanks for your help.'

He then moved in on Claire, all foreign and smooth, seemingly unaware of the desperate urgency of the situation. He was in for some afters and they embraced, for what felt like a very long time. Lips touched.

And all the while I stood, propping Gerald up, occasionally grappling for a better grip.

'Go, now, my beautiful,' Pietro muttered as Claire stroked his beard.

The situation was increasingly surreal.

I then remembered the Fox's card and pulled it out.

I dialled the number.

'Harrow,' said a voice.

I weighted up my options. Harrow was too far. There was no way he would be able to get to us in time. It was late, but the traffic would still be heavy through town. It was, after all, the thick end of Christmas party season.

Pietro nuzzled Claire's neck, and she groaned. So too Gerald, but for very different reasons. I groped his torso and tried to stand him up.

'Harrow,' said the voice.

I was about to hang up, but as I did so I lost my grip on Gerald and he listed forward. I flapped and grabbed for his shirt and as I did, I grunted.

'Help!'

Claire came up for air.

'Ah the Fox say you call,' said the voice, the English broken and scratchy. 'I come ten minutes. Blue van.'

'Ten minutes,' I said, tentatively.

He then hung up.

I got hold of Gerald and stood up, and stared at

my phone, a little bewildered as to what had happened.

'We have ten minutes?' Claire asked.

'What?' I said, still a little lost.

She turned to whisper something in Pietro's ear, casting a hungry eye towards the shadows. This time it was his turn to groan. She was out of control and I was living a nightmare. Pietro, though, pulled himself away insisting he needed to return to work. The police, he said through his moustache, would be asking for him. He kissed Claire again and disappeared back through the delivery bay hatch.

Ten minutes later, a steamy Claire, a groggy Gerald and I were speeding away from the Marriot hunched together in the back of a blue van driven by a man who, even in the orange glow of the streetlight, had clearly been born many time zones from North West London.

We were finally safe.

CHAPTER X

I put the phone down and looked over at Blanchard. He was typing, his hands laboured over the keyboard, heavy, remorselessly bashing out another email. I wondered who to. I noticed his hair was shorter. He had also lost weight.

We had been back at work for several weeks, but I had yet to properly talk to him. I had sent him an email.

'Good to see you back. All ok?'

He had not replied.

Dominique sat next to him, she too, busy tapping away, her posture stiff. I had not spoken to Dominique much either. We had slipped back into a tepid exchange of the occasional greeting. I had emailed her as well.

'Fancy a coffee?'

She too, though, had not replied.

Silence.

What happened that night in the Marriot remained then something of a mystery.

Gerald wasn't at his desk, but I had seen him earlier in the atrium. I hadn't spoken to Gerald at all. He seemed to have retreated into himself. He had been in the office, but he had rarely been at his desk. His screens often remained blank. And he seemed distracted.

Distant.

I had spoken to Claire but only on the phone as she had gone on sabbatical. I didn't know the company did sabbaticals, but she told me they did. If HR deemed you suitable.

She was deemed suitable; hence, she was in Mexico.

'Have you seen Pietro at all?' I asked her down a scratchy line.

'Yes,' she said.

'I saw him a few days afterwards. He sent me a message. He said he had a present for me.'

'Did he?'

'Yes,' she said, the emphasis too long on the vowel.

I paused.

I didn't want to know what kind of present Pietro had given her.

'Did he say anything about Blanchard?'

'Yes,' she said, 'the police think it was an accident. He slipped. As he fell, he must have hit his head on the steps. Hence all the blood.'

I tried to think back to the scene, but my memory of it was hazy.

'Are they not going to investigate further? Did they not think it odd he was wearing black gloves?'

'No. He said they closed the case. There were no witnesses. And there was no CCTV, as we know.

Blanchard had twenty stitches in his head and was released the next day. They questioned him, but he couldn't remember anything. Nor Dominique. She said she hadn't been there. She said she had just found him.'

'So that was it?'

'Yes. The police weren't interested, and the Marriott management wanted the whole thing closed. They told Pietro they would make it worth his while to make it happen. And so, he made it happen and they made it worth his while.'

It seemed that, for the record at least, it was all just an unfortunate accident.

'An accident,' I mulled aloud, 'maybe it's for the best.'

'Yes.'

I thought some more.

'How did he find us?' I asked. 'Pietro. How did Pietro know we were in the laundry? Did you ask him that?'

Claire paused.

'Yes, I did,' she eventually said.

'Well, what did he say?'

'The laundry was on a different CCTV system. He said the police asked him to pull the tape of the spa, and so he had gone into his office. He didn't know that I had cut the CCTV as I didn't tell him. We didn't have time.'

'Yes, I can imagine,' I said.

It was surprising they had time at all.

'Anyway, he saw us in the laundry, on a different screen.'

'Why didn't he tell the police?' I asked.

Silence.

There was some more static on the line.

'Claire? Hello? Are you there?'

Silence.

'Hello?'

'Yes,' she said.

'Why didn't he tell the police?' I asked again.

'My tongue,' she said, with no trace of embarrassment.

It was not what I was expecting.

'Oh. Yes. Umm. Well done.'

It was all I could think of saying.

More silence.

'So, when are you back?' I finally asked, hoping to get the conversation back on to something more comfortable for all.

'I'm not coming back,' she said abruptly.

'What?'

'I've resigned. I emailed HR yesterday. I've met someone out here and I'm going to stay in Mexico.'

I was taken aback. The news hit me hard. How could she do that to me? Claire was my only real friend on the trading floor. She was the only one I trusted. And without her I was vulnerable.

'Who?' I asked.

'My instructor,' she said.

I didn't ask what he instructed. Claire had exotic tastes. She could have been kite surfing or doing yoga. But then she could have easily been doing something else.

'What's he like?' I asked.

She paused and giggled a bit.

'Who said it was a *he*?' she said, and then hung up laughing.

I sat staring at my phone. I felt empty, but deep down, I knew it was for the best. At last her spirit was free.

And then my phone rang again.

'Tell me you're joking?' I said.

And yet it wasn't Claire. The voice was cold. Clipped. It was the curt voice of a female secretary. I recognised it but couldn't place it.

'Please could you make your way to the sixth floor. Gerald would like to see you.'

The words hit me between the eyes, they meant only one thing.

I was getting fired.

That's how they did it. There was never an announcement, never a gathering in a corner office to be gently told that there was going to be some 'rationalisation' and that people should not worry, the EU had ensured that they had a right to be treated with dignity. Instead people were picked off one by one. As if by sniper. They would be invited up to the sixth floor, the floor of quiet meeting rooms, pot plants and discreet staff in starched white uniforms. They would then go up, and never return.

Like many before me, I never saw it coming.

I shut down my computer and surveyed my desk to see if there was anything worth salvaging. Nothing. It was littered with papers. Newspapers, analyst reports, an electricity bill. Nothing of any value to me. I opened the drawer and took out a golf ball and a bottle of cough syrup.

I left the rest.

I thought about saying goodbye to the Fox, but he was hunched over his desk muttering into his phone, and so I slipped out, just like that. Never to return. I would later become a talking point and then someone else would get fired and I would fade from the memory. Like a stale Twitter trend. Within a week or two I would be forgotten. The man with no name.

I took the lift to the sixth floor alone; alone with my thoughts. I never thought it would have come to this. Perhaps that was why no one was talking to me. Perhaps they knew. They were all in on it.

'I've come to see Gerald,' I said to the lady on the reception desk.

She tapped on her computer. Her hair was tight, scraped back in a bun and she had too much make up on. Her eyebrows reminded me vaguely of one of my baby's toys.

A wooden toucan.

'Room 12,' she said, without looking up.

I made my way down the corridor and knocked on the door and heard a muffled voice. Gerald was sitting at the table, his hands in his pockets. He had a glass of water in front of him.

'Take a seat,' he said.

I sat down.

The room had no windows and the lighting was low. It was a gloomy setting. But then the occasion was no tea party.

'This is difficult for me. But I'll get straight to the point,' he said.

I stared back, mulling our full circle. Here we were back in a meeting room, albeit a different meeting room, back to where it had all started. An image of Gerald lying on the masseuse table flashed up in my mind. Indeed, our full circle was perhaps more of a figure of eight.

A metaphysical figure of eight.

Perhaps I could use the time to go away, I thought. Reconnect. Recharge. Maybe Sri Lanka. Take a family break. We could rent a place on the beach. Or the alps. Taste some early spring snow.

So many options.

As I sat there gazing at Gerald, I felt my spirits lift, thinking about the possibilities. The sand. The snow. A glorious beam of sunshine lit up my mind, dispelling the gloom. Dispelling the negativity of the past few months. Getting fired would be a release. A second chance. I realised I wanted it.

I wanted out.

Gerald had his hands on the table and was turning the glass between them. I didn't notice it at the time, but there was no paper on the table. I should have realised it, but I was already mentally in a pair of speedos wondering whether factor fifteen would be enough to prevent skin cancer.

'I wanted to thank you,' he said.

Maybe I should go with factor twenty, just to be safe.

'I don't know what happened that night at the Marriott.'

And no one wants skin cancer.

'I can't remember. But Pietro tells me that you got me out. So, thank you, I owe you my career.'

There was a clash of symbols in my head and I forgot about skin cancer. Sri Lanka wasn't going to happen. Nor, too, the Alps.

'Umm, well, yes. That's no problem,' I said, my mind scrabbling to re-appraise the situation.

'My drink was spiked,' he said.

I nodded.

'I had some tests done on my blood and they said it was probably a painkiller. It also had properties of horse tranquiliser.'

I nodded some more, wondering if Claire really suffered period pain.

'The Doctor said that if I had had any more, I would have died.'

And so, five was indeed the magic number. The killer dose. Claire was right. Murder, like elite sport, was all on the margin.

'Maybe it was one of those girls who was with us?' I suggested, sensing I needed to say something.

Gerald ignored me.

We sat in silence.

'I'm tired,' he said, eventually.

It was an unexpected turn.

'I'm tired of the bank. Tired of this job. I feel like I am suffocating. I have no friends. Half my team want my job, the other half want me out. I think some might even want to kill me.'

I let his words go.

He did though. He looked tired. His shoulders sagged as he sat. He looked old. The ram rod back, the cock sure air: they were gone. Gerald was a different man. A sadder man. A man who had lost his way. And then, in that small stuffy room, I saw something that I thought I'd never see.

Gerald started to cry.

*

I didn't see the email coming.

I was on the phone at the time, peddling the ins and outs of owning the shares of a pub group.

'Wage growth is better,' I said.

'What?' my client mumbled, perhaps balancing a piece of toast on his upturned fingers, licking the jam off the top.

Perhaps.

'Wages. The Bank of England are saying wages have gone up.'

'No, they haven't,' he said.

I paused.

I was reading the press release; it was on my screen. In front of my very eyes. Wages had gone up 2.3%.

'They have.'

'Haven't.'

'They have.'

Silence.

'If the man in the street is being paid more,' I ploughed on, 'then he is going to be drinking more. It's been sunny too. Very good news for pubs.'

'He's not,' my client spat.

'Who?' I asked.

'Barry.'

'Barry?'

'Yes, Barry.'

'Who's Barry?'

'My gardener.'

My client then gruffly explained that he hadn't given Barry a pay rise in ten years and didn't intend to start now. I thought about saying something but didn't. And so, we found ourselves once more in the familiar cul-de-sac of mutual contempt. Nowhere to go.

And then, *ping,* the email.

'My other line is ringing,' I said.

'You don't have another line.'

I hung up, cutting him off, which was satisfying on many levels.

The email was from Blanchard. There was nothing in the subject box, and so I opened it up. And yet I opened it up with mixed feelings, as I had still not spoken to him and a couple of months had now passed. Eye contact too, had been awkward. And now the email, an email with one clear instruction.

'Sauna, 5 p.m.'

It could mean only one thing.

I guessed his sudden engagement was related to his bonus. Or lack of a bonus. The word was out that he had fired a blank. He had been squeezed out of the money and his bonus cheque had carried only zeros.

A doughnut.

If it was true and Blanchard had had to buy a new kitchen on credit, then Blanchard now had a very real motive; a motive that was hot, a motive that was likely to smoulder and smoke if left alone. The bonus was his right.

I felt uneasy.

I felt uneasy as I was beginning to think that Gerald wasn't the man we all thought he was. The reason that I thought this was that Gerald had asked me out to coffee shortly after our meeting on the sixth floor.

I was reluctant to go, but as he had sobbed in the sixth-floor meeting room, I sensed something had changed. There was a vulnerability to him.

We had gone to a coffee shop near the office, that was situated in the back cloisters of an old church, hidden away. Quiet. There were candles and a soft air of contentment that sat in sharp contrast to what we had all gone through since the ill-fated Christmas party.

The choir were rehearsing. It felt holy and calm. Nourishing. Warm soup for the soul. And we had talked. I say we, Gerald had talked, and I had listened.

'My father worked for a bank,' he had said, after we had exchanged the usual humdrum pleasantries of two colleagues out for coffee.

'He did?' I asked, haltingly, a little surprised the conversation had turned personal.

I was still wary of him.

'Yes. He made a lot of money. But he was mean. My poor mother. She had to scrimp and save. He made her re-use the teabags. How mean is that?' he asked shaking his head.

I shook my head.

'Yes, that's very mean.'

Given his father was so mean, I had expected him to say that he never saw him, that he was absent. That his childhood was long and lonely.

'And so, you never saw him?' I asked, taking a sip of my coffee, only half-interested.

'No, not at all. I saw him a lot. He was always there. He didn't work too hard. He was at home. We went on holiday. He took me to sport. We always had supper at the kitchen table together.'

'Oh,' I said, surprised. 'I guess nothing wrong with being frugal! There is a Scotsman in all of us.'

I grinned but he looked at me, his eyes dark, darker than his Americano.

'My father was a cold, mean man but mean in a different sense. He was mean with his attention. Mean with his time. He was there, but he wasn't there. And he never praised me. Nothing. Never. I don't remember him ever giving me one positive comment.'

I grimaced; we do all like praise.

Gerald continued. 'And he showed no interest in me. As a child, we never played together. We never talked. We never did anything. And I didn't know why, or what I had done wrong. I felt like I was a burden to him. I felt like I was a chore.'

Grim.

No wonder Gerald was so emotionally cold.

'My father kept butterflies,' he said, after a time.

'Butterflies?'

'Yes.'

'Where?'

'In the library.'

'How cruel,' I whispered.

'They were dead,' Gerald said.

'Oh, yes, yes of course,' I replied, compromised.

Of course. I didn't think. All I had in mind were wings. Bright, fluttering wings.

Anyway, he said his father had kept an ornate

collection of preserved butterflies in the library. All he ever wanted was to help his father with his butterflies, but he wasn't allowed to. He could watch, but he could never help.

He could never touch the butterflies.

'I used to go and look for butterflies in the garden,' Gerald said, slowly stirring his empty coffee cup, his mind lost in the gloomy vault of childhood. 'I'd then pull their wings off and burn their bodies.'

'Alive?' I whispered.

He nodded his head.

I gasped.

'I'd then write in my diary what I had done and how it had made me feel. I hoped one day my father would find my diary and read it.'

'Did he?' I asked, knowing the answer.

Gerald shook his head.

And so, the pain never stopped.

'He lives in Marbella now,' he said, his tone distant. Like Marbella. 'I see him four times a year. But never at Christmas. He likes to Christmas alone.'

I had sat and played with the sugar pot. I needed something in my hands. A distraction. Anything. The exchange had left me a little off balance.

Silence.

'What about your mother?' I asked.

'Dead,' he said.

'Any siblings?'

'No.'

It was an awkward situation, and I sat and watched the choir.

Gerald's past was one thing, and he clearly had issues, which perhaps explained all the bullying, but the only thing I wanted to know was why had had betrayed me.

'Why did you do it?' I asked, quietly.

'Do what?' he said.

'Throw me under a bus,' I said, my voice rising, 'the Tribunal. Do you remember that? You screwed me.'

He grimaced.

'Yes, sorry about that,' he said, 'I was under a lot of pressure. I felt bad, but I had no choice.'

I wasn't buying it.

'What do you mean no choice?' I fumed.

He looked at me, his eyes still dark.

The Choir started up again with a haunting take on *Faure's Requiem*.

'I know you own that strip club, too,' I said. 'I'm sure HR would be interested to know you have been taking clients to a club you own.'

I wanted to turn the screw.

'I'm sorry,' he said, his voice now barely a whisper. 'You don't understand. I had to do it. I'm sorry it was you.'

'Do what?' I asked.

'Debt,' he said abruptly, 'the club has debt. Loans. And we were not making enough money.'

'What's that got to do with me?' I asked, a little lost.

'I thought the publicity would be good for business,' he said. 'I knew the journalist and suggested it to him. He took it to his editor and she went for it. We just needed someone to take the fall.'

I thought I would have been angry, but I saw the logic to it. I could see that I was just convenient.

A pawn.

'I owe some nasty people a lot of money,' he said, 'I'm so sorry.'

His body crumpled.

'I can't take much more of this.'

It was an uncomfortable exchange and the ensuing silence felt awkward, as I had seen a side to Gerald that had always been hidden. And our relationship had changed. There was more honesty, less pretence, but so too I needed to think.

Re-pitch the tent.

I flagged the waitress down and asked for the bill.

Later as I played back our conversation and Gerald's surprising confession, I saw his sticky pickle. I could see how debt and fear could distort his sense of right or wrong. How his options might have narrowed. I saw too how his childhood had cut him into the vile man that we saw every day on the trading floor.

I also realised – deep down – that I didn't really want to kill Gerald.

Yes, he could be an obscene, abhorrent, bully; but whose fault was that? He had never had a chance. He had been fighting all his life. It was the only way he knew how to survive and now he was out of control. That he behaved as he did, was only a reaction to how he had been treated all his life.

And yet, despite seeing Gerald for what he was – a sad and scared man, broken by his parent's neglect and society's indifference – at 5 p.m. I found myself in the sauna.

Blanchard had called.

The astonishing riddle of Blanchard in speedos.

I had not been down to the sauna for a few months, and so I was off guard. I was lazy. My mind was distracted, preoccupied by a torrent of awkward thoughts stirred up by Gerald. My bold entrance into the sauna left my senses ill-prepared for the startling sight of not one, but two, naked men.

'Guten abend,' I muttered.

Neither moved.

I shuffled in and sat down as nonchalantly as I could, given the astonishing show of pubic hair, and quietly cursed Blanchard.

He was late, again.

Always late.

*

He was out of control.

Sweat flicked off the end of his nose. His arms flapped. His belly was a blur. I started to fear for his heart. It was hot in the sauna, and not the place to have a tizz.

'Calm down!' I said.

He was furious, as his state inferred. A sweaty state, barely able to finish his own sentences.

Blanchard had finally arrived, flinging the sauna door open and marching in, as if taking to the stage. Confronted with two meditating, naked Germans, he had stood in the doorway, brooding, eyeing the scene.

The audience, had there been one, would have gasped. His stance was square and solid, and his hips were thrust forward in a manner that would have had the playwright squealing with delight.

The Germans remained detached.

Motionless.

Naked.

If they were aware of Blanchard's thunderous brow, they did not show it. There was not even a flicker.

'Get out,' Blanchard had said.

Neither moved.

'Get out. Out, out. GET OUT!

Blanchard had then approached the skinnier of the two Germans, who was still lying motionless on the lower bench, bent over, paused, and then, in an astonishing show of peace time bravado, flicked the man's penis.

Just like that.

There was, as you can imagine, a commotion. A moist, fleshy, hubbub. The Germans were swearing in

German, Blanchard was swearing in English. Fingers were jabbed. Egos were ruffled, tackle swayed this way and that.

Indignation stiffened.

The Germans though, perhaps put off by Blanchard's breathlessly tight pair of nut-hugging pants and puce expression, decided to err with caution and skirted the conflict by grabbing their towels and scuttling away for a cold shower.

Tempers hissed.

Blanchard encouraged them on their way with a slow hand clap, wholly indifferent, it appeared, to the fact that both Germans would be able to participate in his end of year, peer group evaluation. He had then sat down.

'You ok?' I asked.

Silence.

All I could hear was his breathing. Heavy breathing. He sat slumped on the bench; his head bowed. A minute passed, maybe two.

'Nothing,' he finally whispered.

I sat across the sauna from him. He was still steaming, and I needed to be near the door in case his moorings came loose again. It was a small sauna and I needed to tread carefully.

'He paid me nothing,' Blanchard said, his voice, as you might well imagine, a little hoarse.

So, the bonus. Or, specifically, the lack of a bonus. It appeared the kitchen had indeed needed the grubby offer of six months' interest free credit.

'You have a job,' I offered, quietly, with the disposition of a self-help guru. Sunny and positive. A little desperate, perhaps, in its intonation not to appear condescending. 'And it's been a bad year. It's not as if you were the only one.'

'I don't care,' he said, his words were sharp and cruel, foreboding even. They were words that belonged to a man in a hooded top who loitered by stagnant canals, embittered and lonely. Vengeful. Hatred burning his core.

Quite frightening.

He then really got going again.

'Do you know how much commission I have made this year?'

I shook my head.

'Millions,' he said, 'millions. I have attacked the profit pool of my clients. I have had it. Decimated it. I own it. I OWN THEM!'

He then started yelling, cursing Gerald, running through the clients, detailing who he had called, who had paid what. He ran through each deal he had done, every line of stock he had placed. He thumped the wall with the side of his fist. He fumed. His puce colour returned.

I knew, then, it was coming.

'Sit down,' I said, worried about his heart.

He didn't. He paced the sauna. Two steps, turn. Two steps. The playwright by now would have been beside himself and even the critics would have had to have put their pens down and marvel at the performance. It was some show.

'I'm going to kill him,' he said, 'I'm going to put right the wrong. Finish off what we started.'

He looked like he meant it too.

'Sit down. You don't want to kill him,' I said, hoping a firm tone would pop his bubble. Ground him. Bring some reality to the situation.

There was, by the way Blanchard snarled in response, no question about it.

'I do,' he said, like a late thirty-something bride in a church. The words, both bold and confident, but said with just a hint of menace.

'Gerald's not that bad,' I said, 'maybe he doesn't deserve to die.'

Blanchard stood and swayed, his eyes glazed. I couldn't tell if he was there or not.

'He's a bully, yes, we know that,' I continued. 'But why is he a bully? Ask yourself that. Maybe it's not his fault? Maybe there's stuff we don't know about.'

More silence.

'What he needs to do is let go of the insecurities. He needs friendship. Support. He needs help. He isn't a bad man, he can change.'

There was hope, I thought, there was always hope. Blanchard sat down, his breathing now slower and I let him breathe. I let the silence settle.

'What happened that night at the Marriott?' I finally asked, taking advantage of the lull, gripping the conversation further.

There were pressing issues to hand, but I needed to know. Blanchard closed his eyes. His head was perfectly still, and his breathing slowed right down. He was no longer at immediate risk of popping, which was a relief.

'I don't know,' he eventually said. 'I remember going down in the lift. I remember the reception. I remember the girls were there and then they weren't there. They disappeared. Gerald might have gone with them, I don't know. I don't remember seeing them in the pool. I remember thinking it was so quiet. So, very quiet. Dominique was there but she did not get changed, she was just standing by the ferns.'

He stopped; his lips moved but nothing came out. It was if he was searching for the memory, but he couldn't find it. There was nothing there. It had been lost, gone forever, perhaps mixed up in the bowls of potpourri.

'Did she say anything?' I asked, sensing a question might help him sift through the dried leaves. Perhaps he could find a scrap, something, anything but he shook his head.

'No. Nothing. I can't remember a thing,' he said.

We sat in silence for a bit, I for one, unsure of how to take the conversation forward. He eventually stirred, reaching for the bucket of water to douse the stove.

'I have a plan,' he said, almost nonchalantly, as he scooped the water onto the stones with the long wooden spoon.

I started to sweat.

Death was back in the room and I didn't know what to feel. My speech had failed. He hadn't heard it. He told me about his plan and, as he spoke, I grew worried, more worried with every detail. The problem was that the plan was clever.

And it was so simple.

There was a very good chance it could work.

'Can you trust him?' I asked feeling as though I needed to say something.

'Yes, I think so,' he said, 'although I haven't met him yet.'

'Where did you find him?' I asked.

Blanchard looked at me. His black hair was now wet with sweat. His lip curled down.

'A friend of a friend,' he spat.

Blanchard had a motive.

And now, he also had a very real plan.

*

'Some days I am filled with the Holy Spirit, I feel like… I feel like it is in me, deep in my soul, and all I want to do is tell the world!'

'Thank you, Pauline,' said Canon Chris, his voice calm and measured, Vicar like.

I shot my wife a look. This was not what we had expected.

With Blanchard's tight plan ringing in my ears, I had hurried home to meet my wife as we had to go to Church. The reason we had to go to Church was that we had decided to get our boy christened. This involved an early evening meeting with the Vicar. We thought it would entail a quick hello and a casual enquiry as to whether the organist would be up for tickling the ivories.

That, at least, had been the plan.

Yet now we were in Canon Chris' small, but well-appointed office, with Pauline and Canon Chris. I didn't catch Pauline's role in the holy set up. She had a zealous air and an eager face. She wore velvet trousers and had the slight whiff of a sardine sandwich about her. She breathed brine. If Canon Chris ever itched to run off script and set up a cult, I sensed Pauline would take little persuasion in cancelling her direct debits and packing a bag.

There was a sofa, on which my wife and I had squeezed. And then there was Canon Chris who was sitting in his swivel chair and who had swivelled away from his desk to face us and form a group, completed as it was by Pauline who was sitting in the one other armchair, directly across from Canon Chris.

Only Pauline wasn't sitting in the armchair.

Pauline was perched on it, her buttocks barely finding their natural equilibrium on the edge of the chair. For me, it looked dangerous, for Pauline's buttocks had enjoyed the cake party of late middle age and required, perhaps, a little more commitment to the chair. Were she to list forward, the Canon's terrier, who was lying on the floor seemingly devoid of any holy spirit of his own, would possibly die. Pauline would simply carry too much momentum. He would be crushed.

Like Bruno.

God rest his soul.

I looked at my wife and nodded my head Pauline's

way. I then looked at the dog. My wife's eyes bulged, and she frantically reached down to try and pat the dog awake but the dog was having none of it.

'And how do *you* express God?' Canon Chris asked me, his eyes, locking my own.

He had inquisitive eyes, but they were eyes too, that demanded truths.

How did I 'express God'? It was a tough question, a good question. I tapped the pencil I had been given on my pursed lips. We had each been given a pad and a pencil, although we had yet been asked to use it and I now used it as a prop to buy myself time. I felt my wife shift uncomfortably on the sofa beside me, knowing she was up next. She continued to try and coax the dog from harm's way.

The dog growled.

Express God? It was a difficult question and yet it in the context of my boy's christening, it was a valid question: how *did* I express God?

'Is he with you?' asked Pauline earnestly, reaching out to pat my arm.

Yet as she did so, she realised she had misjudged the distance, I was further away than she thought, and as she came at me, slowly at first, she picked up speed. She tipped. Basic physics did the rest. I scrambled forward as best I could, handicapped somewhat by the depth of the sofa. My hips were too deep, too low, but I leaned forward as best I could. I extended my arms, straining, sinews tight, my body, my whole body braced for the impact.

'Jesus Christ,' I heard Canon Chris mutter, 'watch

out, Puddles!'

Puddles raised his head begrudgingly, idly, opening one eye. Yet one eye was all he needed. Fear iced my core. I tell you, you haven't seen terror until you have looked into a dog's eye and in a flash seen it — the dog — understand it was about to die.

I pushed further, I pushed harder, my chest all but touching the top of my thighs, my buttocks still too deep. One last effort. I didn't quite catch her, in fact, I didn't even come close.

But I did save Puddles.

At the last moment, I realised there was no way I could have taken her weight in my arms. The angle she was coming at me was all wrong. There was a real risk she would have grabbed my arms and taken me down with her. And, so I had pushed her, violently, with my foot. I had the leverage. I had the angle. I found solid purchase on her hip bone and had enough power in my leg to divert her fall. She had crashed into the ornate set of fire pokers, finally coming to rest at Canon Chris' feet.

It had been outrageously violent, but it had also been, I felt, my only option. No one spoke and the grandfather clock in the hall struck a quarter past the hour. I looked up at Canon Chris not knowing what his Godly reaction would be. He had Puddles in his lap and he was beaming. Grinning. Grinning from ear to ear.

'Thank you,' he mouthed, stroking Puddles' tummy, his eyes welling up with tears. 'Thank you!'

Pauline groaned.

I never did have to share my thoughts on God, as we all went home shortly afterwards.

Canon Chris emailed me later saying that the Holy Spirit was in all of us, and that sometimes actions spoke louder than words.

Vicars, I was fast becoming aware, were not quite what they seem.

CHAPTER XI

Blanchard's plan was clever, and it was very much in vogue. As with so much of modern life, his plan involved simply outsourcing the actual grubby act. He had hired a hit man.

An assassin.

He had stumbled upon a man who, if the price was right, would, with a moody look, go and take care of Gerald and dump the body in a skip. Blanchard, himself, would do nothing, other than sit at home and wait for the text message saying business had been taken care of.

Blanchard said all he had to do was provide a photograph and an address.

For several days after Blanchard's sweaty revelation in the sauna, I had found myself restless, fidgety, my spirits ruffled. I couldn't concentrate. I didn't know why, but there was something about the plan, it was too neat, it didn't fit with Blanchard, it just wasn't his style.

It was too subtle.

Too clean.

One uncomfortable explanation, and one I kept going back to, was that Blanchard was now conspiring with someone else. A someone who remained in the shadows. It was most unsettling and at supper one night, my wife noticed my restless mood.

As she always did.

Nothing got passed my wife.

'Everything ok?' she asked.

I chased a pea around the plate, too buttery to skewer; elusive, much like the words I needed to explain my mood.

'Fine,' I said.

My heart, though, wasn't in it, and she knew it.

'You sure you're ok?' she probed.

I put my fork down and closed my eyes and without thinking about the consequences, I just said it.

'There is a guy at work who told me the other day he has hired a hit man to kill our boss, Gerald.'

It would sound preposterous, I knew that it would, but it felt so good to say it. To share it. To unburden my worry. I knew that she would have questions, lots of questions, but I needed to say it. I couldn't keep any more secrets from her.

My wife laughed.

I didn't.

Hit men, I knew, were no laughing matter. And Blanchard was serious. He had not been paid a bonus.

She soon stopped laughing.

'Are you serious?' she asked, her voice surprisingly steady for hearing such outrageous news.

'Yes, I'm afraid so,' I said, solemnly.

I choked back on the words though. There was more, so much more. And yet I knew, I couldn't tell her everything. I knew I couldn't tell her that murdering Gerald had originally been my idea. I knew that I might then drown in her questions and so, I told her what I could.

I told her about Blanchard, about his love of boutique hotels and gold watches; about his taste for carrot cake and his long clammy climb up the corporate pole. I told her about his hunger for an ever-bigger bonus: new gadgets and gizmos, hotter holidays, more money, more influence. I told her about his deep-set eyes and taste for trousers too tight in the groin.

'Square-toed shoes?' she whispered.

I nodded.

'O M G!' she mouthed.

I told her about the deal, about the Fox's sabotage. I explained how IPOs ran, about fees and commission. I explained how the bonus pool worked or was supposed to work. I told her everything I could. And I told her that Blanchard had been paid no bonus.

'How did he buy his kitchen?' she asked.

'Credit,' I muttered.

Her eyes grew large.

And then I told her about Gerald and our unlikely friendship. The coffee shops. The morning walks and conversations in the tranquil grounds of a nearby Church, where the priest had been so thrilled that some bankers had finally graced his gates.

I told her about his father.

'How awful,' she said. 'The poor man. He never stood a chance.'

'I know.'

I skewered the elusive pea and popped it in my mouth.

Silence.

'You have to stop him,' she eventually said, 'you have to stop Blanchard. You have to save Gerald.'

She was right, I knew I did, only I couldn't quite absorb the irony of it.

Me.

The man with the original plan, and yet now, a full U-turn. I knew that I had to do something, I knew as soon as a sweaty Blanchard had finished telling me about his plan in the sauna. I knew then that I couldn't stand aside and let that happen. I had to stop him.

'I know,' I said.

The image of Blanchard in speedos, with sweat dripping off his bits, was still too fresh in the mind though. He had been out of control in the sauna. And the man was dangerous. I sat and stared my plate. I knew what I had to do; I just didn't know how to do it.

'Do you want some tea?' I asked, getting up to clear the plates.

I needed to move. My mind had started to wander, to plan, to prepare. I needed to mobilise, think. I knew I'd need gloves, and a balaclava. And maybe some cheap sunglasses. Perhaps even a beige mac.

'I can help if you want?' she asked as the kettle boiled.

The steam hissed.

'What?' I said.

I'd also probably need a wrench.

'I can help!'

'It's ok,' I said, 'I'll do it. You cooked supper!'

'Not the tea!' she said, 'Gerald. I'll help with Gerald.'

'What?'

'I can help you stop Blanchard kill Gerald.'

I paused and turned and stared at her.

'Are you serious?'

'Of course, I am. This Blanchard sounds like a horrible man. What sort of person actually wants to kill their boss?'

I stood, and stared some more, the tea bag balancing precariously on the end of the spoon, much like Gerald's life. Indeed, I mused, gazing at my wife, what kind of man?

I knew then, there were some secrets I could never share, no matter how much wine.

Murder being one.

Bruno, perhaps, being another.

*

Blanchard withdrew.

He stepped back.

It was clear that, whilst he had told me about his plan, I was not part of the plan and I started to get the sense that he was avoiding me. I tried to get close, to find out more details, but it was as if he sensed something. He clammed up and I grew frustrated, and worried. Worried that the wheels of his plan were spinning, and that his hit man was waiting in bushes, watching, biding his time.

The days ticking down.

Death looming.

Walking back from a client meeting a few days after the surprising offer from my wife, I decided to nip down through an old cobbled alley which took me round to the back of the office. It was a short cut. I wasn't late for anything, but it had started to rain, and I was wearing a woollen suit.

This time with pants.

My thoughts, though, as ever, were a foamy mix. A cocktail of woe. Death, I had come to rue, was playing too prominent a role in my life and it needed to stop.

With my mind so pre-occupied and distracted by the prospect of dead bodies, I almost missed them. As I turned to walk back around the front of the building, I caught sight of two figures down behind the big recycling bins; the bins that were stuffed full of the shredded memos of stale, ill-fitting deals.

I stopped and peered through the drizzle.

Blanchard.

And talking to Blanchard, was a gruff, moody looking foreigner.

I gasped.

The assassin.

I walked quickly down towards the bins, hugging the wall, careful not to make a sound on the wet cobbles. I needed to get close enough to hear what they were talking about. I knew it was dangerous. Blanchard was dangerous, and the hit man ought to have been more dangerous still. Fortunately, I had undies on under my increasingly damp woollen suit and as I slipped in behind a bin, I crouched down and listened.

'We agreed a price,' Blanchard said, 'I'm not paying you a penny more.'

'I need more,' the assassin replied, his voice gruff and foreign.

'No more,' said Blanchard 'nothing more until the job is completed.'

'I need lead piping,' said the assassin, 'lead piping is expensive.'

And so, lead piping was to be the instrument of choice.

A traditionalist.

'We agreed. I'd pay you half upfront, and then half when you finished. And no mess. I don't want any mess. You have to clear everything up.'

Blanchard, I knew, didn't like blood which might be difficult to avoid given the choice of lead piping.

'The price has gone up,' the assassin said, his words catching Blanchard back on his heels.

He moved forward, closer, easing himself into

Blanchard's space. He was a big man too. Hairy, as you'd hope, and tattooed. A bonus. His black beanie hat framed a mean face and the eyes were cold and cruel.

'Out of the question,' said Blanchard, although his voice was hesitant as he knew the hit man had the better hand in this negotiation. He was just in shirt and suit trousers. He was soft and vulnerable.

A banker with no memo.

'Then I don't do the job,' the assassin said, pulling out a crumpled packet of counterfeit cigarettes. 'You "do-it-yourself", as you like to say in this country!'

The assassin laughed, a deep throaty laugh. He coughed. And spat some phlegm on the ground.

Menacing.

Blanchard stood, weighing up his options but he knew he had no choice. He was in too deep now.

'Ok,' he finally said, 'how much more?'

'Five thousand.'

'Fine,' he said, 'I'll drop it off tonight.'

The assassin smiled.

'It'll be worth it, my friend, I do good job. No mistakes. No mess.'

He held out his hand and, as Blanchard shook it, I quickly slipped back and out, and round to the front of the building. I pulled out my phone to text my wife the exciting news that I had found the evil assassin. I texted that I would also be late home as I was planned to follow Blanchard after work and find out where the assassin lived.

I could then confront him.

Or call the police.

She replied with an enthusiastic run of thumbs up and asked if I could pick up some more nappies.

*

'59?' my wife asked.

'Yes,' I said.

'Are you sure?'

'I think so.'

'I've just seen a man walk in, but he was small.'

'Did he have any tattoos?' I asked.

'No, none that I could see,' she said.

'That's not him. The assassin is a big man, with tattoos.'

'I think it's the wrong house,' she said.

'Damn it,' I cursed.

I was sure it was number 59, but it had been dark. And after the dog had barked, I had quickly scuttled away, anxious not to be seen.

I had, as planned, followed Blanchard after work. I had been on the phone when I saw him put on his jacket and walk towards the lifts, holding a thick brown envelope and I quickly hung up on my client. It was abrupt and rude, but the market was closed, and I knew there was no order to follow. I knew that I could apologise in the morning and blame it on the fickle whim of a new phone system.

In any case, it didn't really matter.

He would soon forget.

I followed Blanchard to the tube and stood as he stood, all the way down the escalator. It was harder than I thought, though, tailing a man at rush hour. Bodies were everywhere. So many bodies. All tight faces and sweaty top lips. We changed line once and went deeper underground and rattled through stations I had not seen for years. We eventually popped up in the quiet surrounds of South London.

Norbury.

I followed him through quiet streets, keeping a safe distance behind him. My brogues, though, were too hard on the wet pavement, and I took to walking on the balls of my feet. Had a gang of idle, feckless teenagers seen me, they would have bayed like hounds. But there were no teenagers. It was too late. And cold. And they were all at home eating fatty snacks and bullying each other online.

Blanchard had then stopped outside of a small house and knocked on the door.

I ducked in behind a tree.

He knocked again and waited, staring at his phone. The street was quiet, suburban, and after a long wait the moody assassin had finally opened the door holding a small baby. It was hard to tell, but the baby looked the same age as mine. The contradiction was hard to take in. A father.

And a killer.

Blanchard handed him the envelope and they stood chatting. It looked easy. Friendly. Blanchard laughed and tickled the baby's chin. It was all so normal.

And then the dog had barked.

It was near me and they both looked over in our direction. I cursed and turned, and quickly started walking, pulling my collar up, striding down the street away from their prying eyes. I had the cover of dusk, but I still felt conspicuous. I did not look back, but as I walked I made a note of the house numbers. I was in the fifties, walking ever lower and I counted back in my mind, 56, 57, 58.

59.

The assassin lived at number 59, and as I reached the main road, I glanced at the street sign.

Wedgewood Road.

59 Wedgewood Road.

My wife and I had stayed up late talking, throwing ideas around. She had suggested that she go down in the morning and case the street. The baby, she claimed, was the perfect foil.

A wily woman.

Like so many.

And I had foolishly agreed.

And now she had phoned to say that I was wrong. The assassin didn't live at number 59, a small man with no obvious tattoos lived at number 59.

'What shall I do?' she said.

I closed my eyes and tried to picture the door.

'59 Wedgewood Road,' I said aloud, 'I'm sure it was number 59.'

As I opened my eyes I saw Blanchard, who had

been sitting at his desk, turn and stare right at me. He had heard. He had heard me say the address and my heart started to thud.

'Hang on,' my wife said, 'I think I see him.'

'Who?' I asked, my panic rising under the intense gaze of Blanchard.

'Oh no, he's seen me,' my wife said, her voice now a little too shrill for my liking. 'It's him. Tattoos! He has tattoos. And he's seen me. He's coming.'

'Run,' I said, 'get away!'

There was the sound of a car horn.

'RUN!'

I heard a man shout.

And then the line went dead.

I stared at my phone and then I looked up to see the whole desk was watching me.

Including Blanchard.

Thud.

Thud.

Thud.

My heart hammered my chest.

I couldn't stay and stare back at them all, and so I quickly turned tail and walked, heading straight for the nearest door. An exit. Any exit. I found the lifts. I pushed a button. I needed to get out. My mind was buzzing. Some doors opened, and I slipped in.

Up.

And up.

All the way up to the sixth floor. I turned right out of the lift, catching a glance at the beady eyed toucan on the reception desk. I saw that her hair was still clawed back, her eyes still beyond pity or care. The same eyes I saw when I had last been on the sixth floor. The day that Gerald had cried. I walked quickly down the corridor, down to the end. I knew where I was going.

Space.

Fresh air.

I pushed through the door to the roof terrace and phoned my wife.

As the phone rang, I gazed out across the cityscape, south, across the river to where my wife and baby were in trouble. I felt helpless and angry. Angry that I had so nonchalantly agreed to her helping me. Blanchard, I feared, was a psychopath; and the assassin was a killer, and yet I had just let my wife and baby step into their world.

The phone rang out to voicemail and I let out a throaty scream.

Frustration.

And fear.

'Is everything ok?' a voice said.

I spun around.

The toucan.

Her face caught the sun, dazzling the brilliant whiteness of her thick foundation. Her hair was so taut it lifted her eyebrows so that her expression was one of near constant surprise. It dawned on me that she had seen a banker, and a roof. She knew, too, that bonuses had recently been paid. And she had been trained.

Keep the voice steady. Calm. Make no sudden moves.

Talk.

'Yes,' I said, 'I mean no. My wife. My wife and baby are in trouble.'

She moved forward, relieved perhaps, that my being on the roof was not bonus related. She took my elbow and as she effortlessly guided me to a nearby bench, her features softened.

'What's happened?' she said, after we sat down, 'tell me.'

'My wife …' I started.

And yet I didn't know what to say. The whole thing was preposterous, Blanchard, the assassin, the whole thing. It was absurd. And yet it was true.

'My wife,' I said, regaining a scrap of composure, 'is being mugged.'

'Where?' said the toucan, putting her hand in her pocket.

'Does it matter?' I asked.

'Where?'

'Norbury,' I said.

She pulled out her own phone and found a number which she dialled.

'Hello, love, yes it's me,' she said. 'Where are you?'

I couldn't hear what was being said.

'Can you get to Norbury?' she said.

She lowered her phone to talk to me.

'Do you know what street?'

'Wedgewood road,' I said.

'Wedgewood road,' she relayed to the mystery phone-a-friend. 'A woman is there with a baby, and she is being mugged.'

My phone rang.

It was my wife.

'Are you ok?' I yelled.

The toucan hung up.

'I'm fine,' my wife said. 'Why are you yelling at me?'

'What? I said.

'You were yelling. You sound mad.'

'I am! I thought you were being mugged? The man. The man with tattoos, you said he was coming for you?'

She chuckled.

'Oh yes! Sorry I was wrong. It was the postman,' she said. 'I didn't see the uniform. He did have a lot of tattoos though. He wanted to know if I lived on the street.'

'Jesus Christ,' I said, 'I was worried sick!'

The toucan cocked her head.

'It's ok,' I said, lowering the phone, 'it's my wife. She's fine!'

I grinned, although my grin felt a little forced.

Which it was.

'I have his name though,' my wife whispered.

'You have what?' I asked.

'His name, the assassin's name. The postman told me!'

'That's great, honey!' I said, smiling, 'I'll call you back.'

The toucan was too close and the information too sensitive.

I hung up.

'It's fine,' I said, smiling.

Relief.

'Turns out I over-reacted a bit! I have been a little tight of late. Work!' I said, rolling my eyes in a theatrical manner.

'No problem,' she said.

'And thanks for your help,' I said, as she got up to leave. 'By the way, who did you phone?'

'My husband,' she said. 'He's a copper. He said he'd send a car around.'

A copper.

Given my wife's real mission south of the river I knew I needed to tread carefully.

'Wow, thanks!' I said. 'Thank you so much. You can tell him she's fine. There's no need to send a car.'

'Oh, I think he will anyway,' she said. 'He told me that they know Wedgewood road very well. They think the Moldovan mafia is run out of some houses there. They've been watching it for some time.'

I nodded.

And smiled.

'Is he in surveillance?' I asked.

'No,' she said, 'he's CID. Murder squad.'

I kept smiling as she got up to go.

Murder squad.

How very interesting.

*

My wife had indeed found out the assassin's name.

Bogdan.

The postman, as they so often are, was happy to talk. He had worked Norbury for years. He said he knew everyone, although not so much now, not since the Moldovans moved in. They kept themselves to themselves, he had said.

My wife then told the postman she was looking for one, a Moldovan, a big one with lots of tattoos. She had pulled her phone out of her pocket and told the postman that she had seen it fall out of his bag on the bus. She had tried to follow him, but she had been slowed by a pram and crying baby. She had lost him, she said, somewhere around the fifties.

The postman posted a rueful smile and told my wife he knew the man. And then he told her his name.

My wife was one, wily woman.

The man, he said, lived at 60 Wedgewood Road.

Whilst we now knew the name of the assassin and

knew Blanchard had hired him to rid the world of the now supine and introspective Gerald, I knew that we didn't have enough hard evidence to take to the police. We needed more. For the next few days I kept a low profile at work. In and out of the back door. I arrived late and left early. I kept a busy diary, one that frequently drew me away from the desk.

And away from Blanchard.

I saw him watching me, though, his jaw slack, his fingers slowly stroking his neck. But nothing happened. There were no words. No spittle flecked exchanges in the inky surrounds of the print room as photocopiers hummed and whirred, spewing out more reports. More memos bound for the big hungry bins out back.

I was sat at my desk one morning, mulling our next move, when my phone rang. Distracted, and with the market falling hard off the back of some unexpectedly weak economic data, I answered it, expecting an order from a frazzled client. Orders often flowed when screens were red and yet it wasn't a client, it was my mother-in-law.

'I've been trying to get hold of you,' she said.

'You have?' I asked, as innocently as I could.

'We have a problem,' she said.

I looked around the desk to check no one was listening.

'What kind of problem?' I asked, sitting down.

I had been standing, like any broker would in a market meltdown. Posture mattered.

'The central heating system is down,' she said.

'Have you checked the pipes?' I asked.

'Yes. It was the first thing we checked.'

'What about the thermostat? Are you sure it is turned up?'

She didn't dignify me with an answer.

I knew that if they dredged the oil tank and found Bruno, there would be questions. Perhaps an autopsy. Dates might follow. Diaries checked. Indeed, the weekend the son-in-law first stayed. Eyes would flicker. The Gestapo's imagination might be gripped with feverish thoughts and suggestions of bizarre, whimsical conspiracy. I knew I would quickly be fingered as a suspect. I need to breathe, to stay calm. There could be many other reasons why the heating system was broken.

'A man is coming to check the boiler today,' she said, 'I'll keep you posted.'

I hung up, imagining the Gestapo in his shed, a stained heating manual spread out on the work top; his expression furrowed, vexing, cursing the manufacturer's recently expired guarantee.

My mobile phone buzzed on my desk and I picked it up to see a message from Gerald. He said he wanted to meet. The icon in his message was the normal one, the church, and I glanced at my watch: too late for early communion. The Gestapo's heating system was a problem, but it wasn't an immediate priority. It would have to wait for Gerald's life was in ever-increasing danger.

I slipped down the back stairs and out of one of side exits and walked quickly to the small church tucked in the shadow of our own shiny, angular temple; one that was devoted to a God who eyed the collection with a bit more zeal. We had taken to meeting in the church grounds. To talk and walk. I knew where he would be sitting. Where he always now sat, gazing at the gravestones, his mind drifting, stewing, flailing for answers to the intangible questions of life.

He was a different man.

And a man, I had found myself slowly realising, I had come to like.

The outsider, the boy, the man whose life had been distorted by a dysfunctional society and a cruel, distant father. A man who lived alone, deep within himself, too frightened to open himself up. The pain too raw. I saw the battle he had been waging all his life, the blackness, the spiritual and physical isolation. The absence of love, and intimacy.

And yet I was now pulling for him, we were fighting together. He deserved better. He deserved a second chance. I saw in Gerald the damage that can be done to small boys and I thought of my own boy and vowed one night as I stared into the bathroom mirror, eyes bloodshot from too much whisky, that I would not consign him to the same fate.

Time.

And love.

There was no limit to each.

Gerald was, as ever, sitting on the bench staring into space. I sat down next to him and savoured the silence of the graveyard. The peace. It was a world away from the tetchy, fractious surrounds of the trading floor, and somewhat ironic that we came to reflect on life, in a place that was stuffed to an inch of its topsoil, with dead bodies.

Lives lived.

But of a distant age.

A different age.

We swapped pleasantries, as we always did, tip toeing around the real conversation we had come to have. Getting comfortable. Soon, though, the small talk was done, and Gerald deemed it time.

'I think I am being followed,' he said, with a frown.

I paused, to reflect. I had learnt not to thrash out at his secrets, however shocking. The best response was a measured response, however shocking the secret.

'When?' I asked, lightly.

'Last night,' he said.

And so, I mused, our assassin was doing his homework. He was preparing, building a picture. Annotating maps and getting to know the habits and routine of his ignorant victim.

'Did anything happen?' I asked.

He shook his head.

'No, but something feels wrong,' he said. 'I don't know what. It's odd, but I think I'm being watched.'

I should have told him then and there. I should have told him what I knew, but I didn't. I couldn't find the words and so, we talked a bit more before he abruptly announced that he was going.

'Where are you going?' I asked.

'To see my lawyer,' he said, standing up and walking away before I could ask why he needed to see his lawyer.

I watched him go, his shoulders slumped, a broken man; and the phone call I would receive later that night confirmed that his suspicions were very much on the money.

CHAPTER XII

'Are you going to answer your phone?' my wife asked.

She was still awake. I wasn't, I had been dozing, and I had no intention of answering my phone. I glanced at the clock.

11.23 p.m.

My phone stopped and then it started buzzing again. When phones start buzzing, having stopped buzzing, something is up. And something was indeed, very much, up.

'Can you please answer it?' my wife had said.

I knew that tone. And it wasn't one to ignore. And so, I picked up my phone.

'Hello?' I said.

'It's me,' said a distressed voice.

'Gerald?' I asked.

'Please come,' he said. 'Please come now.'

'Where?'

'My house. Please come right away. I need to see someone.'

He then started to jabber. Words falling out of his mouth. They were scrambled. They didn't make any sense. It was obvious that he was in a real state. My wife looked at me, concerned, her eyes wide with worry. She knew what was at stake. I had told her about my meeting in the churchyard with Gerald. We had talked late, with wine, weighing up our next move. We agreed we needed to do more, we needed to act, now that he was being watched. The killer could strike at any time.

And now a phone call.

Events were happening too fast.

'Please can you come around?' Gerald asked.

'Now?' I said.

'Yes, I really need to see someone,' he said.

He sounded frightened. I knew it had to be related to Blanchard's plan. And yet, had the assassin done his job, Gerald would have not been able to make any calls. That was the point of the plan.

'Of course. I'll be there in twenty minutes,' I said.

As I pulled on some trousers, I was surprised at how much I cared.

'Something's happened,' I said to my wife as I recycled some socks.

'Did he say what?' she asked.

I shook my head.

'What do you think has happened?' she asked.

Her wily mind, I could see, was whirring.

'I don't know but he sounded in a bad way.'

'You think it has something to do with the assassin?' she asked.

I nodded.

'I think so. It has to be connected.'

'Be careful,' she said.

I bent down and kissed her.

'Of course, I will. I love you,' I said. 'Don't wait up.'

*

I parked outside Gerald's house. All the lights were on despite the late hour. It was well past midnight. I was apprehensive, I didn't know what I'd be walking into. I rummaged through my bag in the boot and found a can of deodorant. It wasn't pepper spray, but it was all I had. Were it needed, a little pish-pish of some 'dark temptation' body spray might be enough to buy me some time and so I slipped the can into my pocket and took to the steps at a good pace and knocked on the door.

'Who is it?' said a voice through the intercom.

It was crackly and remote. Even through the static I could tell it was scared.

'Gerald, it's me,' I said.

The door buzzed, and I pushed it open.

Inside, the house had a whiff of polish to it. The wooden floors perhaps having been given a buff that morning. I walked through the hall and into the kitchen where I found Gerald slumped on the table a bottle of whisky open, half-full. Or half-empty depending on one's disposition. For Gerald, judging by his dishevelled appearance, most likely half-empty.

He looked like a ghost.

'They want to kill me,' he said.

I poured myself some whisky and sat down.

'Who do?' I said, knowing full well who did.

'Someone at work,' he said.

'That's crazy!' I managed to say.

It was all I could say, and it was too, it was crazy. I was relieved, though, that he now knew, however distressing the news. If he knew, that meant I didn't have to tell him.

We sat in silence.

I sipped my whisky and waited for him to talk.

He had those big bulbous, industrial type lights over his kitchen table, three of them, all flooding the room. Aesthetically pleasing, but sitting under them, with the subject of murder hanging in the air, I got hot. So hot that I stood up and removed my jacket. Eventually I prodded him with a question.

'What happened?' I asked, adding a cube of ice to my whisky.

He slowly sat up and scratched his chin.

'I was having supper when the doorbell rang,' he said quietly, gazing at the fridge. 'I wasn't expecting anyone. I thought it might be the neighbour or someone. They want me to sign a petition to stop a basement project. They think I can help.'

He looked at me, as if contemplating whether to continue.

'Go on,' I said.

'I opened the door and there was a man. He was

big. Dark hair. Tattoos. And he was holding a gun.'

'A gun?' I asked, surprised. 'What kind of basement project is it?'

'No, this was no neighbour. I had never seen him before. He told me to go inside.'

'What did you do?' I asked.

'I did as I was told.'

I gulped more whisky, knowing now Blanchard's plan had failed. Gerald said the man was foreign and gruff. Like many of them are. He was pale too, as criminals, or those still in crime at least, also tend to be and his tattoos jarred with the cream décor and clean lines of the hall. Off-putting.

So too the gun.

'He told me to go into the kitchen. I assumed he was a robber and so told him to take anything he wanted. Anything at all. I even offered to help get the TV off the kitchen wall. I told him there was a tool kit under the stairs.'

'What did he do?'

'Nothing.'

'I thought he didn't speak any English, so I started gesticulating for him to take the things he wanted. It was like some sort of high-octane game of charades. He then told me to sit down. His English was perfect, with a slight accent. I thought it was Eastern Europe, but it could also have been Glaswegian.'

'Crime statistics suggest either is plausible,' I offered.

Gerald said the man had then put his gun on the

table and rubbed his eyes and explained to Gerald that he was a contract killer. He had been offered a large sum of money to kill him. This offer he had been forced to take. He explained that he rented a small apartment in Norbury and the landlord had just hiked the rent. He had a wife and small child.

'Norbury!' he had said to Gerald, 'it's not even Clapham!'

Gerald, terrified, had nodded in agreement.

'Did you ask him how much he had been paid?' I asked.

'Yes, but he didn't answer. I thought I was finished. But he then said that if I offered him a bit more, not much, five maybe ten grand, he would shake hands and go back to Norbury.'

'No way?' I said, 'deal or no deal?'

'Deal,' he said, smiling.

He poured himself some more whisky.

'How extraordinary,' I said.

I didn't know what to feel. It was over. Blanchard's plan had failed, and yet something didn't feel quite right.

'Thanks for coming over,' he said, 'I really needed to see you.'

He stared at me.

'No problem at all,' I said.

His stare, though, was intense, and a little uncomfortable. And his tone had shifted. It was colder. It was a subtle change, so very subtle. What was I even doing there? I shifted in my seat and played with my empty glass. There was a question on my lips, but one I couldn't bring myself to ask. The implications were too significant. I did though, finally, I asked him. I had to.

'Did the assassin tell you who had hired him?' I asked, attempting as best as I could, to keep my voice calm.

'He did,' he whispered and drained the rest of his glass.

It was then that I saw it on the dresser.

Half tucked in behind the laptop, there was a gun. I looked back at Gerald who was now gazing at me with a look that had my gonads on the run. His late-night call now made perfect sense. I saw it, I saw what had happened.

Blanchard.

Blanchard had hung me out to dry. He must have given the killer my name, knowing that there was a risk the killer would be caught. I had been double crossed. I sat stock still. I couldn't move. My body refused to move. All I could do was watch as Gerald slowly reached out behind him and picked up the gun.

*

It was humiliating, watching him on the ground like that. He was a mess. Under pressure, he had crumbled, like so many of us do. Men. Pathetic. And useless. Extinction remained a plausible end game, within just a few generations.

'Poor chap,' Jim muttered.

I didn't know Jim, but I knew where he was

coming from as it could have been me, or Jim. I had just met Jim because waking up on a glorious sunny Saturday, I had been told that we were going to the park to meet the mummies and their husbands, from our boy's baby group. The mothers saw each other each week, they caught up over coffee, they swapped toys. They gossiped. They gossiped so much that in the end they then thought it would be fun to all meet up one weekend so that they could run beady eyes over each other's husbands.

As we walked through the park, my wife told me who was who. Which mummies would be there. The names of the babies. And which babies belonged to which mummies. Snippets. But bits of information that I immediately forgot. I forgot as she had then vented, as wives are sometimes prone to do.

'Dad's in a foul mood,' she said.

I tightened my grip on the buggy. It was a reflex. Involuntary.

'Why?' I asked, fearing bad news.

'The central heating system is broken,' she said.

As my mother-in-law had said.

'Do they know what's wrong?' I asked, cautiously.

'No, they think it could be the boiler.'

I breathed.

The boiler was not the oil tank.

Bruno remained safe, for now.

When we arrived in the park, I smiled, I shook hands, I smiled some more and made sympathetic noises about the lack of parking.

The man in question, the man who was now taking his own buggy apart, I didn't know. He was well turned out in a blazer and a shirt with expensive looking cufflinks. His brown cords and brogues suggested he too felt slightly out of place.

He had a professional air to him. A man who was a head or co-head of some large department. He looked important. And yet now he was on the ground, his eyes wild, his side parting split. His blazer was off. Sweat patches had appeared on his back and his knees were muddied. He would have been unrecognisable to any work colleague.

The mothers murmured quietly behind their bug-eyed sunglasses; the fathers continued to gulp the warm white wine on offer, happy that it wasn't they muddying their own knees and slowly popping apart at the seams. The reason that he was on his knees was because the sun had come out. And when the sun had come out his wife had barked at him to fetch their little girl a hat.

He had jumped to it.

But could he find the hat? No, he could not.

'In the bag!' his wife had said.

And he had rummaged through the bag.

No hat.

'I said the nappy bag!' she had then said, her tone now, as you might suspect, scratchy and impatient.

Conversations stopped. Everyone turned to watch, eyes devouring the scene. There is nothing quite so delicious as watching another couple having a very public, domestic spat. I looked at my wife and grinned. She too was enjoying the show. It was impossible not to. And yet despite the show, I was a little detached. Distracted. For I was still trying to get over the previous day's events at work.

*

As it turned out the gun had been a fake.

'Look, it's a fake!' Gerald had said to me. 'Christ, you looked as though you thought I was going to shoot you.'

I mumbled something; I don't know what. There had been too much adrenalin in the system. He threw the gun across the table to me, and I picked it up.

'It feels real,' I said. 'Heavy.'

'Yes, I think it's a replica. They use them for police training. Very easy to get on the internet.'

It felt very real, only it wasn't.

Like so many things in life.

Gerald had then explained that his gruff assailant, having checked that the money had been transferred into his account, had softly put his hand on his shoulder.

'God be with you,' he had said, much to Gerald's surprise.

And with that he had disappeared, leaving the gun on the kitchen table.

There had been no Amen.

'Did you try and cancel the payment?' I asked.

'No. I thought about it, but I didn't want him coming back.'

'What about the police? Why not call the police?'

'I don't know. It was odd. He seemed like a nice man. He had a manner to him. Almost caring.'

'Caring?' I said, 'he threatened to kill you?'

'I know. But he clearly just needed the money. He's just trying to do his best for his family. Put food on the table. And no one should have to live in Norbury.'

He had a point.

Gerald had then told me it was Blanchard who had hired the killer. I had been wrong. Either way, for Gerald at least, it appeared that it was Blanchard who had wanted him dead. Not me. This was a relief, but something I already knew. And whilst I was relieved, what still bothered me was that the plan was so unlike Blanchard.

And I started to worry some more that someone else had to be involved.

*

'A hat! We need a hat!' the wife shrieked.

The man, I noticed, was now on the brink. He was on the edge and it was a long way down. He had taken everything out of every bag. He had emptied them all on the ground but had found no hat. He had now started dismantling the buggy. His wife, sitting on the rug like some sort of Buddha, had swivelled around on her substantial backside and was now shouting at him. By her manner, she too thought he was pathetic, but she was too deep in her own buttocks to do anything about it.

It was ugly.

'You packed the hat!' she yelled, 'tell me you packed the hat?'

The man looked broken. There was no hat. That the sun had now eased itself back in behind the clouds didn't matter. They were now having a domestic. A spat that was being consumed by the deep matter of its own black hole. Their weekend was over. It was no longer about the hat. It was now about him and her, and them.

They would not be having sex any time soon.

'Twiglets?' asked a woman.

'Thanks,' I said, as I made for the packet.

'Awful, isn't it?' she said, looking at the man, now slumped on his own, slowly putting clothes and nappies and rubber toys back in the assorted bags. He had the solemn air of a rescue worker.

'Indeed,' I said, edging away, with a fistful of twiglets.

It was the events of the Friday afternoon, though, that really dominated my thoughts. They were still too fresh in the memory to offer the baby fest my full attention. The implications were too great.

It had happened about three o'clock.

Like any typical Friday afternoon, it had been commercially quiet and the hum on the floor was, as ever, expectant. The weekend beckoned, what with the pungent prospect of cocktails and bare flesh. Anticipation tingled, as it always did, for those still eking out the week, those now planning nights of hedonistic, illicit escape. A weekend of masks.

It was all very normal.

And then the doors to the trading floor had been flung open and two burly security guards had marched in flanking two, equally burly, police officers in standard, high visibility jackets. Bringing up the rear was a small, impish man in a Barbour jacket. It would have been easy to miss him, tucked in as he was behind his burly entourage.

'What the…. who the hell is that?' muttered the Fox, who I had been talking to at the time.

It turned out the man was CID.

Murder squad.

And he was the one who had read Blanchard his rights.

*

The picnic in the park had been a success. It had been a little awkward to start, the conversations stiff and stilted, but in the end, people loosened up. The Dads gathered around a buggy and swapped gritty tales of domestic misfortune. The wine helped. That said, I didn't get a sense that there was any great need to do it all again, anytime soon.

'Weekend is family time,' I had suggested to my wife as we walked through the park back home.

'Yes, but it's nice to see other people,' she countered.

I watched the ducks on the pond.

Such a simple life.

They didn't even have to forage for food given the stale bread that was so frequently lobbed their way. I imagined their only real fear was of teenage boys trying to pick them off with rocks but, as was the fashion of the virtual age, those same teenage boys were all contorted in their own bedrooms trying to get the right angle to photograph their genitals to send to girls in their class.

'Maybe,' was all I could say.

'Coffee?' my wife asked.

I nodded, and she went off to the café. I stayed with the boy, loitering by the entrance, wondering how Blanchard had fared overnight in the cell. That Blanchard had been arrested was a mild concern. I knew he'd blub. He had something of the canary about him, a wobbly top lip. He would be yabbing before the Detective had even unzipped his Barbour.

I knew I'd need a defence.

And I was prepared.

Denial, the petty criminal's natural go-to state, would be, I thought, as good a place to start as any. There was, after all, no evidence. Nothing to connect me to the hiring of a sullen, cash-strapped assassin. There were emails between Blanchard and I arranging to meet in the sauna, but I could explain that away through work. We liked talking stocks in the nude. It freed up the thinking. It inspired creativity. Nudity, I would tell the officer, offered a sense of 'liberation.'

It would then be his word against mine.

I quickly discovered that standing in the entrance with a buggy though, was a bad idea. There were too many people, and so I turned the buggy around to go out to the seating area by the lake. I parked next to a table near the edge of the water and sat down. The baby was asleep. As my defence started to take shape in my mind, I caught sight of a distinctly uncomfortable sight.

There, sitting at another table, sitting with a buggy of her own, was Dominique.

It felt odd seeing her. The context of the park was so at odds with our normal relationship; a relationship that was rooted in work. The office. And the surrounds of the office. It jarred seeing her outside of that environment, more so in jeans and a thick red jersey. Normally she just wore black.

It was also odd seeing her, given that Blanchard was now locked up, twiddling his thumbs, awaiting bail. I thought about going over to say hello. I thought maybe away from the office the guard would be down and that she would be more inclined to talk. Perhaps the informal setting would help loosen her tongue. The park. So innocuous. Informal. Safe from the politics and pitfalls of the trading floor.

And yet, as I continued to consider my options, a man approached carrying a tray with two coffees and a croissant. His back was to me, and so I couldn't see his face. But they were together. He put the tray down and then reached into the buggy and pulled out a baby with possibly the biggest head I had ever seen.

It was huge.

'Jesus Christ,' I muttered.

'That baby has a massive head,' my wife said.

Absorbed in the scene of Dominique and her man, I hadn't noticed my wife return. She put our own coffees on the table and sat down, her back to

Dominique. She, after all, didn't know that I knew Dominique. I wondered whether I should tell her.

'Did you talk to Ginny?' she asked, before I had a chance.

'Ginny?' I said, my attention still half on Dominique.

'Yes, Ginny. She is married to Jeremy.'

'Jeremy?'

'Yes, the parents of Toto.'

She looked at me.

'Are you ok?' she asked.

But I was far from ok, I was in shock. Speechless. Behind my wife, the man had given the baby to Dominique and had then stood up to do some more rummaging around in the buggy, and in doing so he had turned around, and I had seen his face.

Pascal.

I was astonished to see them together. And, given his easy manner with the baby, on apparent speaking terms.

'What's the matter?' my wife asked.

'Nothing, no, nothing at all,' I said quickly, trying to mask my obvious discomfort.

I tried to think, to play it calm, but I couldn't. There were too many unknowns, uncertainties. Too many shadows. All whispering. My mind was trying to piece together the implications of seeing Pascal and Dominique together. I had no feel for what was going on. Lurking in the shadows was the truth. But I couldn't see it.

'We should get going,' I said, making a move to get up, 'let's walk. I think we should walk.'

I needed to think.

'Sounds good,' my wife said, 'and you're sure you're ok? You sound a bit distracted?'

I was.

'Listen, don't look now,' I said, 'but the couple with the baby – the one with the massive head – I work with them.'

She immediately turned and looked over at them.

'Do you want to go and say hello?' she said.

I shook my head.

'No. Not now. We should go,' I said.

My wife shrugged, gazing at the baby.

'That baby has a massive swede,' she said.

I grabbed the buggy, turning to push it out of the exit and, as we crossed the picnic area, I stole one last glance at them. Dominique was busy with the baby. But Pascal wasn't. Pascal was sitting, staring, staring right at me. He then casually reached into his pocket and pulled out a packet of cigarettes. He lit one and exhaled, blowing smoke full in the face of himself, and the baby. Neither he, nor the baby flinched.

It all felt odd.

Odd and wrong.

So very wrong.

*

I eased into work on the Monday morning, unsure of

the mood. Blanchard's capture had likely given the PR office a nasty turn. The arrest of an employee was not good news, however which way it was spun. The trading floor though, was alight. Buzzing. Rumours blended into fact, facts that had themselves been squeezed out of rumours. By the time I had reached my desk, I had been told that Blanchard had been arrested for various reasons: embezzlement, funding a Nazi website and flashing a group of schoolgirls. All of which were possible, but none of which were true.

I knew they weren't true as I alone knew the reason for Blanchard's ignominious exit.

I also knew why the police had so happened upon him as he had idly eased through what he had assumed would be a forgettable Friday afternoon. I knew because it was I who had told them. I did. I had emailed them. I knew there were shadows involved, figures I could not yet see. Dark forces that played a part in Blanchard's conniving, but a part that I was not party to and so, before it was too late, before I was sucked into the quagmire of blame, someone needed to take the fall.

Blanchard.

It was always going to be Blanchard.

Late one night, when my wife had gone to bed and the baby was sleeping, I sat at the kitchen table and set up an email account in the name of Bruno. I still felt bad. I ached at the pain and sadness of Bruno's ignominious end and I wanted his death to mean something, and so, Bruno shopped Blanchard. I sent the email to the toucan's husband. It was easy to find him. The police had on their website a list of detectives and I found his name. He looked intense. And dogged.

Just what was needed.

I had put in the email as many facts that I could remember from the night at Gerald's house. I gave the assassin's name and address. I also made up a few more to bulk up the cache, hoping that it would be enough for them to pinch Blanchard for questioning. One click with the mouse, and it was done. I had then sat back and waited and was quietly thrilled when the burly scrum of high visibility jackets had bundled through the doors of the trading floor to take the man down.

Power.

I had tasted power.

I was in early, and the desk was still largely empty. I walked across the trading floor and saw that Dominique was at her desk.

'Morning Dominique,' I said.

She slowly looked up, but her expression was blank. It was also somewhat unsettling. It was the way she cast her eyes, and the way her head hung low off her shoulders, slightly twisted, looking up at me, as I passed. She looked like a witch. Or a troll. Or a maybe a bit of both.

It was an alarming sight, so early in the morning.

The Fox was also in, whispering down his phone already and so I left him to it and logged on. The email was hard to miss. It was labelled urgent and it had a red flag next to it and capitalised instructions in the subject box.

READ ME!

I looked back at Gerald's desk which was still empty, which meant he had sent the email from his phone.

'MEET ME IN THE SAUNA' it had said.

The sauna, it was always the sauna.

I glanced at the clock. It was not yet 7 a.m. but I knew the gym would be busy. I knew too that the sauna meant one thing. The irony was not lost on me as I headed down, knowing it was not going to be good news. It seemed the sauna was never the place for sharing good news. And I couldn't shake the sight of Dominique. She looked so cold, so menacing.

Something was up.

Something had changed.

I slipped down the back stairs to the gym and quickly peeled off once again to my crumpled boxer shorts and opened the sauna door. For once no naked Germans. No Germans, just Gerald, who was sat in the corner. He had a towel draped over his shoulders and looked a little agitated. I sat down and stared at the stones, but Gerald remained silent. Perhaps he too was holding back. A minute passed. Maybe two. I had neither the time nor the patience. I stood up and poured some water on the stones, hoping the heat would loosen him up, which it did.

'Someone else is involved,' he said quietly.

'You didn't tip off the police?' I asked, playing games.

He didn't know it was me, he didn't know Bruno.

He shook his head.

'Someone else tipped off the police,' I said in the manner of a man thinking aloud. 'I have to say, I thought that too. Blanchard would never think of using a hit man. It had to have been someone else's idea.'

'Yes,' he said, 'it's obvious when you think about it.'

'It was too clever for Blanchard,' I said.

'And there are others.'

'What do you mean others?' I asked

'At work. People. Here. People I have, I don't know, perhaps treated badly in the past.'

'Who?'

'Lots,' he said, his voice laced with a little sadness.

Silence.

And then it hit me.

How had I not seen it before?

A stray memory.

A fragment.

I hadn't thought anything of it at the time given all that was going on, but it had stuck deep in the mind. I remember thinking it had just been a little bit odd. Something wasn't quite right. It was the way she had been standing. And the scream, the scream had not been natural. There had not been enough of a shriek about it. The blood too. It was too patchy. It was as if someone had dabbed it on themselves.

She had staged it in the hotel lobby.

And then the look that morning.

It wasn't aloof or moody or tired.

It was evil.

Pure evil.

I knew then who had been pulling Blanchard's strings all along.

'My God, I know who it is,' I said to Gerald.

It was so obvious, I felt embarrassed.

'It's Dominique!' I said.

He looked up but said nothing.

'Dominique! It must have been Dominique! She has been working with Blanchard all along. The assassin must have been her idea!' I said, spitting the words out, giddy from the heat and the duplicity.

And it was then that we both saw it. It exploded in front of our eyes. It was why I had such a strange feeling in the park. It was them. Together. They were a team.

Pascal.

He was the criminal mastermind.

He had to be.

He had put the Fox up to scupper the IPO, it had to have been him. It was the way he had arrived late to the meeting, in time for the Fox to hole the deal with the information that he had been given. And Dominique would have told him about the events at the Marriot. Pascal would then have seen the opportunity, to go hard, to do one on Gerald and get revenge for all the times he had been belittled and pushed out by him at work.

All because he was French.

Foreign.

And if Pascal knew that I had ratted on Blanchard to the police, I was now also in danger.

I had interviewed without wearing any pants in a woollen suit, I had nearly drowned in a lido, I had even forgotten my wife's birthday; but it was only then, in the heat of the sauna, that I properly tasted fear.

*

It was carnage, utter carnage, there was blood across the trading floor; blood and feathers and fur.

'BANKERS BLOODBATH' bellowed the headlines.

And it was too, it was the biggest jobs cull the bank had ever seen. The omens were there. They had been for some time. The industry was under pressure. Revenues were falling and there were just too many people. The surprise, though, was the timing. It was a storm that was expected, but the clouds were assumed to be distant, and then one morning the storm broke.

Sitting at her desk, at least two hours before she normally did, was the secretary of the boss, the big boss. The boss who had a perpetual look of a man under siege, who was pulled from meeting to meeting. Meetings in which he was expected to sign off strategy, risk and fend off the advances of wet-lipped subordinates desperate to sell him their own personal brand of snake oil. The big boss who always looked tired.

And a bit sad.

I had spoken to him man-on-man only once, in the elevator, shortly after I joined.

'Do you have big firm balls?' I had asked, innocently.

He had looked at me with the expression of a four-year-old on being told there were dragons in the garden shed. It was a face of fear; fear and disbelief. It had, though, come out wrong. I had meant balls, as in social occasions with dinner and dancing and posh frocks. And I had meant did the firm, the bank, did the bank have big social events.

That, nevertheless, had been the extent of our relationship.

That his secretary was at her desk so early was the clue. It meant he was up on the sixth floor with his bullets out. She would have a list of names and she would have been able to see when the victim was at his or her desk. She would then dial the extension with her long, cold fingers.

Eddy had been first.

Gone before breakfast.

The Fox was next.

The Fox was old and knew it was coming. He wanted it. When his phone rang, I saw him smile, relief stamped across his face. It was what he had been waiting for. He, having been at the bank so long, would have been looking at a windfall; a redundancy package that would mean he and his wife would never have to take an economy cabin, when cruising the Turks and Caicos, ever again. He even came over and shook my hand. I wanted to say something to him. I wanted to ask him who his Chinaman was in the blue van who had rescued us from the Marriot, and how he knew I would call him.

The Fox, though, remained a mystery, like so many, and I knew I would get no answers.

'Golf. Soon,' he had said softly and walked off looking five years younger already.

I had sat there mulling my fate, knowing it didn't look good.

My phone rang.

'Hello?' I said, prepared for what was coming.

'It's me,' said my client, his voice as brusque and bad-tempered as normal.

The familiarity was surprisingly reassuring.

'Good morning!' I replied, wavering a little as I had little information to hand. I glanced at my screen and saw the Nikkei was flat, gold was up, and the car giant Ford was cutting ten thousand jobs.

Ford too.

Tough times.

'So, you're still there?' he asked.

'I am,' I said.

'I was just checking,' he said and hung up.

Word was out.

The City would be buzzing at the news. The first shells were still smoking on the floor and already the vultures were circling, eager to pick over the carcasses. Still, maybe he cared? Deep down, maybe he enjoyed our unconventional relationship?

Maybe.

A few more faces disappeared and never came back. Some traders too. Traders whose jobs were being taken over by machines, machines that didn't read the Racing Post, or grumble and moan, or scratch their groins in public. For them at least, it was a blessing. They needed to be fired to move on, to find another skill. For the traders, the robots had already arrived.

I saw Gerald sitting at his desk with the look of man who knew it was time. It was over. His movements were laboured. He sighed and pouted. He chewed on the edge of an empty coffee cup and tidied his desk. He shuffled some papers and drifted over to talk to a trader with whom he owned a racehorse. He had one leg; the trader had three.

I forget which leg he owned.

He had told me over coffee once that he had been introduced to racing through his grandfather. The old man had taught Gerald to ride horses, to care for them, and to love them too. Gerald had said it was the only time that he ever remembered feeling happy as a child and was why he had been so distraught when he, aged nine, had found his grandfather in the stables, hanging from the rafters.

Dead.

The gambling debts had been too many.

I waved at Gerald and he nodded, although I wasn't sure if he saw me. Since our exchange in the sauna he bore a haunted look, the look of a man on the run. I had told him he should quit, resign, do something else; go count penguins or build a loo for some tribe deep in a tropical jungle. But he had told me he couldn't. When I asked him why he had just rubbed his temples and looked pained.

There were some things I would never know.

The day dragged by. By mid-afternoon I had had enough and logged out and went down to the gym to kill time and, as I pounded the treadmill, I wondered if my wife would be happy. Or sad. Or angry. With a child though, I felt the splintered yoke of responsibility digging into my neck. I now had real obligations.

When I returned to my desk, the floor was all but empty. I quickly checked my messages and was surprised to see nothing; no missed calls, no post-it notes, no urgent emails. The boss' secretary was also no longer at her desk. It appeared that I had survived the cull.

So too Gerald.

As I skirted the floor to leave, I saw him sat at his desk, his head down hidden behind his bank of screens, tapping furiously on his keyboard. I let him be and walked on, out towards the lifts.

I didn't know it then, but it was the last time that I would ever see the man alive.

CHAPTER XIII

Dead. A full stop. The end.

At least, as far as Gerald was concerned, it was the end.

I knew something bad had happened, I knew it. The day after the jobs cull, Gerald had not turned up for work. People assumed he had been fired, like all the others, only I knew that he hadn't. I had seen him at his screens, long after the big boss' pistol had been holstered. Had he been fired the security men would have taken him down the stairs and dumped him by the rubbish with his own bin liner of possessions.

I phoned his phone.

Voicemail.

I emailed him, but nothing came back. I called my wife and told her something bad had happened, and she needed to go around to his house and see if he was there. When she got there she knocked and knocked, but no one came to the door. After work, I too, went to his house. It was late, well after dark, but the lights were off. A parcel sat neglected by the front door, tossed aside by an indifferent courier, a corner soft and wet from the afternoon rain.

My wife suggested she go down to Wedgewood Road and sniff around. Hang out in the park, scope the play areas. See what she could find out from moody Moldovan wives who had been sold London, not Norbury.

I refused.

It was too dangerous.

She flared her nostrils and stormed out.

It had been a restless night.

The next morning, there was still no sign of Gerald. And then the chatter started. Gossip fed rumour. Stories flowered. The floor buzzed with sightings, lies morphed into facts and idle minds ran riot. Come the afternoon, there was still no murmur from Gerald and his phone continued to hit voicemail.

The following morning the mood soured, and there was a looming sense that something bad had happened. My wife disobeyed my wishes and texted me from the playground near Wedgewood Road, but she said she had nothing. The Moldovan wives did not speak English.

And then Pascal had shuffled out of his office and announced to the trading floor that Gerald was dead. He mumbled something about there being a memorial service, as the police had said that there was no chance of ever finding a body. The current, they said, had been too strong.

I sat down and rubbed my forehead, events were spinning out of control.

Gerald dead.

And Pascal.

Pascal?

How was it that Pascal was the bearer of such tragic news?

Pascal was the killer. He was the man who had been deftly plucking Blanchard's strings, dispassionately whispering Gerald towards his grave. Blanchard, though, continued to pick his nails in jail. Pascal, I presumed, must have taken matters into his own hands and murdered Gerald himself. Or vaulted the moody assassin into a different pay bracket.

I couldn't think.

And the stunned silence of the floor was deafening. I had no proof that Pascal had been involved; but he had to, it had to be him. I watched him closely as he stood talking into the microphone. He was calm. His voice soft and steady. His hands gripped the podium and he paused when he should. It was too polished a performance. It had to have been rehearsed.

Expected.

I knew it was him.

And, deep down, I feared he knew that I knew.

Only there was no proof.

None.

The police later announced to the press that they saw nothing sinister in Gerald's death. It was sad, and tragic, but sometimes there are no answers. The Chief Constable expressed his condolences to the family but said that there would be no further investigation.

*

The reason that Pascal had delivered the news was

because Pascal had been promoted. He finally had his corner office. The office that was tucked into the corner of the human battery farm with extravagant floor to ceiling glass walls, from where he could watch and plot and swivel, in the plush leather chair of the Head of Global Research.

A man who wielded real power.

A man who could break careers.

And men.

It was as he had always wanted.

The seat was vacant as the previous Head had left. Suddenly. The day after the jobs cull, with Gerald's disappearance still unnoticed, he had announced that he was leaving: leaving to become a she. He was, though, not leaving the business for ever, for management had, instead, insisted he take a stay; see it as a mere leave of absence, whilst his bits got sorted.

The reason was that HR had got themselves into a proper lather when they heard the news and phoned New York. They were beside themselves with excitement at what delights, as a she, she could bring to their diversity agenda, and yet they were also worried he might leave and not come back. They demanded New York do something, and so New York did. They phoned back with an offer of a nebulous role in 'client communications', and a pay packet that he could not refuse.

And so, he agreed to stay, but first he had to go, to become a she.

He gave a speech to a small gathering outside of his office. His voice faltered, and he smudged his mascara wiping away fat tears from his eyes. The representatives from HR cried. It was a happy scene.

As one life ended, another had begun.

Pascal had immediately taken over as an interim Head of Research, but everyone knew he would be no interim. The office was now his, so too our souls.

Or those who still had one.

By mid-afternoon he had stripped the office of personal bric-a-brac and turned the desk around to face the door, a symbolic move to shift the *ying* of the room's power source. Those that walked in now had to stand, vulnerable. Like elk. There to be picked off and mounted.

He immediately fired the Deputy Head of Research, and several analysts, some of whom had been his senior. He was purging the ranks of dissent and he barely drew breath. The list had been assembled long in advance. And then when he had called the trading floor to quiet, we had expected him to talk in strident tones about his new strategy, a freshly minted approach that would bewilder our clients with its ferocity of focus.

Their dollars would be our dollars.

Instead he announced that Gerald was dead. A lone sob pierced the silence. He said that he didn't have much in the way of details, but the management team had felt we had a right to know. A phone rang but stayed ringing.

The market was open but, for once, there was no appetite to take the call.

*

Over the next few days, details leaked out of the police, via quiet briefings, in tune with the PR team's 'employee-dead' narrative.

After Gerald had failed to turn up for work for the second day, the police had been called and they soon found out what had happened.

Gerald had jumped.

They said that he had climbed to the top of a bridge, where only the seagulls and maintenance men went, without fanfare or scene. The CCTV footage had captured him slipping the gaze of the security guard and he had climbed to the top, via ladders and perilous railings. He had then taken off his shoes and laid out his wallet and his phone. Tucked under his wallet they had found a crumpled photo of a man in speedos standing next to a small boy.

Gerald and his father.

And all was explained in the email. He had written an email to his father. A note. What the media was later told to be, a suicide note, explicitly laying down the pain. The years of hurt, it appeared, had finally broken Gerald's spirit. No more. Life had beaten him. He was, he wrote, tired of being alone. He was tired of trying to fit in, tired of judgement, tired of fighting for the love and attention of his father. A fight that over the years, had formed such a large black hole in his life, his only option he had – or so he had thought – was to jump into it.

Into the black abyss.

To finally stop the silent pain.

And so, he did.

He jumped.

The police said that there was no way a person would survive from such a height. He would have jumped, his arms spiralling in the air, his jacket and shirt billowing in the wind. Cold. Chops taut. Down into the darkness. The water would have been like concrete. And the night that he had jumped had been a stormy night, as they so often are, and the river was swollen after weeks of rain. The barrier was open, the currents too strong. The experts confidently predicted his body would have been swiftly swept out into the North Sea.

Lost.

Gone forever.

The coroner, minded to her own year-end targets, had seen nothing in the evidence to persuade her otherwise.

Suicide.

It was ironic and sad – tragic even – that despite our best efforts to drown him, he had ended up drowning himself.

A few days later, I went to the memorial service, we all did, or those that were left. We all sat, a quiet, uncomfortable mass, each lost to their own thoughts and quiet reflections of a man who had figured so prominently in the bleak and breathless struggle to mollify the displeasure of spouses and bank managers. A man who we had long resented, hated even, for the years of bullying and torment. A man who, with such ease, had been able to add or discard zeros to year-end bonuses.

I had arrived late and slipped in at the back, anxious to avoid Pascal who I suspected saw me now as the one remaining loose end. I had taken some leave of my own after he had announced the news. I claimed grief, knowing HR would be sympathetic. I scanned the congregation for Gerald's father and spotted him at the front, shaking hands, mixing with well-wishers and distant relatives; the latter eager for news on Gerald's estate. He was smaller than I had imagined, but then old people are, they shrink, more so if they live in the heat. They shrink and shrivel as their pension pots slowly run dry. Families back home, long forgotten. Shortly before the end of the final hymn he had turned around and our eyes had met, and I saw what Gerald had seen all his life.

I saw nothing.

He was a ghost.

Devoid of any feeling.

Devoid of any love.

I stood and swayed. No words came out of my mouth as the organist drove the tuneless horde through the bars of the final chorus, and I finally understood Gerald's pain.

God rest his soul.

*

I woke up with a little yelp.

My dream was the same, it was always the same. I had been naked. Again. And running. Always naked and running. Running through thick brambles which cut my legs as I stumbled through the dark. There had been no moon. There was never a moon. I didn't know where I was going, but then I didn't care. I just knew I needed to get away. He had been after me again. There, but always shrouded in shadow, his breath hot on my bare buttocks. And I remember falling, knowing he would get me. He always got me. As I lay on my back, on a bed of brambles I stared back up into the ferocious jaws.

Open.

Covered in drool.

Bruno.

I woke up with my son's face inches away from my own.

I looked at my boy, relieved it was him, not Bruno, although reality meant I was back facing the unsettling prospect of having work colleagues wanting me dead.

Still, for now at least, I was safe in my own home.

Darkness had fallen.

I looked at my boy.

One-year old.

Where had the time gone? A whole year. And so much had happened.

'We should have a party,' my wife had said.

'Why?' I asked.

'For his birthday,' she said.

'He's one' I said. 'He doesn't have any friends.'

'He does.'

'Who?'

She had then listed a long list of names I had not heard of. I had my doubts, but I was to be proved wrong. We did have a party on a Sunday, and it turned out that he did have friends. The floor at its busiest, had been littered with babies, all licking things they would, later in life, see no reason to lick. I had been standing in the middle, slowly surveying the scene when a baby had started to cry. I didn't move, I couldn't move, I was alone, lost in a parallel world, drifting on the eddies of my own mind.

The only escape I had.

That and liquor.

'Pick him up!' my wife yelled.

I looked down and saw the baby was crying. The face was red, contorted, and wet with tears. And yet in my tranquil, detached state, I did nothing. I just stood and stared. My immediate reaction was relief. Relief the baby wasn't mine. And then, wallop. There was clap, a sharp sucking of air, and I landed back in the present.

Action.

My wife wanted action.

'My man!' I yelled.

'I've got him!' yelled his mother.

So much yelling.

And yet she beat me to it. She was too quick. She dived in and scooped the baby up and retreated to a corner to coo and shoot me dirty looks.

I smiled.

She didn't.

SOLD SHORT

Eventually, though, the party broke up. Tears became hysterical and they all started drifting off. I grinned and shook their hands and thanked them for coming through glazed eyes. After tidying up, I had then sat on the floor with my boy. And a beer.

Another beer.

And stopped grinning.

I stopped grinning because now it was just me, my wife, and my in-laws. We were all that remained. My mother-in-law had caught my eye several times during the party, but I couldn't escape. There had been too many adults wanting drinks and nibbles. I sensed, though, she had news.

'You'll be glad that's over,' the Gestapo said, easing himself into a soft chair as I picked marzipan out of the carpet.

He sighed and rubbed his ankle.

'You ok?' I asked, looking up.

He nodded.

'Getting old,' he said, smiling.

I fetched him a beer.

'How's the central heating?' I asked, sitting down on the sofa, 'I heard it's been down.'

I saw my mother-in-law slowly drying some glasses by the sink.

She looked concerned.

'Still down,' the Gestapo grimaced.

'A problem with the boiler?' I enquired, gently, edging into the conversation.

Interested, but also somewhat reluctant to hear the latest news.

'No, the boiler is fine. We had it checked out.'

I nodded and sipped my beer.

So too, he.

And then the fist.

'We think there's a problem with the oil tank.'

A punch to the midriff.

I wheezed dry air.

'We have someone coming to look at it tomorrow.'

I stared back at him and tried to breath normally.

The end.

Bruno was going to be exhumed from his oily grave, his matted body startling the engineer sent out for what, he assumed, would be a routine job. I turned away from the Gestapo. I couldn't let him see my face. I knew I had gone white. I could feel it. I then stood and made some excuse; I don't know what. All I could hear were dogs barking. My vision was blurred. I stumbled on a rug, picked up some empty crisp packets and shuffled through and into the spare bedroom.

Away.

I lay down on the carpet, my breathing now heavy. I wanted it all to end and closed my eyes. After that I must have drifted off to sleep. For how long, I don't know. Possibly minutes. Maybe longer. With darkness falling outside, lying next to the radiator, I felt safe.

I was safe.

But that would not last.

Come the morning, as I walked through the lobby into work after a week on leave, wrought with fear over what the Gestapo's engineer might find, I was hit again, square between the eyes.

Not possible.

I feared I had started to hallucinate, but I hadn't. There, standing on the escalator easing his way into work, was a sight that would once more pitch my addled mind into the fiery pit of emotional hell.

The suit was as tight as ever.

The gut, still fabulous.

Blanchard.

*

It turned out that Blanchard had been released without charge.

He had been released without charge, because there had been no evidence. Nothing. The police had found absolutely nothing. As far as they could establish there was no hit man. He didn't exist. As Blanchard had smugly insisted all along. With no evidence and no assassin, the police had to sheepishly admit there could have been no attempted murder.

And the one man who could provide proof, was now dead.

Within days of being back at work, Blanchard had been appointed Head of Sales, replacing the now stiff and bloated Gerald. I had no friends on the trading floor anymore. Claire had left, and the rest had been fired, but I picked up in the canteen that the management had felt vulnerable to some bad press having hung Blanchard so publicly out to dry. They felt that they owed him, and the vacant Head of Sales job was to be his prize, and the cost of his silence.

The irony was exquisite, as was the plan all along.

And then, on my first day back Blanchard had asked me out to lunch. An email – *ping!* Just like the old days. Only not. This time no sauna. This time an upmarket French restaurant. And I had to go, I knew it. There was no way I could put it off.

As I was about to leave my phone rang.

I picked it up.

'It's me,' said my mother-in-law.

My heart started to thud. It was late morning. The engineer would have been.

'They found the problem.'

I sat down heavily, resigned. Despite knowing what was coming, I felt calm. It would, perhaps, be a relief.

The truth.

Aired.

Bruno could then perhaps be buried with dignity.

'It was a broken valve in the boiler,' she said. 'It seems the boiler man didn't do his job properly. The engineer checked the pipes and noticed it. He didn't even need to go outside.'

I breathed out and rubbed my forehead.

Relief.

Our secret remained a secret.

I glanced up at the clock on the wall.

'I need to go,' I said, 'thanks for letting me know.'

'Of course,' she replied, soft, maternal. 'Any time.'

I hung up.

*

I turned up at the restaurant and was shown to a small booth in the back where Blanchard was sat. The waiter dithered with menus and napkins and fussed over our order. Blanchard waited until we were alone.

'Why?' he asked, softly.

'Why what?' I said, pouring some water.

'Why did you do it?'

'Do what?'

'You know,' he said, his tone sharper.

I picked up my glass and swirled the ice around it, buying myself time, thinking, trying to put the pieces together.

'I know it was you that sneaked on me to the police.'

'Sneaked?' I said. 'What do you mean?'

And yet we both knew.

The restaurant was quiet, plush, the tables generously spaced out and the carpet thick. So thick the waiters ghosted over it silently. Conversations murmured. I shifted in my seat and eyed up the fire exits as the scallop starters arrived.

'My lawyer demanded to see the email that the police had received,' Blanchard said, after the waiter left. 'He had a geek look at it, decode it. Fiddle about. And do you know what the geek found?'

He forked a scallop.

I knew what was coming.

'No,' I said.

'He found out where the email had been sent from.'

Blanchard dipped a scallop in butter.

I shrugged and frantically thought through my options. I could deny it. I could throw my water at him and run away. I could admit it. Or I could plunge my butter knife into his neck and hope the waiter was due a cigarette break.

'A block of flats,' Blanchard said, chewing his scallop, his mouth open. 'The geek found the block of flats the email was sent from.'

I topped up my glass of water.

Running was still an option.

'Do you know where block of flats was?' he asked, violently skewering another scallop.

'Where?' I asked, innocently.

Blanchard stopped.

'Your block of flats,' he spat. 'What a coincidence that is?'

He smirked, but it was a nasty, angry smirk. He chewed and swallowed.

The scallop disappeared.

As I weighed up my response, the waiter arrived with more bread rolls, breaking the conversation.

If Blanchard had evidence that I had sent the email, I knew that I was in a bit of a stew. There was no denying it, I had sent it. But unless he had hard evidence, it struck me as a little light, circumstantial at best. It was a big block of flats. I made a mental note to lob my laptop in the communal recycling bin; dispose of the hard drive and all its leaky secrets.

'So, why did you do it?' he asked, after the waiter had once again, disappeared.

He slowly nibbled another scallop off his fork, this time his body pitched forward, his elbows on the table.

I sighed.

'Does it matter? I mean Gerald is dead, and you are Head of Sales. Job done, no?'

'No, it's not job done,' he said, putting his fork down.

I stared back.

'What do you want me to say?'

'Admit it.'

'Admit what?'

'Admit you sent the email.'

'I don't know what you're talking about.'

'My lawyer is going to skin you alive,' he spat.

'Your evidence is circumstantial,' I said, contemptuously. 'It won't stand up in court.'

My tone was confident, it's all I had left, and my eyes never left him.

'Who is Bruno?' he then asked, changing tack.

'Bruno?'

'Yes, Bruno.'

'I don't know. It sounds like a good name for a dog,' I said.

There was no way the police would make the connection between me and Bruno. It was too random. And I knew the Gestapo would not talk. Despite our differences, he wasn't the sort. I was, though, worried. Blanchard had an obsessive air to him. And he was angry. As he might have been.

I watched as he slowly dabbed his mouth with the crisp linen napkin, all the scallops now gone. So too the chorizo crisp. A stray stretch of pear puree had flecked his suit lapel. I knew he was unpredictable, and I needed to be ready. I reached for my butter knife, ready in case he lunged. Hands out. Flapping. Grappling for my throat.

I knew how hard he could squeeze.

And then, before he could answer, or work himself up again, it happened.

Blanchard started to squirm in his seat. He loosened his collar and reached for his glass of water. He shook his arm and massaged his hands and then slowly turned the hue of beetroot. That rich, vivid, puce colour that I had last seen in the sauna. He said something, but his speech was slurred.

'Heart attack,' I whispered, the words barely escaping my mouth. They were almost inaudible. The words themselves, shocked but thrilled, almost disbelieving of their own meaning. Rapt, I sat back and watched Blanchard have a heart attack in front of my very eyes. It was quite gripping, seeing it happen so close.

And I felt nothing.

No fear.

No shame.

No nothing.

Instead, I leisurely forked a scallop of my own.

Eventually, after a minute of gasping he slowly toppled off his seat narrowly missing the cheese trolley. As he panted on the floor, I felt detached, peaceful, completely unmoved by his plight. I felt no part of the tragic act. I was but an idle spectator. Absorbed, but powerless to stop it.

And yet, as I dipped another scallop in some pea purée, I knew that I had to do something. There was a risk I would be seen and so, I slipped out of the booth and found myself once again leaning over Blanchard, trying to feel for a pulse. His bloated, red face looked engorged; his eyes small.

Desperate.

Piggy.

'And squeeze,' said a voice in my head. 'No one would ever know.'

And yet I couldn't.

'Help!' I shouted, knowing there was little more that I could do. 'Un Docteur!'

And the staff descended on the scene. There was a din of activity. Tables were moved, windows were opened. Light flooded the room. And I slipped back into the booth to watch the scene unfold. Within minutes an ambulance had arrived. The paramedics did their best, but they were too late, nothing could be done. His heart had had enough. There would be no more scallops, and no more Blanchard.

He too, was now dead.

*

After the paramedics had wheeled Blanchard out, in a big black bag, I had sat back in the booth and ordered a coffee from the ashen-faced waiter. He was as white as a Frenchman might go on being told he had to work the weekend. And as I waited, I softly hummed *La Marseillaise*.

The turn to our lunch had been stunning.

The prospect of jail time, or even death, had been staring me in the face before Blanchard's besieged heart had reprieved my lot. One butter-glazed scallop too many. As I got up to leave, I saw Blanchard's phone on the seat. It must have dropped out of his pocket when he made is final, tragic, fall to the floor. Without thinking I grabbed it and slipped it into my pocket.

I walked out of the restaurant and meandered through the streets, heading south, heading home; home to see my wife and my boy. I couldn't go back to the office. News travels fast and they would know. There would be too many questions. Too many people watching me, interested. Interested to see my state.

My manner.

They would whisper and squint.

Two deaths in two weeks.

SOLD SHORT

It was all turning a little fishy.

I turned down alleys, through courtyards and hidden squares, and emerged by the river and saw that I was not far from the bridge. Gerald's bridge. I looked at the water and felt Blanchard's phone in my pocket. It was obvious. Life often had a symmetry to it; so too it, death. There was no better place to dispose of the phone.

The river.

I pulled it out and as I waited for a boat load of bug-eyed tourists to chug past, I tried to unlock it. I was just killing time. Waiting. I had no motive, no great urge to crack it open. I just idly punched in some numbers, as I waited.

Zero, zero, zero, zero.

It was silly.

Nobody was that dim.

And then, ping!

I was in.

The photo that stared back was of a small poodle. I cursed and wondered whether it would be fed that night. Blanchard, I knew, had a mottled history with dogs. My fingers continued to move, as if on their own accord, and I flicked open the messages. My curiosity was now all consuming. Reading a dead man's text messages had an illicit feel. It was wrong, and possibly illegal.

And then I saw a message from Bogdan, the mean, surly faced assassin.

Adrenalin coursed my body.

How come the police had missed it? Did they not seize his phone? I breathlessly opened it up to find a long string of messages with Bogdan. I read them all. I scrolled and scrolled and yet it didn't make any sense.

I stopped and stared out across the river.

They talked in some sort of code. They talked about Blanchard's basement. They talked about pipes and plumbing. They talked about interiors. Bogdan wanted to know if Blanchard wanted the skirting boards painted white, like the kitchen walls.

I stared out over the river and tried to think.

Once again, I couldn't see what was happening. The fog was back. And this time it was thick. Just as I had thought I had worked it all out, I felt that familiar pitch of unease. Everything was not as it was. My interpretation, my understanding of it, was all wrong. I turned the phone over in my hands, trying to find an explanation, and as I did, it rang.

I flipped it over and saw that the number was withheld.

It continued to ring.

And then, I answered it.

Impulsively.

'Hello?' I said.

'Congratulations,' a voice replied, 'I read about your promotion. The plan worked, as I said it would.'

I said nothing.

Something was very wrong.

I tried to slow my breathing, my mind racing, and

as it raced, the fog started to clear, and it started to make sense, such perfect sense. I stumbled back and collapsed on a bench and closed my eyes.

It was so obvious.

How had I not seen it? I had been played, we had all been played. The assassin had been a mirage, a hoax, a puff of smoke to distract and confuse. I couldn't believe it, and yet it was true. I racked my brains, to think back, to try and remember. I tried to recall the phone calls, the emails, the quiet meetings in saunas and cafes where I had been softened up and seasoned; where I had been fed lies about both mood and motive.

And the voice.

Unmistakable.

And yet, impossible.

'Are you still there?' it said.

I couldn't speak.

I couldn't move.

There *was* someone else involved, but it wasn't Pascal, or Dominique.

And however hard they looked; the police would never find Gerald's body.

Unlike Bruno, there was no body.

'Blanchard, it's me...' the voice said, 'it's Gerald.'

THE END

ABOUT THE AUTHOR

The author lives quietly in the countryside, and has enjoyed working with all the people he has ever worked with. Bar one, or two.

www.hepburnsays.com

Printed in Great Britain
by Amazon